FINDING YOU

A SMALL TOWN ROMANCE

Havenport Series Book 2

DAPHNE ELLIOT

Published by Melody Publishing, LLC

Editing by Happily Editing Anns

Cover design by Kari March Designs

DEDICATION
To my loving husband. Who once gave me a sledgehammer as
a gift.

PROLOGUE
ASTRID

March

Just my luck. The day I realized I was in love was also the day I got arrested. When I woke up this morning, I did not expect this day to end with me getting my mug shot taken, but given how my life had been going, it was not a shock.

I was a planner. I carefully examined every decision and its statistical implications before implementing and executing with precision. Needless to say, I had never imagined getting myself into a situation that culminated in my arrest. On the bright side, I was wearing a gorgeous evening gown and had professional hair and makeup done, so the odds were good it would at least be a decent photo. I wonder if I could get a copy of it? I could post it to my Instagram.

Getting arrested sucked. And I was pretty sure it would ruin my career and reputation. But damn, it also felt really good. After years of taking other people's shit and smiling politely, it felt good to finally fight back a little. To do what I wanted to do, what I needed to do. It was about time I reclaimed some of the dignity that had been stolen from me. And if a criminal record was the consequence, so be it.

The holding cell was pretty gross. There were a bunch of other women in here with me. Everyone seemed like they were keeping to themselves. Yes, I was dressed like a beauty queen, but I was also pretty tall, and years of being a lawyer had helped me develop an excellent "don't fuck with me" face, so I was fine. I knew I would be bailed out soon. I was only going to get slapped with assault and battery, nothing crazy. Even murderers made bail sometimes.

If anything, the greatest tragedy of the night was the loss of my shoe. My new friends Christian and Dante had given them to me as a gift, and they were sparkly Louboutin perfection. A four-inch platform stiletto with a delicate sling back, the toe box was covered with small crystals that created a purple and blue ombre effect. My toenails were painted a perfect purple to match, and they set off my eggplant gown beautifully. They were the most perfect shoes I had ever seen. And now I only had one of them. Apparently, my right shoe was evidence, so the odds of me getting it back were slim. As I sat in the grimy holding cell, wearing one shoe and waiting to be bailed out, I realized that this had been one of the most memorable days of my life.

1

ASTRID

JANUARY

"Are you sure you're okay up there? You can come here if you want." I looked around my new home. It wasn't bad. It was a far cry from my luxury apartment in downtown Boston, but on the plus side, it had a lovely ocean view.

"Thanks, Emily. I'm fine," I replied. "The cottage is perfect."

The little cottage was charming in its shabby-chicness, bursting with pillows, paintings, and tchotchkes. A worn, plush couch faced a brick fireplace in the tiny living room, and there was a small kitchen in the back, stuffed with every possible kitchen tool and gadget known to man. Not that I would be using any of them, but even I could appreciate the value of a well-stocked kitchen. It had a small porch that looked out over the bluffs, and as I stood there, freezing my ass off in the January cold, a sort of calm settled over me. I wasn't in the city anymore. And I wasn't necessarily mad about that.

"What can I get you? Do you need anything?" Her kindness meant a lot to me. Emily was my first cousin. We were nothing alike. I was quiet and serious, and Emily was zany and adventurous, but somehow our childhood bond developed into a genuine adult friendship.

I briefly saw red. I was still so angry. How could they treat me like this? After everything I had done for the firm? I could feel the lava travel up my esophagus. I had to unpack and find my heartburn medication. "I'm good. I have everything I need to kick back and unwind for a couple of days."

The cottage belonged to my aunt Connie. She was my father's younger sister and the only extended family I had any contact with growing up. She was an eccentric sort, an artist who had fled the city for the idyllic small town of Havenport, Massachusetts sometime in the 1970s. Here she had found some success, opening a gallery and marrying her first husband. Emily and her sister, Grace, grew up here, among the bluffs and the dunes and the charming small-town festivals. I associated this place with fun and freedom, which may have been the reason the first call I made after being fired from my law firm was not to my mother, but to my aunt.

As a kid, I would come visit Havenport in the summer, and I loved every second of it. My cousins lived a few minutes from the historic downtown, and after dinner we would walk to get ice cream cones and watch the fishing boats unload their daily catch. It was an idyllic sort of place—safe, clean, and everyone knew everyone. My cousins had lots of friends, participated in fun activities, and had the kind of free-range, charming childhoods I longed for.

My childhood, by contrast, was one of strict discipline and formality. I was raised in a historic mansion in Brookline, Massachusetts by my mother and a series of nannies. My mother, the right honorable Justice Mary Wentworth, was a judge on the Massachusetts Supreme

Judicial Court. She was consistently ranked by Boston Magazine as one of the most powerful women in Massachusetts.

She had been nominated to the bench when I was in middle school and worked her way up the courts to her current position. She was widely regarded as a legal genius and a fair and tolerant jurist. Her life was a series of high stakes legal decisions and grand parties and networking events. All of which I hated.

She devoted her life and career to public service and the pursuit of justice. That left very little time for being a mother, a role she outsourced as much as she could. When I was a kid, she never came to parent-teacher nights or to school plays or concerts. She did begrudgingly attend my graduations, but only because I was graduating from prestigious institutions.

I attended private school and left home at fourteen to attend Miss Farmer's Academy in Connecticut, the preeminent prep school for the daughters of Boston and New York elites. After Miss Farmer's, it was on to Yale and then to Harvard Law School, where, to the embarrassment of my mother, I only finished fourth in my class. Then I spent one year clerking for a federal judge before starting my career at Burns & Glenn, one of the world's largest law firms. I had spent six years chained to my desk, churning out billable hours and getting yearly pats on the head. I had skipped vacations, friends' weddings, holidays, and countless meals, workouts, and nights of sleep. I had one goal— partnership. The brass ring. The ultimate validation of all my hard work and sacrifice. Every minute of my life to date had been precisely calculated to help me achieve my goal.

And it was all for naught. One day I was the hardest-working, highest-achieving senior associate at the firm, and the next I was a liability who required an investigation.

Emily interrupted my thoughts as I stared out the window. "Do you want to tell me what happened? I'm happy to listen."

I took a deep breath, but it did nothing to calm the angry fire inside me. It wasn't just my stomach. Every cell in my body burned with rage, and I didn't know what to do with it. I had spent my entire life with a mask of calm on my face. I sat and negotiated with opposing counsel for hours without so much as a yawn or a pee break. I could pull an all-nighter and charm clients at a seven a.m. breakfast meeting the next day. I was a stone-cold badass and yet it wasn't enough for them.

Nothing I did was enough for them. Because I was a woman and the deck was stacked against me. Everything I'd worked for since middle school had disappeared in the last seventy-two hours and I was too shocked to cry. But the rage. The rage that had simmered on the periphery for years was starting to bubble up inside me. The volcano of anger and disappointment had been dormant too long, and I knew I was going to blow soon.

"It's complicated, Em. They fired me."

"What? Fired you? You are the hardest-working associate they've ever had, and your mom is a goddamn judge."

"I know." I had given them six years of my life. I had never made a mistake, my reviews were excellent, and my client relationships were strong. I had the makings of an exceptional partner and everyone there knew it. I volunteered for client pitches, wrote academic articles in my nonexistent spare time, and represented the firm at professional conferences and law school recruiting fairs.

And yet, in a few short months I had gone from all-star to pariah. "They said I made a mistake. They said I accidentally sent a confidential document to opposing counsel, jeopardizing negotiations in a billion-dollar merger."

"What?"

"I know I didn't. I couldn't have." I paced around the tiny living room. "And when I asked for proof—the emails, the metadata, screenshots—they couldn't give me anything." As attorneys we were trained to always organize the evidence before making accusations. We were trained to know the answer to questions before you asked them. So why did they come at me with such flimsy accusations and no evidence?

"That is total bullshit...oh crap, I meant caca," she spat. I heard one of her kids laughing in the background and assumed she would be making a healthy donation to the swear jar tonight.

When the managing partner had sat me down, he seemed so disappointed. "We never expected this from you, Astrid. It's a shame—you have been such a bright spot in your associate cohort." John Waterson was a sharp-looking man in his sixties who built his reputation on his aggressive tactics and take no prisoners attitude. He was rich, elitist, out of touch, and just a little bit mean—the perfect BigLaw partner. When I pushed back on him, he acted shocked. Like how dare I ask for concrete evidence of my career-ending mistake? If he was looking for me to sit there and take it, then he was sorely mistaken. I was many things, but a doormat was not one of them.

"When I asked for more information, he noted the poor review I had received from Max Shapiro and some rumblings within the partnership that I was 'not as committed' as I used to be."

"What?"

"It is total bullshit." My commitment to the firm and my clients was unwavering. "I looked him in the eye and asked for an example of this lack of commitment. He was unable to provide a single one. The real mistake I made was not reporting that smarmy motherfucker Max Shapiro, not anything related to client documents."

"Good for you. I'm glad you didn't back down."

"So I serenely asked him to provide actual facts to back up these assertions, and he told me to 'calm myself.'"

"You have got to be shitting me. He did the old, sexist 'calm down, you crazy woman' play?"

"Yup. Then he suggested that I not get 'so emotional.'"

"OMG."

"I wanted to 'emotionally' punch him in his wrinkled old man balls." But, being the consummate professional that I was, I sat quietly and calmly advocated to keep my job. Total coded sexist bullshit. "He seemed so surprised that I wouldn't go quietly into the good night with the generous severance package and an ironclad noncompete."

"What happened?"

"I refused to sign the liability waiver that they require before they pay you severance. Basically you waive all your rights to sue the firm."

"So you don't get severance?"

"Nope. I have ninety days to sign it, and if I don't, not only do I not get severance, I won't get a recommendation from the firm. Which I need if I have any hope of getting another job."

"I am so proud of you for standing up for yourself!" Emily yelled over the sounds of screaming and a dog barking in the background. The four walls of her house could barely contain the chaos most days. "So they want to prevent you from suing them?"

"Bingo. They are trying to cover their asses. The good news is, I didn't screw up the merger, and they will know that once the investigation begins. The bad news is that Max Shapiro badmouthed me and ruined my reputation after I repeatedly rejected his sexual advances, and I don't know if I'm ever going to recover from that."

"Astrid. What happened?"

As if the rage and heartburn weren't bad enough, a runaway tidal wave of shame crashed over me. I didn't want to talk about this. I didn't want to relive it all. But Emily was family, and I hadn't been able to confide in anyone about this.

"He came on to me several times, and I politely said no. The intensity increased and I remained professional and pleasant, just as I was taught to." That wasn't the whole story but it was all I could manage right now. He was a creepy, persistent asshole who terrorized me with texts, emails, and comments for months. Eventually it stopped, and I assumed that he got the message and things would go back to normal. "I thought that was the end of it. But he was sabotaging me behind the scenes for months before I caught on. Blaming this mistake on me was just one of the many things he did to undermine my position at the firm."

"That motherfucker. That's retaliation."

"I know."

"So what are you going to do? We could burn his house down. I've always been up for a little light arson."

I made a mental note to check in with Emily's husband about her firebug tendencies at a later date. "No, Em. I need to trust the process. Without a recommendation, I won't get a job at another firm. So I need to wait for them to complete the investigation. Once they realize I didn't do this and he unfairly blamed me, I'll be able to leverage that for a recommendation for my next job."

"But what if they don't? Shouldn't you sue them or something?" I wasn't ready to confront that reality. That everything I had spent my life working for was over. And while suing them for sexual harassment and retaliation seemed an attractive option, it would kill any chances I had of getting a position at a rival firm. Law firms may pretend to be bastions of equality, but there was nothing people hated more than a squeaky wheel. Especially when that wheel was a woman.

"I don't know what I'm going to do yet. But right now I'm going to enjoy my break and figure out my next steps."

"Let me know what I can do to help!"

I laughed. "I'm fine, really. Just need some time and space to think. Actually," I said, feeling super awkward, "what I need is a date."

"A date?"

"For this legal gala. I am receiving an award for some pro bono work I did. And, I could skip it…"

"Stop right there. You are not skipping this. You worked your ass off, and you are not going to go run and hide after being fired. You are going to attend and show everyone there what a stone-cold badass Astrid Wentworth is. Got it?"

I smiled. Emily was fiercely loyal, and right now, I needed all the loyalty I could get.

"Yes. But I don't want to go alone."

"We can take care of that, Astrid. You are gorgeous, and there are loads of single men out there who would happily squire you to your fancy event." I doubted that very much. I had never had much luck in the dating department. "In fact," she continued, "you should join some dating apps. Use this time in Havenport to go on some dates, meet some guys, have some fun!"

I shuddered. Dating apps were my idea of hell. But she was right about one thing—I certainly had the time on my hands to actually meet some people.

"Ok. I'll join one app and see how it goes."

"Sounds like a plan. Oh shit. Jacob is trying to slice his own strawberries again. I gotta run."

Since I couldn't possibly stay in my apartment next door to my office after being fired, I had packed a few bags, called an Uber, and gotten the hell out of the city. What do people do when they are not working? I have slept, gone for a million walks, listened to a few podcasts, and flipped through some of the hundreds of romance novels piled high in the built-in bookcases.

Despite living less than an hour away, it had been years since I had come up here to visit. I forgot how charming this place was. I had only been here a few days, and I could begrudgingly admit that I was already feeling more relaxed. The cottage was outside of the downtown area, but nothing a good brisk walk or an Uber couldn't fix. And walking! Turns out I loved walking. It may sound strange, but for years, I just walked from the lobby of my apartment building across a tiny side street to the lobby of my office building. I rented an overpriced studio at the Greenside, a luxury apartment building for Boston's trendy professionals, because it was located directly next to the office tower where Burns & Glenn had its Boston office. I overpaid for the convenience of having a two-minute commute. It made sense at the time. Time spent commuting was time I couldn't be billing. And billing was the most important and most valuable use of my time. Sleeping? Exercising? Socializing with friends? Nope, my billable time was worth nine hundred dollars an hour, so nothing was worth that much. I spent very little time at the apartment, using it mainly for showering and sleeping. I certainly had never cooked a meal there or even watched a movie, as far as I could remember. Every minute was spent in pursuit of billing more hours, accomplishing more for my clients, and impressing the partners at the firm. Nothing else mattered.

And so there was no time for walks. Or fresh air or exercise. Coming here and just walking had been a revelation. I had been listening to podcasts, reading books, and getting to know the area. I had just signed up for Netflix and was excited to catch up on all the movies and television people had been gushing about for the past decade. I didn't even own a TV. Now I had all the time in the world to kick back in front of the cottage's modest-sized flatscreen. These activities were entirely unproductive and a waste of my sterling intellect, but I was enjoying myself.

Adding to the satisfaction, this morning I caught a glimpse of my hot neighbor. It was dark and cold at five thirty in the morning, but I still got a decent look at him. I woke as I usually do, in a panic around four thirty. My heart pounded and my mind raced as I reached for my phone to check my emails. It took a few minutes before I realized they had taken my company phone and so there were no emails to check.

But still, I was jittery and awake so I decided to take a morning walk and was rewarded with a sighting of one of the most attractive men I've ever seen. He was tall and broad and exuded masculinity. I had no idea what he did for a living, but I bet he worked with his hands. His strong, fit body indicated a physical job, not just time spent in the gym. He was scruffy, with a full beard and long dark hair pulled back into a bun. I couldn't tell exactly how old he was, but I'd guess probably in his thirties. He'd run in sweatpants and a faded Navy hoodie. When he got back to his yard, he stripped off the hoodie and started doing pushups in his T-shirt. I could see the faint outlines of tattoos in the early morning light. If I was a religious woman I would have thanked the good Lord for pushups. It seemed like he could do them for ages and ages. And I watched. I watched his arms, back, and shoulders contract and his firm, round ass in those sweatpants. The men in my life never wore sweatpants, so I was not familiar with their allure. Even across the street, they were the hottest thing I had ever seen. He was dirty and sweaty and oh so hot. Not my type at all, of course, but I could appreciate a fine specimen of man when I saw one.

My hot neighbor was one of the only bright spots in the past few days.

But as I stood on the tiny porch, the winter wind burning the skin on my cheeks, I knew coming here was the right decision. My world had completely shifted on its axis, and I needed to regroup and make a plan. What better place than a secluded oceanfront cottage in some small charming town where no one knew who my mother was or about the mistakes I had made?

2

DECLAN

IT HAD BEEN A LONG DAY AT WORK. WINTERS WERE hard—there was little sunlight, and storms made navigating to and from our fishing grounds even more treacherous. People got sick, people got depressed, and everything got exponentially more difficult to manage. Our business continued to grow, and all the pressure rested squarely on my shoulders. I was in charge of protecting the legacy built by my great-grandfather, and sometimes, I dragged that legacy around like a weight. Today was one of those days. I was driving home, listing to some Arcade Fire and looking forward to seeing my dog, Ginger, when my phone rang. I clicked the Bluetooth link on my steering wheel. "Hi, Mom."

"Hey, sweetie. How was your day?" My mother was relentlessly cheerful and organized. She had to be, raising three wild boys. She sounded sweet, but underneath that sweetness was a steely backbone that we knew not to mess with.

"Great, Mom. How's Dad doing?" My dad had suffered a massive heart attack back in November. He was improving every day but still faced a long recovery. My mom managed his health like a general, so I had a lot of faith he would be back to his old self soon.

"Your father is a pain in my behind, but other than that he's great. They have him walking on a treadmill at physical therapy now. He's ahead of schedule!"

"That's great, Mom."

"And I know it's because of the plant-based diet we're doing. You should consider it, sweetie. We both feel amazing. And I am so regular."

"Mom, please. TMI. Just stop." If I didn't stop this line of conversation soon, who knows what kind of awkward questions she could start asking me.

"Okay, okay. Sorry I brought it up."

"I am actually just driving home from work, Mom. Anything you need?"

"Oh no, sweetie, I just wanted to say hello. I am so sorry you were stuck working late."

"It's fine. Business has been great, so I've been busy."

"But while I have you. I was at the salon today getting my hair done, and I ended up chatting with Mrs. Zimmerman in the waiting area. Do you remember the Zimmermans, sweetie? They lived in town for a while and then moved to the South Shore. After retirement, they came back. She was filling me in on her kids. Her son, Bruce—I think he was a year or two below you in school—he just got married to a woman he met on some website called Bumble. Have you heard of it?"

And here we go. Annie Quinn could not keep her nose out of my dating life. "I haven't, Mom."

"You should go home and google it. It's apparently for people who want to meet their special someone. Not for hookups. Like that Timber."

"It's Tinder, Mom."

"Whatever." I could hear the disdain in her voice.

"Anyway, I would sign you up, but I am no good with technology. So you can do it later tonight?"

"I'll think about it. I'm not sure I'm cut out for that sort of thing."

"Nonsense. Sweetie, you are going to do great. You are so handsome, the girls will be lining up to go on dates with you. Especially if you get a haircut. So you'll do it? Awesome." Typical Mom, steamrolling me every chance she got.

Suggesting I join a dating site was at least marginally better than the blind date she set me up on last month. She twisted my arm into meeting Stacy, a realtor from West Haven, who my mom met at a meditation workshop. I met her for dinner, and within five minutes it was clear we both wanted out. Stacy was twenty-five and obsessed with TikTok. She babbled on and on about followers and engagement and how her real goal was to be an "influencer," whatever the fuck that was. I tried to feign interest but gave up by the time my dinner arrived. It felt like I was talking to a member of another species. At one point she whipped a small light box out of her massive purse so she could light her dinner better for the photo she was taking. Going out with her confirmed what I had long suspected—that I was only interested in women over thirty.

Yet as soon as my mom brought up dating, my mind flashed to a woman I saw this morning. I was out for my morning run in the cold, and I saw a gorgeous woman walking down my street. I had never seen her before. It was dark so I couldn't make out a lot of her features, but she was tall, with mile-long legs, and wore a large red knit hat. We made eye contact briefly while I jogged by, and I felt something strange happening in my chest. I returned to my run and went about my day, but now, heading home and hearing my mother nag me about my lack of girlfriend, my mind wandered to her. Who was she? Did she live nearby? Maybe she was just visiting? And why did I care? I saw good-looking women all the time and never spared them a second thought.

I turned into my driveway, and the automatic lights flipped on. In the window, I could see Ginger, my sweet dog, looking for me. I usually brought her to work, but today I had meetings with some suits so I had to leave her at home. The odds were pretty good she was pissed at me and would let me know it, but I was still happy to see my girl.

We had been together almost eight years. I found her at a kill shelter in Virginia after my honorable discharge from the navy. I was twenty-seven, had known nothing but military life, and desperately needed a friend. I walked into the shelter and saw dozens of happy, affectionate dogs, but Ginger caught my eye.

She was guarded and wary, even for a puppy. The volunteer at the shelter told me that no one wanted to adopt her because she wasn't friendly. That stuck with me. I wasn't friendly either. We formed a tentative friendship and have been inseparable ever since.

Ginger was a cat in the body of a dog. She was aloof, didn't easily give affection, and preferred to do her own thing. Most of the time she acted like I was annoying her with my presence. But she was loyal, protective, and the best roommate a guy could ask for. When I adopted her, they said she was a poodle mix and would likely be medium sized. They were wrong. Ginger was over seventy pounds of badass with soft gray fur. She got monthly haircuts at the fancy pet place in town, because I only wanted the best for my girl.

I dropped my bag and keys and hung up my coat. The house was warm and welcoming, but sparse, just how I liked it. This area of town, a tiny peninsula overlooking a rocky ocean bluff, was prime waterfront real estate. For decades it had been a campground with rows of tidy cottages and areas for fires, volleyball courts, and horseshoe pits. The family that owned it, the Lawsons, decided to sell a few years back, and hating slick real estate developers, insisted on selling the plots individually to people they knew and liked. One of the Lawsons' grandsons worked for me on one of my boats and put in a good word. They sold me an acre at the end of the peninsula for a song, and I got to work building my dream house. In fact, there were only three other homes on the street, mostly smaller cottages and craftsman-style bungalows. It was quiet and secluded, and I loved it here.

I was just filling Ginger's food dish and debating what to cook for dinner when my phone pinged. Another text from my older brother, Callum.

Callum: Coming out tonight? Grabbing drinks at the Whale with some friends.

I loved Callum. He was probably my best friend. But there was no way in hell I was going out to the Whale on a Thursday night. The Tipsy Whale was a local bar where most Havenport locals hung out. Thursday nights were jam-packed, and I wanted no part of that. The last thing I needed tonight was to see a ton of people I know and be forced to make small talk over the sounds of loud pop music. No, thank you.

I decided to text him back and make sure he got the message. I sent him a photo of my middle finger next to a glass of whiskey I had just poured myself. That should do it.

My older brother, while my best friend, was also my complete opposite. He was the clean-cut corporate type who loved to socialize and have a good time. He was polite and outgoing and beloved in this town. He was a great student, athlete, and citizen. He couldn't walk down the street without multiple people saying hello. He fundraised for charity, volunteered as a coach at the high school, and was the kind of all-around good guy that everyone loved. But recently something had been going on with him. He wasn't exactly himself. I don't know if it had to do with Liam getting engaged on New Year's Eve, but I wasn't sure.

My younger brother getting engaged was wonderful. We loved Cece and she was so good for him. Seeing them together, it was so beautiful. They really understood and loved each other. And they had to get through some stuff before it worked out—but it was worth it. Seeing them together was sometimes difficult. I had recently begun to experience a weird feeling around them. I wasn't jealous, per se. It was more a longing. A longing for that love, that support—the satisfaction of knowing you'd found your person out there in the big wide world and your life was better for it. Maybe Cal had been feeling this too? I could try to talk to him, but that wasn't really our style. We were more the drink too much and work out too hard instead of dealing with our feelings type.

I had been on my own for a long time. And I liked it. I loved my home, I liked my job, and I had Ginger. My family was nearby, and I always had the wacky, loving town of Havenport if I needed them. Things were stable, they were good. I had no complaints. Given my personality and my dislike of socializing, I was likely going to die alone a grumpy, old bachelor, and I was generally fine with that.

I was pretty lucky that I didn't have to try very hard to attract women. As I've gotten older, I've found the quiet, surly type can sometimes attract ladies like moths to a flame. I've dated, had flings, and a couple of one-night stands. I've always enjoyed women, and it seems like they enjoy spending time with me. But nothing has really stuck. I haven't met anyone I could see myself settling down with. For good reason. I'm a grumpy, moody pain in the ass. I wouldn't marry me, so how could I expect some poor woman to?

This weirdness was compounded by the constant, yet loving, nagging from my mother. Now that Liam had "settled down," in her words, by popping the question, she wanted to see Cal and me "settled" too. This meant frequent and unsubtle hints about dating. In her defense, she was stuck at home with my father, so it wasn't surprising that she busied herself with trying to engineer our happily ever afters.

So what if I was thirty-five and happily single? I was employed, I owned my home, and I didn't live in her basement and play video games all day. Most mothers would think I was a prize. My mother acted like I was the sad spinster of the family. It wasn't a shock, as I was generally the black sheep of my family. My parents were loving and supportive, but I found it challenging to live up to their expectations at times.

I gazed out the window and noticed the lights on in the cottage across the street from my house. That was strange for this time of year. It was owned by Mrs. Jensen, a friend of my mom's, and she rented it out in the summer to tourists. It was usually empty in the winter. I knew because I blew the snow from the driveway for her, so she didn't have to drive up to this side of town in the snow.

January was not a popular time for tourists in Havenport. Actually that wasn't entirely correct. The annual Christmas Tree Burn always drew decent crowds, but it was nothing like the summer tourist traffic. Good for Mrs. Jensen if she was getting renters this time of year. For a flaky artist type, she had really become quite the local real estate mogul.

I decided to take Ginger out for a little stroll before hunkering down for the night. As we walked up the street,

I stared at Mrs. Jensen's cottage to see if anyone was in there. The lights were on, but there were no cars in the driveway. Strange.

We rounded the corner and I saw her. The woman from this morning. She was standing on the deck of the cottage staring out at the ocean. Her blonde hair was flying around, and she had a knit afghan wrapped around her shoulders. In the moonlight I could sort of see her face, and she looked like a gorgeous angel, but she looked unhappy. Who was this sad, beautiful woman, and what had brought her to Havenport?

3

DECLAN

It had been a great weekend. The weather had been clear, I hadn't had to work much, and Ginger had been in a great mood. We went for a run this morning and then I built some shelves in my hall closet. There was nothing I loved more than a quiet weekend at home, working out and enjoying myself. My family made fun of me and called this my fortress of solitude, but it was the truth. I spent years building my dream home on my dream property in my dream town, so why would I want to leave?

I even decided to treat myself and smoked some ribs today. I considered myself a decent cook but an excellent griller. A couple of years ago I splurged and bought my baby—a Big Green Egg. It was a giant ceramic smoker that required a lot of work but made some of the most amazing food ever. Every few weeks I'd take an afternoon, a six pack, and a good book and cook something amazing. My brothers were so jealous and were always trying to get me to smoke things for them. Liam once showed up with a ten-pound brisket and expected me to cook on demand. Needless to say he hasn't tried that again. But I do occasionally share the fruits of my labor with them. I would never say this to them, but I like cooking for people.

Callum had been making me work out with him a lot lately—he was going through something and trying to deal with it by lifting weights—so I felt like a decadent meal was in order. I prepped my ribs this morning, removing the membrane and rubbing them down with maple syrup and barbecue rub. It would take hours, but would be so worth it.

The best part of smoking meat? It forced you to sit and relax while it cooked. So I took a book, my dog, and a glass of good whiskey out to my deck to enjoy the delicious smells and the cold ocean air. It was only in the midforties. Practically summer weather.

I threw a tennis ball for Ginger. She walked toward me and then veered off in the other direction to pee on some shrubbery. I don't know why I bothered. We both knew fetch was beneath her. For all her attitude, I loved her to bits. We made a good team, and she was far smarter and better company than most people. We had a great life together.

I noticed my new neighbor walk by with headphones on. I hadn't introduced myself. I wasn't a nosy neighbor so probably wouldn't. But it didn't stop me from wondering about her. What brought her here in the middle of the winter? Was she okay? She seemed fine. Some people would feel bad for the beautiful young woman stuck in an oceanfront cottage in the middle of winter, but not me—that was basically my dream. I figured if she needed something she would say hi.

For now, I just pretended to read my book while watching her walk by. She was tall and lanky with a blonde ponytail and rosy cheeks. Even in a winter coat she was stunning. I found myself staring at her, mesmerized.

She walked with purpose, as if she was actually going somewhere important. And her face looked serious and a little bit mad, not that I was one to judge. I wondered again what brought her to Havenport.

Thirty minutes later I was checking my ribs that were close to being done and had forgotten about my mysterious neighbor when Ginger started to bark. She wasn't an excitable dog, so I immediately looked up and saw my neighbor.

Up close, she was younger and prettier than I expected. Her cheeks were flushed pink, and she wore a gray beanie over her blonde hair. Her green eyes shone in the winter sunlight. It was clear that the ocean air agreed with her.

Her face was serious, but her body language was friendly. Ginger continued to bark, banging her tail against the grass. I waved in what I hoped was a friendly way.

"Hi," she said.

"Hello."

"I just wanted to introduce myself. I've seen you out here a few times. I'm Astrid. I am staying at my aunt's cottage across the street." She gestured to Mrs. Jensen's house. Her voice was low and husky, not at all what I expected.

She offered her gloved hand and I shook it, momentarily surprised by the firmness of her handshake. "Nice to meet you. I'm Declan."

She shifted her weight back and forth, looking at her feet. "Your home is lovely."

"Thank you?" I replied. I was never much of a talker, but this pretty girl in my backyard was scrambling my brain. It was in the forties, but I instantly felt hot and off balance. There was something about this woman that got under my skin.

"Can I pet your dog? I really love dogs." She looked at Ginger who sat beside me, tail thumping.

"Sure. You can try. But she's not super friendly."

Astrid gently unlatched the gate and walked through. She sank to her knees and offered her hand to Ginger who sniffed her eagerly. She began to scratch her ears, and Ginger nuzzled her hand. Huh. That's weird. Ginger hated most people and was especially wary of women.

Astrid stayed on the ground petting her and talking to her. "You are such a good girl. Look at you, so regal like a queen. What a good girl you are!"

She looked up at me. "What's her name?"

"Ginger," I replied, slightly dumbstruck.

"Aww, Ginger, you are a gorgeous girl. And so friendly! What a good girl you are."

I was officially lightheaded. This was not where I expected this day to go. I stood, dumbfounded, watching this lovely stranger with the moss-green eyes play with my dog, who liked people even less than I did.

After two minutes or two hours—I was not in a place to quantify time—Astrid stood up and brushed herself off. "Thanks," she said. "I really needed that."

I smiled in what I hoped was not a goofy way. I wasn't a smiler, I was more of a brooder. Generally this worked well with the ladies, but with Astrid, I couldn't seem to wipe the goofy grin off my face. *Speak, dumbass. Say words to the pretty lady. You are being a weirdo.* Unfortunately, no words came.

She clearly sensed my awkwardness. "What are you cooking? It smells incredible."

"I'm smoking," I answered. "Smoking some meat." Clearly I had lost my grasp on the English language.

"What are you smoking?"

This I could talk about. "I'm smoking a rack of ribs, actually."

"Wow. That sounds amazing. I could smell them across the street. I don't know the last time I ate ribs."

Don't do it. Don't do it. Don't even think about it. "Do you want some? I have plenty to share."

She seemed embarrassed. "No. I couldn't impose. Sorry I even said that. I don't have a car, and there is no grocery delivery in Havenport, so it's been a while since I had a home-cooked meal, that's all. So sorry to be so forward."

She was giving me an out, and I should take it. "Not at all. I'd be happy to share. I've been cooking these for a few hours, so it would be nice if someone else appreciated my work." *Dumbass.*

"If you're sure…"

It was as if my mouth was operating independently of my brain. "Yes. Of course! We're neighbors. These need to come off in about thirty minutes and then need to rest. Want to come back in an hour?"

She nodded and smiled. Her smile was big, slightly crooked, and really beautiful. I got the sense she wasn't a natural smiler, so it made me feel pretty good. I still didn't know what I was doing, inviting this random stranger into my home. I didn't invite people into my home ever. My family just showed up some times and barged in, but I wasn't exactly the dinner party type. But I couldn't say no to her, and she seemed lonely and it was always nice to have someone to cook for.

"I would offer to bring something over, but all I have is booze. A lot of booze actually. I'll bring you something nice. What are you drinking?"

"You don't have to do that. I'm fine. I have plenty here."

"No, I insist." She reached over and grabbed the glass out of my hand. As if living in slow motion, she brought the glass to her lush pink lips and took a long sip. "Ooh.

Irish whiskey. I like." She took another sip and handed the glass back to me. She tapped her nose. "I have something you will love." And she turned on her heel and walked back to her cottage.

I stood there, dumbfounded, watching her hips sway as she walked up the driveway into the house. Ginger stood beside me, watching her go inside. She cocked her head and gave me a hopeful look.

"I have no idea what just happened, girl. But I think we are going to have a dinner guest."

4

ASTRID

So I just forced my way into dinner with my hot neighbor. How did that happen?

My natural inclination to be blunt sometimes led me into weird social situations. It did not, however, result in lots of dinner invites. So this was a first.

I would be lying if I said I hadn't been watching him for the past week. I had noticed him jogging and almost tripped over my own feet. Up close he was even hotter. The long hair, the full beard, the height. Being five feet ten, I was used to looking most men directly in the eye, but he was so tall and broad that I felt tiny. I was intrigued by his scruffy, Jason Momoa vibe.

When I saw him playing fetch with his dog in the yard this morning, I was even more intrigued. For a big, strong, serious looking guy, he was so adorable rolling on the ground and playing. It also helped that I had a perfect line of sight to enjoy his very round, very firm ass in a pair of gray sweatpants.

I had always wanted a dog growing up. My mother despised pets and forbid me from even considering it. My half siblings had an old golden retriever, and my dad sometimes showed me photos of him. I always swore the minute I was an adult with my own house I would get myself a dog. Unfortunately I was never home enough to take care of one. The minute I got out of law school and started practicing, it became clear that I would be a terrible dog mom. I was never home, and when I was I was either working or asleep. I couldn't keep groceries in the house, never mind a living thing. So sadly, my dog dreams never materialized. But watching him cavort around with his dog was reigniting them.

I was doing nothing right now. Maybe I could get a dog? That would be fun. I could train it and take it on walks. I wondered if there were any shelters in Havenport.

But then reality set in. Even though I was bored at the moment, eventually I would be going back. Back to the city, the office, the pressure, the all-nighters, and the endless travel. This was just temporary while I worked out how to get back what I deserved. Because I couldn't lose sight of my goal. After a little pit stop in Havenport, I was going to get my career back.

Suddenly, I was filled with panic. What had I done? Did I just invite myself over to a random man's house? What if he was a serial killer who wanted to wear my skin as a suit?

Shit. Shit. Huh. One of the benefits of a small town is that everyone knows everyone else. I grabbed my phone and called Emily.

"Hey, lady, what's up?" I heard screaming in the background. Emily was the mother of three kids under six, and every time I spoke to her there was some degree of chaos in the background.

"Sorry if it's dinnertime. I didn't mean to bother you."

"No, no. I'm thrilled to speak to an adult today. Derek is traveling." Emily married Derek, her college sweetheart, and moved back to Havenport. Derek was an architect and a proud Texan. He had embraced her hometown wholeheartedly, but still insisted on wearing his cowboy hat and boots everywhere. He occasionally traveled for work, and I know it was hard on Emily.

"Hey, why don't I come over tomorrow and hang with the kids for a bit?"

"Seriously?"

"They are adorable. Maybe you could run some errands or something."

I could hear Emily exhale on the other end of the phone. "You don't know what you're agreeing to but yes, please yes. I am going to take a shower and then go get a fancy coffee at High Tide. Thank you, Astrid." The enthusiasm in her voice made it worth it. I loved kids, and Emily's, while insane, were super cute. I could handle them for a few hours.

"So did you just call to rescue your crazy cousin, or is there something on your mind?" Emily knew me too well. I was never the kind of person who called just to chat.

"Do you know the guy who lives in the house across the street from my cottage?"

"Declan Quinn?"

"Yes."

"I've known him since childhood. What about him?"

"I met him today."

"Hold on one second." I heard her shouting in the background and then a large crashing noise.

"I'm back."

I didn't dare ask what the crashing noise was. "And he sort of invited me over for dinner. I accepted and then realized I didn't know him, and it's probably not smart to go to a stranger's house for dinner when I'm new in town." I was rambling.

"Time out. He invited you? Into his house?" Emily sounded shocked. Ugh, maybe he was a serial killer.

"Yes."

"I am not sure he has even invited his own mother over for dinner. Very few people have been invited inside the fortress of solitude. I have to text Cece. She will be so shocked."

"Wait, can you back up a minute? I called because I want to make sure it is safe for me to go over there."

"Yes. Totally safe." She laughed loudly.

"I'm not following."

"He may be a broody jerk sometimes, but he is harmless and kind. His family is lovely and everyone knows him."

"Okay…"

"But your vagina may not be safe." It sounded like she was smiling on the other end of the phone.

"I don't know what you are talking about." I feigned ignorance but I knew what she was getting at. Emily was very blunt and tended to have no qualms about discussing personal stuff. The last thing I needed was her talking about my vagina.

"I assume if you spoke to him you also saw him? His face? His body?"

I didn't say anything, too afraid she could read my voice over the phone.

"Let's just say very few women are immune to that broody lumberjack charm." She was right, of course. He was impossible not to notice. I had been drooling over him since I saw him running the other day. I never should have walked over and introduced myself. Up close he was so much hotter.

"No, no. It's not like that," I protested. "I was walking and we got to chatting and I mentioned that what he was cooking smelled good so he invited me to dinner."

"That doesn't sound like Declan. Are you sure it wasn't one of his brothers? They are both personable and polite."

"No, it's him. I've... noticed him a few times since I've been here."

"Oh really!"

"Not like that."

She snorted. "Of course it's like that. Let's not lie to each other, Astrid. So what are you wearing?"

"I don't know? Is it formal?"

"I should think not. But then again, I have never been invited to his house. And you and I have very different definitions of formal." That was an understatement. Emily, while beautiful and whimsical, had a very distinct "overwhelmed mom" style these days.

I laughed. "I don't have much. Just some leggings and my suits."

"Why did you pack your suits?"

"I didn't pack all of my suits. Just a few in case."

"In case there was a random legal emergency?"

"Exactly."

"I'll take you shopping this week. But for now, just wear something comfy. Don't dress up. He would probably think that was weird."

"I should go. Now I'm stressing about my outfit and I need to find something."

"Fine. But you need to call me tonight! I need to hear about this. I can't believe you're going to have dinner at Declan Quinn's house. My high school self is freaking out."

"Shut up. You are happily married."

"Yes, but my sweet husband is in California right now, and the time zone makes FaceTime sex a bummer. Call me tonight and give me the deets."

Oh Jesus, that was way more than I needed to know about Emily and Derek.

"I want to know everything. You and Declan... I would have never guessed that one. But, I suppose it actually makes sense, since you probably hate people more than he does."

I was desperate to get Emily off the phone. This was turning into a way bigger deal than I initially thought. "Then, it should be an interesting night."

5

DECLAN

WHAT DID I DO? WHY ON EARTH DID I INVITE A strange woman into my house? I never invited people to my house. My parents and brothers just sort of showed up sometimes, but certainly not because I wanted them there. This was my sanctuary, my place where I could just be me. I never invited people here if I could help it, especially women.

I ran around furiously picking up and trying to make everything look presentable. My time in the navy had turned me into a little bit of a neat freak so I tended to get anxious if things were out of place. I carefully folded the knit afghan my grandmother had made for me over the couch and fluffed the throw pillows. Everything in my home was carefully and deliberately chosen. Unlike most guys, I wanted to live in a real home, not some glorified frat house with a big-screen TV and no couch. My house wasn't fancy, but I took a lot of pride in it.

It had taken years to build this place. After I bought the land, it took a while to save enough to start building. I did some work myself and just waited until I could get things exactly right. I painted and sanded and built some basic furniture and waited while my dream slowly came together over the years. This house was a labor of love. And it was my special place. Ginger was the only woman in this house. My mom dropped by occasionally, usually with baked goods, and sometimes Cece, my future sister-in-law, stopped by when Liam was working late. She was cool and didn't force me to talk too much, so I didn't mind.

Why couldn't I have offered her some to take home? Why did I invite her to eat dinner with me? What was it about this girl that made me act so strangely? Also, eating ribs was the last thing I wanted to do with a pretty girl. They were messy and required the use of your hands. I was going to feel embarrassed the whole time.

But there was something about her. On the surface she looked like a supermodel and carried herself like a CEO. But once she started talking, she seemed lonely and kind of bored. I was intrigued, which doesn't happen often.

I could lie to myself and say I was just being neighborly. But, I had lived here for six years and never entertained my other neighbors, the Shulmans. They were a nice retired couple that spent the winters in Florida and hosted big parties in the summer for their grandkids. I liked them well enough, but we certainly didn't hang out. And let's face it, I wasn't exactly the neighborly type.

The good news was that it was just one dinner. And it wasn't like anyone was going to find out. If my mother got wind of this she would be thrilled. Then, once she took a look at Astrid and confirmed she was a woman under the age of eighty, she would be trying to schedule a wedding. The good thing about living up here on the bluff was that no one knew my business, and I liked it that way.

———

"So I brought you something." Astrid thrust a very fancy bottle of scotch into my hands and immediately bent down to greet Ginger.

I took a step back to hang up her coat and got a whiff of something feminine and spicy and a bit bold.

Desperate for something to do to keep me from sniffing her again, I stared at the bottle. "Wow. Lagavulin 16. This is really good stuff. Thank you."

"You're welcome." She slipped off her boots and walked breezily into the living room. "I debated what to bring you. I have a bunch of nice stuff. Including a small batch rum that was flown in from Haiti on a private jet. But I pegged you for a scotch guy." She turned around and smiled at me, and I noticed a dimple in her left cheek.

"Yes. It's great."

"I have lots of fancy booze. Every time we closed a deal or fixed a regulatory filing for a client, they always sent expensive liquor. I never had any time to drink it."

She walked around my house looking at the photos of me and my family that hung on the wall across from the fireplace. "And so, when I was packing to come here, I threw a bunch of it in a duffel bag."

I had no idea what to say to this blunt, random, and beautiful woman who was currently performing an FDA-grade inspection on my living room and apparently traveled with duffel bags full of booze. "Thanks. Would you like some?"

"Sure." She kept walking around. "So you live here alone?"

I watched her as I grabbed a pair of glasses from the cabinet. She walked with such purpose, I half expected her to pull a white glove out of her pocket and start swiping all the surfaces. "Yes. Just me and Ginger."

"Wow. Then I'm impressed."

I poured the scotch and shrugged. I don't know what was so impressive to her.

"This is not a bachelor pad. This is a real home. Did you hire an interior designer? It definitely screams manly, but it's homey too. You have throw pillows! And framed photos."

"It's not that big of a deal. I spent a long time building this place and getting everything the way I wanted it. I did it all myself. But those frames... my mom bought those. But I did hang them."

"It's like a magazine spread in here. I don't read magazines, so I don't know which one. But one of the fancy home decor ones, definitely." She shrugged and continued to stare at the photos.

I walked back toward her with our drinks.

I gestured to the couch. "Have a seat."

She stopped her inspection long enough to sit on the deep leather couch and crossed her long legs. Her white-blonde hair glowed in the firelight. Ginger approached and sat in front of her, gently nudging her hand. Astrid responded by scratching Ginger's ears and nuzzling her neck.

I couldn't help feeling a bit betrayed. It had taken months to get Ginger to even tolerate me. And after years together, I was the only person she really liked. Seeing her open up to this complete stranger was jarring. But also cute. I wanted to be annoyed, but they were pretty adorable together.

I handed her a tumbler and sat down on the opposite side of the couch. She held up her glass.

"To neighbors who invite themselves over," I said teasingly.

She glared at me, and I thought I felt my balls shrivel slightly. "To neighbors with extra meat." I choked back a laugh, but she kept a straight face. We clinked and took a sip. Damn, this was good. We sat silently for a few minutes, watching the fire and enjoying our drinks. It felt nice. I couldn't remember the last time I had sat quietly and contentedly with a woman. Most women I dated felt the need to chatter and fill every silence. Astrid was confident and seemed to value the quiet just as much as I did.

I studied her profile as she gazed into the fireplace. She had a cute upturned nose and long, dark eyelashes. Her hair hung like a shiny curtain to her collarbones, highlighting a long, graceful neck. She was wearing a sweatshirt, but one of those fancy, expensive sweatshirts that hung off one shoulder exposing a tantalizing triangle of flesh and what looked to be a pink bra strap.

I tried to keep myself from staring, focusing instead on Ginger, who got bored of all the human attention and walked back over to her dog bed. Thanks, Ginger.

As much as I loved the silence, I needed to know more about her. I wanted to know everything about her. That thought scared me so I started to babble. "So you are Connie Jensen's niece?"

She nodded.

"What brings you to Havenport?"

She shifted away from me and suddenly looked uncomfortable. I instantly felt guilty for asking.

"It's hard to explain." She twisted her hair around her fingers, and I saw her poker face begin to crack. "I am taking a little break from work and didn't want to stay in my apartment in the city, so Connie, my aunt, offered me this rental property for a while." I got the sense that was not the whole story, but I was not one to push.

I took a sip of whiskey and chose my words carefully. "Welcome. It's much nicer in the summer, but January is a quiet month here."

"That's what I'm looking for," she said eagerly, "some

peace and quiet." She stared at the fire as if she wished she were a thousand miles away from here.

"I'll drink to that."

———

"Oh my God, this is so good." She groaned, licking the barbecue sauce from her fingertips.

I smiled and tried to stay focused on my food and not the sex moans coming out of her mouth. I thought the moans were bad, but watching her lick her fingers had me shifting uncomfortably in my seat, grateful I had worn jeans and not sweatpants.

"I can't believe you made this."

"It's not that hard," I replied.

"Um, don't sell yourself short, dude. This is incredible. This is easily the best thing I've put in my mouth in years."

She was not making this easy.

"And this jalapeño cornbread? You baked this?"

"Yup. My mom's recipe. It's super easy."

"A man who cooks. Goddamn, you are a catch." Her smile was so big and genuine, so different than the cold, formal woman who had shown up an hour earlier. Perhaps it was the second glass of scotch or the barbecue, but she was warming up and I liked it.

I could feel my face heat. Thankfully my beard concealed my blush. As the night went on, I found myself getting more and more comfortable with Astrid. She was serious and intense but had a silly streak. And watching her eat was amazing. I had been on dates with so many women who refused to eat or acted like they were afraid of food. Why did women think men were into that? I hadn't realized how much I liked a girl with an appetite until I saw Astrid destroy a rack of ribs and then lick her fingers.

"Where did you learn to cook? Did you take classes?

Where? I can't even microwave popcorn." She grabbed her smartphone and started scrolling. "Is there a cooking school nearby?"

I stared at her, completely intrigued and yet confused by this woman. "Not that I know of. I learned mainly from my mom and then by watching YouTube videos."

"Huh." She seemed impressed.

"I was in the navy for eight years. A lot of those years were spent at sea where the food options were terrible. When I got out, I vowed to learn to cook really well so I would never have to eat rubbery chicken or boxed macaroni and cheese again."

"You were in the navy?" She tapped her chin, as if assessing me. I sat up a little straighter. "I can see that. You have excellent posture, and your house is really neat. Did you enjoy serving?"

"I did. When I enlisted I was an eighteen-year-old dumbass, and when I got out I was a twenty-six-year-old man. It wasn't easy, but I am grateful for that time and the opportunity to serve my country."

She grasped my hand across the table. "Thank you for your service. I admire the commitment you made."

She was so earnest it made me smile. My skin burned where her graceful hand covered my large, callused one. "Thanks. Both my dad and grandfather served in the navy, so it's kind of a family tradition."

She took a sip of scotch and leaned forward on her elbows, causing that fancy sweatshirt to slide even farther off her shoulder. "So you are a military man, an excellent cook, and what else? Tell me more about you, Declan."

"There is not much to tell. You know Ginger. I have lived in Havenport most of my life. After the navy, I joined my family's fishing business. I am a fourth generation fisherman. Our company, Quinn Fisheries, is headquartered here in Havenport."

"That's so interesting. So you work with your family?"

"Not really. Both of my brothers are in different lines of work. I worked with my dad for years, but he technically retired two years ago. He is still the CEO and works there, just not as much as he used to. I am currently COO, but I run the day-to-day operations."

"So you are not a fisherman?"

"I am, but I'm not. I am frustrated by my role because I like being out on the water, and I like my crews. I hate paperwork and useless meetings and holding clients' hands." What I didn't say was that I hated dealing with people. The ocean, while dangerous, unpredictable, and sometimes downright hostile, was much easier for me to manage.

"And I love working with my dad, but we have different ideas about the future of the business." I didn't want to get into it with this gorgeous stranger, but I was growing more and more frustrated at work. Every year things got harder, and we needed to do more to adapt and evolve as a business. My father, of course, thought this was crazy and we should just stay the course he had set twenty years ago.

She nodded and remarked, "So you're really an executive?"

She had hit the nail on the head. "Yes. It's what I do. But it's not who I am. I am a fisherman. Being out on the water, celebrating the beauty of nature—that's what I truly love." I paused, I hated talking about myself. "You haven't told me anything about yourself."

She leaned back, her body language changing. "There isn't much to tell. I was...I am a lawyer."

"Wow." I could tell she was educated and refined, but I hadn't guessed lawyer, especially for someone so young.

"I'm an associate at Burns & Glenn. It's a massive global law firm." She paused. "I was, I guess." She looked down at her plate. "I do mergers and acquisitions mainly, and some general corporate work, debt and securities, that type of thing."

I had no idea what she was talking about, but I was certainly impressed.

"I live in Boston. I was raised in the area and that's about it." She dropped her hands into her lap. Clearly she didn't like to talk about herself either.

"I don't believe you. What do you do for fun?" I asked, trying to tease a smile out of her.

She laughed out loud. Not a dainty cute laugh but a big honking laugh. I had no idea what was so funny. "Not much. Unfortunately my career doesn't allow much time for fun." She said this matter-of-factly, like it was no big deal. "I like to plan vacations."

"That's cool."

"I don't actually take them. I just plan them. Every time I try to go on vacation I end up having to cancel because of work. But I really enjoy the planning—reading reviews, looking at photos online, scoping out activities and restaurants. That kind of thing."

I nodded, not really sure what to say to that. "What is your dream destination?"

She sighed and played with her fork. "Iceland. A few years ago, a group of associates I was friendly with were planning this big trip to Iceland after a case we worked on wrapped up. We all booked our tickets, and I read every possible book and website about Iceland. I was fascinated. I wanted to hike a glacier, see the Northern Lights, and swim in the geothermal springs. I planned the shit out of that trip."

"What happened?"

Her face fell. "I ended up getting staffed on an emergency bankruptcy filing and had to cancel. The others went and had a blast."

"You will get there someday."

"I hope so. Because I already know everything I want to do there."

She must really love her work. I wondered what had happened, why she was here and not kicking ass in a boardroom somewhere. She seemed sad, and not just about the cancelled trip to Iceland. I tried to lighten the mood. "So you are a corporate lawyer who lives in Boston and can't cook."

"Yup. And trust me, I really can't cook. That's why I am so grateful for your hospitality."

I smiled at her, and then a crashing sound distracted me. Ginger had flipped over her food bowl. There was kibble all over the floor.

"Ginger," I shouted. But my darling dog sat, with her perfect poodle posture, and stared at me.

"What's wrong?" Astrid asked, curiously staring at Ginger.

"Ignore her," I said. "She's just mad because I didn't give her any barbecue."

Astrid snorted. It was cute. "So she knocked over her own food. Nice job, girl."

I rolled my eyes. "Don't encourage her. She's already super spoiled. She would totally eat at the table with a knife and fork if I let her."

But Astrid was ignoring me, already picking some meat off her plate to offer to Ginger, who slowly strolled over and gently took it from her hand.

When she finished, she sat at attention, staring at me for more. Ginger never begged—we both knew it was beneath her. Instead she would sit and stare at me until I gave her what she wanted.

"In her defense," Astrid said, laughing wildly, "it is really good barbecue."

"Fine." I sighed. I started cutting some meat off the ribs to give to Ginger.

Astrid beamed at me, delighted that I was kowtowing to Ginger's demands. "You are a really good dog dad."

I looked up and found myself staring into her gorgeous green eyes. "What can I say? I love strong women."

———

Astrid insisted on clearing the table and doing the dishes while I vacuumed up the spilled dog food. "I can't cook for shit, but I am a halfway decent cleaner," she told me, while scrubbing the cornbread pan.

I believed her. She approached every task carefully and thoughtfully. She considered where each dish should go in the dishwasher to maximize space and easily fit everything in. Was it weird that I was attracted to her superior spatial awareness?

"Can I walk you home?" I asked hopefully.

She pinned me with one of her serious looks. "Across the street? That hardly seems necessary."

I shoved my hands in my pockets. "It's late and it's cold. And my mother raised me right."

She carefully folded the dish towel and placed it on the countertop, taking her time and avoiding my question. "Fine. You can walk me home. But only if Ginger comes too."

Ginger perked right up and trotted over to the door, excited for a late night walk.

It took all of two minutes to reach her front door. She carefully unlocked the door to the small cottage and turned around. "Thank you for dinner. It was delicious."

"You're welcome."

"And the company wasn't half bad either." She smirked.

Kiss her. Kiss her. Grab her and kiss her. My brain was spinning as we stood on the tiny porch. I needed a game plan, and I had nothing. Was this a date? Was she interested? Before I could get my head out of my ass, she gave me a quick peck on the cheek and walked through the open door.

Ginger gave me a look. "I know, girl," I said, walking back toward my house. "I like her too."

6

ASTRID

I LOVED DOWNTOWN HAVENPORT. ALONG THE cobblestone sidewalks, historic buildings were sandwiched between farm-to-table restaurants and kitschy shops. There were people everywhere, even on a Tuesday afternoon. And delicious smells wafted through the air. I wanted to browse all the shops and soak up the lively town vibe. However, I was on a mission. I had to get some normal clothes. Emily had dropped me off while she ran errands, and I had to finish up quickly so she could pick Jacob up at preschool. So I had to stay focused.

I was going to enjoy this time off. I was going to embrace Havenport and all it had to offer, especially if that involved my sexy neighbor.

Jeanius Bar was a large storefront in an old brick building. I opened the doors and was assaulted by more jeans than I had ever seen in my life. The store was huge, with airy cathedral ceilings and large chandeliers hanging over an industrial space. There were colorful couches and tables piled high with denim.

I considered turning around and going home to order stuff online. This was so not my scene. I was not a shopper. I had no time to just browse around and try things on. Twice a year, I met Lara, my personal shopper, at Neiman Marcus, and she pulled a few things for me. I spent twenty minutes trying them on, chose a few things, and she charged my credit card while I was getting dressed. So I had a well-planned wardrobe consisting mainly of black and gray with carefully selected accessories. Every morning I just got up and put on a dark suit or a shift dress. It saved a lot of time and energy and suited my lifestyle just fine.

Before I could escape, a loud, curvy woman appeared from behind a display of sweaters.

"Hello."

"Hi." I tried to give her a smile, but it probably looked like I was having a stroke. Years spent behind a laptop and in meeting rooms had not done much for my social skills.

"You must be Emily's cousin! I'm so happy to meet you."

I gave her a strange look.

She waved a jeweled smart phone at me. "She texted me you were coming in and I had to help you and do it quickly. I'm Nora."

God, information traveled quickly in this town. "I'm Astrid." I stuck out my hand and gave her a firm shake. She smiled at me, clearly thinking I was mentally ill. She was pretty and vivacious. She had a short, curvy body that was highlighted to perfection by a pair of dark wash, high-rise jeans and a pink wrap sweater that looked soft to the touch. She had long dark hair and wore bright red lipstick, the kind of shade I was way too chicken to ever try.

"First of all, wow, you are gorgeous. I am going to have so much fun dressing you."

I smiled weakly. What was I supposed to say to that?

"And second, what are you looking for?"

I laughed. I had no idea what I was looking for. A new

life? A way to get my old life back? A time machine so I could go back and become a dentist instead of a lawyer?

She gave me a kind smile. Maybe Emily had warned her that I was an awkward mess. "Do you want some coffee? I really need caffeine right now."

"Yes." This woman was speaking my language.

"Follow me."

I watched as Nora led me to a lounge area in the back near the fitting rooms. There was an oak-topped bar with a huge copper espresso machine, likely handmade in Italy. Someone who consumed as much caffeine as I did could spot a fine piece of machinery at a distance. "Is that a La Marzocco?" I was amazed. It was a thing of beauty.

"Yes. Good eye. My family owns a bunch of Italian restaurants. I got it through one of their equipment reps. I drink a lot of coffee, plus I think it adds something to the space."

"It certainly does." I was liking Nora more and more.

"What can I make you?"

"Cappuccino."

"Does almond milk work?"

"Totally."

Nora got to work, and I was mesmerized by the sounds and smells. "So what brings you to Havenport?" she asked innocently.

"I lost my job as a corporate lawyer. I'm really not happy about it. And I needed to get away from the city and my office. Anyway, I'm staying at my aunt's cottage, and it came to my attention that all I own are suits and workout clothes." I had no idea how to answer her question, and I was so disarmed by her charm and her five-figure coffee apparatus that I just verbally vomited all over her. I needed to get it together. Wentworths never got emotional, especially in front of strangers.

She nodded at me, and I could tell she had a lot of questions.

"And so I came here because I need some new clothes. I need a change. Something different. I want jeans, and cute tops, and regular person clothes, not high-achieving lawyer clothes."

Nora grinned. She was clearly a very kind and patient person because I was rambling like the village idiot.

"You came to the right place, girl. I will hook you up."

Five minutes later I was standing in a hot pink dressing room, stripped down to my sports bra and undies while Nora piled stacks of clothes on an upholstered bench for me to try on.

"So tell me, what happened with your job?"

I felt oddly comfortable with Nora. Her boisterous personality was disarming, and it had been so long since I had talked to another woman my age besides Emily. "It's a long story. But basically I got fired. I was unfairly blamed for a mistake I didn't make. A partner had been… inappropriate with me for a while and I rejected his advances. He then blamed me for this mistake and here I am." I shrugged, not wanting to get further into this.

"That is both illegal and immoral. Who is the asshole and where can I find him?"

As a woman with a deep well of rage, I admired that quality in others. "Yes. Exactly! You get it," I said.

"So you're a smart, ass-kicking lawyer. Why don't you sue those jerks and own that law firm?" I had certainly thought about it. Many times. But I didn't have enough evidence to make my case. When I was fired I had to hand over my company phone and laptop. Without those, I had no evidence other than my word. No one knew about what had happened with Max, and when I hinted to our practice development manager about it after the fact, she said that I should just put my head down and keep working. She said making a big deal about it would hurt my career more than it would hurt his.

In retrospect I should have kept records, noted all the details. But I never thought in a million years this would happen. I was great at my job. I just assumed things would go back to normal and he would get over it. Apparently, that narcissistic bastard was more evil than I thought.

"It's a little more complicated than that. But I'm currently weighing my options." That was a bit of a lie. Mainly, I was just sulking and flying into fits of rage at the moment, but I fully intended to do a thorough legal analysis to determine the feasibility of any type of suit I could bring against them. But mostly I was just waiting, hoping that they would realize it wasn't my fault and let me come back and reclaim what I had worked so hard to build. It was naïve but it was all I could manage right now.

"You look amazing," she exclaimed. I examined myself in the three-way mirror. Never in a thousand years would I ever think to wear bright red jeans, but she was not wrong. These were killer.

"I love the color red," I told her, smoothing the waistband over my hips. "But I don't actually own any red clothes."

"Oh, we are fixing that right now. You look amazing. Your legs! They go on forever."

I couldn't believe my eyes. I looked cool and young. When I looked in the mirror, I finally saw a thirty-two-year-old woman looking back at me. Not an exhausted husk of a person wearing a black suit and carrying oversized eye bags.

Nora made me pair the jeans with a slouchy cropped black-and-white striped sweater. It was soft and fuzzy and showed off the high waist of the jeans.

"Can I take a photo of you? I am doing a new marketing initiative where I try to show the clothes on real bodies. I mostly take photos of myself and my bestie, Cece, but you look so hot right now I feel like, as a business owner, I need to document this."

"Sure," I said, feeling self-conscious. I was not comfortable having my photo taken. I didn't go to parties or on vacation, so I didn't have many occasions for photo taking. I wasn't exactly snapping selfies while drinking lukewarm coffee in my office at eleven p.m.

She took a few photos of me and showed me. "Do you mind if I post this one on the Jeanius Bar Instagram page?" I shook my head.

"Do you have a photo release?" I asked. Her head snapped up from her phone. Shit. I had inadvertently snapped at her in my lawyer voice.

"No. Why?" she asked, looking nervous.

Smile, Astrid. Don't scare away your new friend.

I smiled. "No big deal. As an attorney, I would recommend you have a document that people can sign which releases you from liability for using their photos. That way you can use customers on your social media and there is no legal risk."

She exhaled. "Thanks. I didn't think of that. I just started doing this."

"No, I get it. I wasn't trying to intimidate you, and it is actually really easy. There are standard forms online, or I could just write one for you."

"No. I can't ask you to do that."

"It would be my pleasure. It will probably take me twenty minutes. Give me your card. I'll email you something tonight."

"That is so kind of you. Thank you so much."

"It's the least I can do. You are the only person on earth who could talk me into red denim."

"Talking people into doing things they don't want to do is actually one of my superpowers."

"I believe that."

"You should."

After ringing me up and giving me a significant discount, I headed toward the door to wait for Emily to pick me up.

"Hey, Astrid," Nora called as I was leaving. "I do this great Krav Maga class down the street. You should come. You seem like the type of chick who would enjoy it."

"What's Krav Maga?"

"It's Israeli self-defense. It's basically a workout class that combines martial arts, boxing, wrestling, and conditioning. It's pretty intense, but you get to punch stuff."

I smiled. This girl clearly got me. "I'm in. I could use a good workout, and I'm not doing much."

Nora jumped up and down and clapped. "Yes! Emily won't take the class with me because it's 'too violent.'" She affected Emily's airy voice, and I laughed out loud.

"I can see that," I said. "But if Emily thinks it's too violent then it's probably just violent enough for me."

"I knew I liked you."

I ended up leaving Nora's store with bags of new clothes and a new friend. She had given me her cell phone number, promised to text me about class, and invited me to her "coven," whatever that meant. It had been a long time since I made a friend. Nora was cool and loyal and had just sold me a brand-new wardrobe at a steep discount. Not too shabby for a Tuesday.

7

DECLAN

"What are you doing here, Captain?" I had a busy day and the last thing I needed was my dad asking me thousands of questions and passive-aggressively questioning my leadership choices.

"Can't a man come and check in on his business? I walked through this door every day for forty-six years, son. I can't just stop." He took off his coat and draped it over my chair. My dad was a big, burly man with a thunderous voice and a larger-than-life persona. He had worked on the water his entire life, since childhood, and I knew he was having trouble letting go.

"But you are supposed to be stopping, Dad. Remember? Scaling back, retirement, handing over the reins?" We had been having this same conversation for years. The man did not know how to be retired.

"I will get there, Dec, I will. But right now I wanted to come in, take a look at the numbers, and check in with Vince."

"Callum reviews all the numbers and keeps on top of everything. Are you concerned he's not qualified?"

"Of course not." He would never speak ill of Callum

or second-guess his business acumen. He saved that for me.

We walked through the processing area to where trucks were being loaded. Several guys stopped working to say hello to my dad, who, in typical fashion, had to check in with everyone.

I wasn't the leader he was. I never would be. We were too different. I was good at what I did and I knew what I didn't know. But Captain Quinn was a giant in this business.

He knew everything about everyone and went out of his way to help all the time, sometimes to the detriment of our business. When I took over there were tons of past-due invoices and old contracts that needed updating.

He was a great guy and a wonderful leader but not so much for details. Which is where I came in. When I joined the business after the navy, it became clear my father needed someone to keep track of the thousands of details that sprang up every year—applying for permits, attending industry groups to keep up with regulatory changes, upgrading our equipment, negotiating with suppliers and customers. An operation of this size was all about the details. And although my personality was not that great, I managed details precisely and efficiently.

Which is why it was still killing me that he wouldn't retire and promote me to CEO. I realized it was a title. And I was currently acting as CEO and everything was fine. Why did I need this? Why did I put so much stock in something so silly? For all intents and purposes, I ran this business. I reported to no one and was responsible for its successes and failures.

But there was a part of me—a part I didn't like to acknowledge—that needed his approval. That needed his faith in me. That needed him to acknowledge that, despite our differences, I would continue to build our family's legacy into the next generation. That was something I craved. I couldn't admit it out loud. I could barely formulate it in my own brain, but it was what I needed most.

I thought of Astrid. Her take-no-shit attitude and her intense focus. What would she do here? She didn't seem like the type of person to let anything get in her way.

I decided to get direct. "Dad, I think it's time to talk about a succession plan."

He sat back in his chair. "What do you mean?"

"Let's go to my office and chat."

We sat on the large leather couch. The main office upstairs had a small balcony that looked out at the shipyard and the harbor. You could watch the fleet come in and out every day. I loved my office. I kept an eye on everything and still had peace and quiet.

"Got any scotch, Dec?" My dad had a few loves in this life—my mother, the ocean, and single malt scotch.

I shook my head at him. "No, Dad. Mom said no booze."

He rolled his eyes. "Declan, son, I love her to pieces but your mother is killing me. Do you know she made me go vegan?"

I laughed. "Vegan? She mentioned she was making you eat plant based, but that seems pretty extreme." I knew how painful this probably was for my dad, but he loved my mom so much he would eat cardboard if she made it for him.

"Now when I agreed to it I didn't really know what that meant. But apparently it means no meat. And no cheese and no eggs. Nothing tasty, Declan. Just nuts and seeds. Nuts and fucking seeds."

I tried to suppress a laugh. I can totally see my mother browbeating my dad into going vegan. "But Dad, the doctors say you are doing great."

"I am doing great. But a man needs a finger or two of scotch once in a while."

"Fine. Give me a minute."

One of the benefits of being adjacent to the restaurant industry was the perks. I happened to have quite a nice bottle of scotch, not nearly as nice as the stuff Astrid brought me, but nice nonetheless, in my office.

Screw it. I guess I was drinking on a Tuesday afternoon. I handed him a glass and poured one for myself.

"Did I ever tell you the story about when I bought this land?" He was trying to stall. I had heard the story hundreds of times. My dad, fresh out of the navy, was working on his father's fishing boat and trying to figure out how to impress my mother, who had turned down his proposal after a few dates.

Thirty minutes and two fingers of scotch later, the Captain had recounted the Quinn family's long and storied history for the five millionth time. I could recite the entire tale from memory and was getting annoyed with his continuing attempts to stall what was a necessary conversation.

"Dad, I think we need to talk about retirement."

My family had been here for four generations, and despite all the places I'd traveled in the navy, it was the only place that truly felt like home. My family had been fishing the waters of Havenport, Massachusetts since my great-great-grandparents immigrated to Massachusetts from Ireland during the potato famine. My father followed in the family footsteps. Over time the operation grew significantly to include a sizable fleet and several waterfront properties. My parents instilled the value of hard work and family and never, as far as I could remember, took a day off. My mom worked just as hard as my dad, raising us, pitching in with the businesses, sweet-talking the zoning board when necessary, and keeping everyone in line. I came back here because I wanted to contribute to the community which had meant so much to me and multiple generations of my family. But I wasn't my father. I had to do things my own way.

"You have been incredibly successful, Dad. And I respect the hell out of what you have built. But we need to evolve. We need to adapt."

"We have a good business here, Declan." His tone was defensive.

"It's not like it used to be. The ocean is not filled with fish. We have to pivot and focus on sustainability. Both for our business and for the oceans. I think we need to increase the variety of our catch and start chasing the sustainability market."

"Not this again." My dad had been very successful. But he failed to recognize that continued success meant evolving our business.

"Back in Grandpa's day the fish jumped into the nets, but it's different now. Climate change, overfishing, everything is evolving day by day. We can't keep running this business like it's 1985 anymore." I wanted to preserve our family legacy, but preservation meant evolution. I decided to pull off the Band-Aid.

"Dad. We both know you need to fully retire. I know it's difficult. You built so much and worked so hard. But it's time to hand over the reins. I can do this. You know I can do this."

"Declan, I feel conflicted about this." He put his glass down on the table and looked at me. "I inherited this business from my father, who inherited it from his father. This is a family legacy, a family line."

I wasn't following. "And I'm your son."

"Yes. And I am very proud of you. You are a great sailor and a decent businessman." Coming from the

Captain, that was extremely high praise. "But what happens after you? You've made it clear you have no interest in being a family man. You say you don't want a wife and kids. So what happens to Quinn Fisheries then? The legacy built by four generations ends? Or God forbid you sell out to one of those big corporate outfits?"

Selling out was sacrilege in the Quinn household. Several fishing families from the area had done it over the years, and my parents swore up and down they would not destroy the family legacy like that. We would own this company forever, at least that's what my dad wanted. He was being ridiculous.

"Dad, I hardly think whether or not I'm going to have kids has any bearing on whether I should become CEO. I am already COO right now, and I am running this place and have been for almost two years. You were supposed to transition into retirement a while ago and yet you keep hanging on."

"I trust you, Declan. I do. I just struggle to think that there may not be a next generation to pass this business on to."

I couldn't believe him. It was bad enough that my mother was perpetually up my ass about dating. But getting some bullshit lineage guilt trip from my father? "I don't see why having kids should have anything to do with it. You are deflecting. It's time to take your hands off the wheel. It's my turn to lead. You did things your way— aggressive expansion—but now it's time to take a look, streamline the operation, and optimize. Things have changed and you need to understand that."

He stood, drawing himself up to his full height. Even past sixty and recovering from a heart attack, he was still an imposing figure. "I understand. Just so much has happened recently. Just give me some time, okay? I have to adjust to this. Adjust my expectations."

"Wait a second. Do you mean to tell me you were hoping Callum or Liam would show interest in the business? Would you really give it away, after I've worked here nearly ten years, to them just because they want kids? Newsflash. None of us have any kids. There are no guarantees in life. I am doing a damn good job and you know it. Don't toy with me because I'm not the family man type." Now I was pissed. I was always the third choice, never as good as golden boy Callum or pampered baby Liam. Despite growing up in the boat yard, neither of my brothers had ever displayed any interest in the family business. I had been preparing for this my entire life. Hell, I even did my time in the navy first.

"It's not about offspring. It's just about stability in the future. You're just not the settling down type. I need a steady hand to guide this business." I got up and paced around my office. Was he serious? I wanted to scream, to punch something. Did he really not trust me?

"Steady? How much steadier could I be, Dad? I have been by your side working for nearly a decade. I built a house in this town. I own a dog. I'm hardly a flake or a rolling stone.

He sat quietly, watching me pace. "That is not it, Declan. Not at all."

I felt pissed. I felt betrayed. He knew how much this place meant to me. How could I prove to my father that I was good enough to take over the business? How could I show him I was responsible, steady, and that I wouldn't destroy the family legacy?

8

DECLAN

I WAS STILL REELING FROM MY CONVERSATION WITH the Captain when I realized I needed to head to the brewery. Our Tuesday night crew at Liam's brewery had expanded over the past few months. I sometimes missed the days when it was just me and my brothers, but the newcomers fit in well. The more people there were, the less I had to talk, so that was a win.

Ginger and I had arrived at six to meet with Liam and Callum about our plans for building a beverage distribution company. After years of rejecting our financial help with the brewery, Liam had approached us recently wanting to expand his business to include distribution of his own products as well as those of other microbreweries around New England. The idea was just taking shape, but each of us brought our own skills to the table. I would never admit this, but I felt proud to be working on something of my own with my brothers. They were the entrepreneurs in the family. I was just a fisherman who worked for my dad. But distributing beer, or other types of alcohol, was in my wheelhouse. Quinn Fisheries delivered thousands of pounds of fresh-caught fish to restaurants and supermarkets around New England every single week. Cold storage, transport, and logistics were a huge part of my skill set. They respected me and my ideas. It was going to take some time, some strategy, and some capital, but we were going to build this together.

After the meeting, the three of us walked to the taproom where everyone was laughing at some story Nora was telling about a date she went on last week.

In addition to my two brothers, Trent, Liam's best friend and assistant brewer, was there along with Cece, my future sister-in-law. Her friend Nora had stopped by as well. She was a bit of a wildcard, way too loud for my taste, but a really genuine person nonetheless. She loved Cece fiercely and helped my idiot brother get it together when they hit a rough patch. She had proven herself to be a good person many times over, so I tolerated her always loud and sometimes shrill presence in our lives.

Nora eyed me sharply when I walked in and took a seat at the bar. Trent immediately poured me my favorite beer, the double IPA, and slid it over to me wordlessly. I really liked that guy.

I took a sip of beer and grabbed a handful of pretzels that Cece offered me. Before I could shove them in my mouth, Nora started up. "Hey, Declan, I met your friend this morning."

All eyes immediately locked on my face. Friend? What was she talking about?

"Astrid? Your neighbor? She came by my store."

"Oh, right." I tried to feign indifference but ended up scowling instead.

I took another sip of beer and tried to ignore the five sets of eyeballs that were staring at me in awe.

Callum broke the silence. "That can't be right, Nora. Declan doesn't have friends."

Nora rolled her eyes at Cal. "Nope. She told me she

was Dec's neighbor. We hung out for a while. She's a really cool girl."

Shit. Shit. Shit. "That's interesting," Cecelia said. "Because Emily texted me that you invited her hot cousin over for a romantic dinner last weekend."

"That's definitely her," Nora said. "She is super hot."

I couldn't argue there. I grunted. Just thinking about her made me smile. I had to suppress it with a frown so my nosy brothers didn't notice anything. But there was no denying I liked her. I liked her curious green eyes, her quick wit, and her sassy mouth. I liked the way she carried herself. Her confidence was incredibly sexy. And I would be lying if I wasn't intrigued by her body. Granted I had only seen it hidden under winter clothes, but she was sexy as hell and I wanted to see so much more.

"Use your words, bro." Liam giggled. I liked it better when he was afraid of me. Now that he was engaged, he was a lot more comfortable busting my balls.

I shrugged. "There is nothing to say. Astrid is staying at the cottage across the street from my house. We have become friends. Even Ginger likes her."

"Ginger doesn't like anyone."

"She likes her."

"What is she like? Are you dating?"

"She's fine. A perfectly fine person."

"Oh please, Declan, don't be too effusive with your praise."

"She is awesome," declared Nora. "An ass-kicking corporate lawyer who looks like Charlize Theron. She is amazing."

Liam and Callum exchanged bewildered looks. "Then she is definitely not dating you."

"Unless she has a weakness for man buns and dirty boots." Liam laughed. Little prick.

I turned and shot Callum a glare. "Pipe down, Fabio.

We all know you are jealous of my luscious locks. Not all of us iron our underwear." Callum was as clean-cut and image conscious as you could get. Liam and I had a lot of fun over the years teasing him about his vanity. In college, he had done a bit of modeling, and we never let him live it down. Tonight he was wearing a dress shirt and slacks and really fancy-looking shoes. We were both tall, with dark hair and blue eyes, but the similarities ended there. It was like we inhabited different worlds.

"Be careful," I continued. "Wouldn't want you to mess up those fancy red shoes."

"They are not red," he huffed. "They are oxblood. And they match my belt." I rolled my eyes.

Nora jumped in. "I like your shoes, Cal. Very on trend."

Callum straightened his collar. "Thanks, Nora."

"So let's circle back to this beautiful neighbor, shall we?" Cece said. I adored the girl, but I wish she would let this go. When she showed up here last summer she was all quiet and shy. Since getting with Liam she seemed to have no problem busting my balls as much as the rest of them. I suppose it's a good thing. She would fit right in with us Quinns.

"Is she going to be your date for our engagement party?" My parents and Cece's mother were throwing a huge engagement party for the happy couple in a few weeks. My mom had been stressing about me bringing a date, which I generally ignored.

"I don't know. Haven't asked her." I stared into my beer.

"Ask her, dumbass. Your mom is already threatening to set you up on another blind date," Trent interjected.

"What? How do you know that?"

Trent shrugged. "We talk a lot. And she's worried about you being lonely up in the big house by yourself."

Trent grew up in foster care and had a really difficult childhood. Since grade school, my parents had always taken an interest in him and helped him out. My mother, especially, had a soft spot for Trent. We joked that he was her favorite son, and he adored her back, always stopping by, helping out around the house, and generally being a model son. Sadly, I was not remotely surprised she was talking to him about this.

I shot Trent a glare. He put his hands up. "Dude, I'm just the messenger. Take it up with her, she's your mom. Plus, what's the big deal if you bring her?"

"Yes." Liam poured another round of beers. "Let's discuss. So are you actually planning to date the beautiful neighbor? Or is she just another one of your tourist flings?"

I curled my fist and tried to suppress a growl. "She's not like that, Liam."

"Like what?"

I didn't know what to say. She wasn't one of my flings. My dating preferences were well known to my brothers at this point in my life. And I wasn't ashamed to say that I enjoyed the company of ladies now and again. And I happened to prefer tourists who would eventually leave, therefore sparing me any need to end things myself. But Astrid was in a different universe than those girls. I didn't have the words to explain it, but she occupied a completely different place in my mind.

"Just shut up. She's a nice person. Don't talk about her like that. Actually, don't fucking talk about her at all."

I prayed this conversation would end soon. I didn't want to fight with my brothers, but the way they were asking questions was making my blood pressure rise.

There was a moment of awkward silence.

"I invited her to join our coven."

"Nora," Cece sighed, "for the last time we are not

converting to Wicca. But good work. Is she going to join Monday breakfast?"

"Yup." The girls high-fived, and I had no idea what the hell they were talking about. I just knew I had to get out of this conversation as fast as possible. I was so confused. Astrid was cool and undeniably gorgeous, but what could I possibly do about it? There was no way she could be interested in a guy like me. Right?

9

DECLAN

It had been a long, weird week. Work had been frustrating, and I had been sleeping poorly. And something was up with Callum. We were so close, most days I could read him easily. But something had changed and I had to admit I was a bit worried about him. He wasn't looking or acting like himself. Normally he was the open book in our relationship, but he wasn't saying anything. I would have to team up with Liam to get to the bottom of this.

I got another text from my mom about Bumble. I honestly didn't even know what it was, but I already hated the word. Bumble. It sounded like a fuck-up, like something went wrong. Like "I caught the pass and then bumbled." Or "I drank too much at the holiday party and bumbled in the cab on the way home." I didn't care how many times Mom texted, there was no way I was joining that dumbass app. I didn't want a girlfriend. And if at some point I did, I would go find one the old-fashioned way.

I needed to get out and clear my head. I decided to stop by The Lighthouse, one of Havenport's fancier establishments, to grab a beer. Perched on a bluff halfway between my house and the downtown area, it was a tourist hub known for fine dining and incredible ocean views. I came here for two reasons. One, because my friend Eric bartended here and always took good care of me, and two, because it was not a place that many locals patronized. When I came here, I knew no one would bother me, and I could sit and watch the ocean or enjoy a bowl of their award winning lobster bisque. Tonight I brought a book and was planning to just zone out and unwind a bit before heading home.

I came in and took my usual seat at the corner of the bar. "Hey, man, what can I get you?" Eric had been a friend for a long time. His older brother Jimmy worked for me on one of my crews and was a really good guy. It was one of the things I liked about Havenport—knowing people and their families. No one was ever really a stranger. You would think a loner like me would prefer anonymity, but I didn't. I liked that most people knew me. It took a lot of the pressure off to make small talk or put effort into interactions. But some nights, like tonight, I just wanted to be anonymous. Which was why I loved The Lighthouse.

"Can I grab a pint of the Helmsman Double IPA and a menu?" My younger brother, Liam, was a brewer. He opened Binnacle Brewery here in Havenport a few years ago, and I always ordered his beers when I was out to support him. The business had been up and down over the years, but he truly loved it. It was actually when his fiancée, Cece, came on board to handle marketing that the place really began to take off. As much as I would never admit it to his face, his beer was excellent and I was so proud of him every time I went out and saw his product stocked somewhere. I was born into fishing, and it was in my blood. He came by brewing naturally—it was just his passion, and I couldn't help but feel proud of him.

The bar was relatively busy for a Thursday. Well-dressed folks were milling around, drinking and picking at appetizers. I was clicking through emails on my phone when I heard a familiar, husky voice. "No, thank you. I'm just enjoying my glass of wine alone tonight."

I peered around the side of the L-shaped bar and spotted a familiar curtain of white-blonde hair. Astrid was standing at the end of the bar, looking like a total knockout in a black sheath dress and sky-high heels. Damn, she was beautiful. But there was more to it. Her attitude, the way she carried herself, was nothing short of badass. Nora was right, she definitely had a Charlize Theron vibe happening. She was tall, blonde, and looked like she could kick my ass and I would thank her later. Her posture and body language said "don't mess with me," yet some bumbling idiot was definitely trying to hit on her. Poor schmuck. If I knew one thing about Astrid, it was that she could probably eat this dumbass for breakfast. But there was no way I was going back to my book now. My interest was piqued.

I moved a few seats over on the bar so I would have a better view of her. And that guy would not take a hint. He kept crowding her and, at one point, grabbed her hand which she immediately pulled away. I instantly stood up to say something. Then I got a good look at his face. Asshole.

I pulled myself up to my full six feet three inches and strode over there like I owned the place. I smacked my pint glass on the oak bar top, spilling some beer in the process.

"Flint. What are you doing here?"

Marcus Flint, my nemesis, looked me up and down disdainfully. Yes, I wasn't dressed up exactly. But I was wearing nice jeans and a vest over my plaid shirt. It was my meeting attire, and it worked for me. I wasn't a suit and tie type of guy, and the people I did business with appreciated that.

We stood, facing each other like two moose about to battle over territory. I hated him with every cell in my body. He wasn't wearing his uniform tonight, thank God, but was all decked out in a shiny suit. Probably trying to score with some tourists. He was such a scumbag.

"Why are you interrupting me, Quinn? Can't you see I'm chatting with this lovely lady?" He waved his hand as if I should walk away.

I looked at Astrid, and she winked at me.

"Sweetie, what took you so long?" she whined. "I have been waiting for more than thirty minutes."

I casually shoved Marcus aside, wedging my large body between them. I grabbed Astrid's waist and leaned down and kissed her cheek. "So sorry, killer. I got held up at work. Please forgive me." She nuzzled into my side, and I pulled her in closer. We fit together perfectly. She was warm and soft and smelled incredible.

She smiled up at me, and my entire body felt warm. For a minute I contemplated kissing her on the mouth, but I figured we had sold the ruse so far.

I looked up at Flint who looked confused. "Were you bothering my girl, Flint?"

He looked at Astrid and then at me, as if he could not believe that we were a couple. "Is there a problem?" I continued.

Astrid playfully patted my bicep. I flexed. I couldn't help myself. "Oh sweetie, be kind. Mark here was just telling me how he is a police officer here in Havenport."

Flint grimaced. "It's Marcus."

"Of course," she deadpanned. "It was so lovely to meet you. But Declan promised me a romantic dinner tonight, so if you'll excuse us." She pinned him with a sharp glare as if to say "move along," and he nodded and excused himself. He walked back to the other side of the bar, muttering and shaking his head. Objectively, I was attracted to Astrid. She was beautiful and interesting, but watching her effortlessly dispatch my mortal enemy gave me chills. This was the kind of woman I could fall in love with if I wasn't careful.

She gave me a patented Astrid glare. "I had that situation under control. You did not have to rush over here like a raging bull."

I kept my arm around her waist. "Sorry, Marcus Flint just makes me see red."

She gave me a dramatic eye roll. "Thank you."

I kept her close, not ready to take my hands off her body. "My pleasure. It's not every day I get to save a damsel in distress and stick it to my mortal enemy in the process."

"Mortal enemy? Tell me more!" She perched her chin on her fist, pretending to be fascinated.

I smiled, thinking everything she did was adorable. "He's probably more of a nemesis really, but basically we've hated each other since grade school. I had a really bad stutter growing up, and Marcus Flint bullied me endlessly." That was a bit of an oversimplification. I didn't speak until I was three years old, and when I did, I had a vicious stutter. My parents sought out every specialist and program for me, but I battled with it well into my teens. Because of it I was always really quiet and barely spoke. I struggled in school and had a hard time making friends. I hated social situations and avoided them at all costs. Even with Callum by my side, I never felt comfortable. It took until high school for me to really overcome it, and still sometimes I slipped when I got nervous.

"Wow. What a dick," she said, sneering in his direction.

"I know. And we've just always hated one another."

"I find it shocking that anyone bullied you. Look at you." A sly grin spread across her face. I didn't know what she meant specifically, but I liked the way her eyes swept all over my body, as if she was impressed with me.

"I got bullied a lot, trust me. Just because I'm big and have two brothers doesn't mean I'm immune. There were plenty of bullies and lots of fights."

She nodded. "I went to an all-girls boarding school. Trust me, I know all about bullying and fights."

That was intriguing. "Plus, Marcus Flint stole my prom date senior year."

"What? How?"

"I had asked this girl, Julie Baranski, to prom." It was a big deal. Asking her took a lot of courage and a lot of practicing with Callum to get it right and not stutter. I had crushed on her for years but never worked up the courage to talk to her. I dated in high school—plenty of girls went for the strong silent type—but she was my ultimate crush. I can remember how incredible I felt after she said yes. "Then Marcus Flint told her I had only asked her as a joke and was going to stand her up, so she agreed to go with him."

"That asshole. And what a bitch. How could she think that about you? You are not that kind of guy." She was fired up and I loved it. Some women, when they got mad, yelled and shouted and got shrill. Astrid was even cooler and eerily calm. She spoke in a low, monotone voice. "Does she live here? Can I pay her a visit and kick her ass?" She looked around the room like she would be here.

I laughed. "Stop. I'm over it. It was a long time ago."

"I'm not over it. Let me at him." She pretended to go after Marcus, and I grabbed her arm. I pulled her back toward me, and she placed her hand on my chest. Every cell of my body lit up with lust. I wanted those hands all over me.

"It's fine. They actually ended up getting married."

"Ugh. Of course they did. So why was he here hitting on me? Gross."

"They are divorced now. She lives in New Hampshire with their two kids. Her mom and my mom still keep in touch."

"That's sad. And he sucks. If I had known what a douche he was, I would have sold the fake girlfriend way harder. I would have climbed in your lap and stroked your beard."

Just the suggestion of her words made me squirm, and I hoped that these new jeans could hide the evidence of my attraction to her.

I had to change the subject. "So what are you doing here?"

She sighed and played with her hair. "I was actually supposed to meet a date here, but I got stood up."

I couldn't believe that. "Who, your boyfriend?"

"No. I don't have a boyfriend. I had connected with a guy on a dating app, and we planned to meet here. He never showed."

I thanked the gods of Tinder and Bumble and whateverthefuck the others were called that some dude was dumb enough to pass on this woman. I stared at her, mesmerized by her moss-green eyes, her high cheekbones, and her full, lush lips. I would probably jump off a bridge right now if she asked me to. How could any guy turn her down? "Do you want to grab something to eat while we are here?"

She smiled a true, genuine smile that lit up her whole face. "I'd love that."

10

ASTRID

I WAS SITTING IN A COZY BOOTH AT A VERY ROMANTIC restaurant with Declan Quinn. He recommended I try the lobster bisque and it was incredible. I wanted to lick the bowl but restrained myself. I didn't know why, but since coming to Havenport food tasted so good. Eating was always something that I tried to do as efficiently as possible, usually while sitting in front of my laptop trying to work. I just shoveled food into my face so I could get back to focusing on work.

But sitting here, with an ocean view and flickering candles, it was nice to slowly savor the incredible soup and sip this delicious wine. It was certainly a novel experience. The smoldering dinner companion definitely didn't hurt either.

I bit into one of the seared day boat scallops and moaned slightly. "This is incredible," I said, embarrassed that I was basically orgasming over shellfish.

Declan smirked. "Thank you. I caught that scallop—well, not me personally, but my company supplies this restaurant."

I nodded. "That's fascinating. So this was caught today?" He nodded. "Why is it called a day boat scallop?"

"It's the method of harvesting. We go out for one day, hence the name day boat, and use a trawler to catch them in nets. The alternative is diver scallops, which are harvested by scuba divers."

I sipped my wine. "That's so cool. So how do you use the nets to get scallops?"

He savored a sip of his beer and explained, "We basically drag them across the sea floor picking up the scallops, sea urchins, and mussels."

Declan came alive when he talked about his business. I could tell how much he loved it. "What you do is amazing," I said. "You feed people."

He laughed and looked embarrassed. "It's not exactly noble, Astrid."

"Yes it is. You go out and accomplish something every day. Today's work can be quantified by my delicious dinner." My work, on the other hand, was quantified in billable hours and how much money I could save my clients. Not exactly the same thing.

He cleared his throat, clearly uncomfortable talking about himself. "So are you going to explain the dating app thing?"

"Don't judge me," I said, but deep down I was judging myself. But what was a type-A overachiever to do? Generally, once I set my mind to something, I was successful. So it seemed logical that if I just applied myself to dating and pursued it in a strategic and professional manner, I would find someone great. But after a few days I was ready to quit. It was simply not possible to apply strategy and professionalism to online dating. It was random, messed up, and completely not for me.

Dating usually felt impossible. Normal people with normal jobs and lives just didn't get it. The work always came first. The deadlines, the clients, and the firm were the priorities. Nothing else mattered. Vacations, kids, birthdays, weddings, everything was secondary to the work.

I knew this was not normal. But this was my world. And it was filled with people who understood the rules. So dating had been tough. People outside the BigLaw world didn't get it and wanted nothing to do with a jerk who canceled at the last minute and hadn't taken a vacation in five years. And the people in my world? They were too busy to date or spend time getting to know someone. Hence my foray into dating apps.

"I would never judge you, Astrid. I'm just curious. You don't seem like someone who would struggle to find dates."

I almost spit my wine out at him. "That could not be further from the truth. I have never, in my entire thirty-two years on earth, had an easy time with guys." Most of my life I had received little to no attention from the opposite sex. I wasn't complaining. I didn't have the time or the interest, but right now I needed to find a boyfriend, or at the very least a date. Because Max may have tried to destroy my career, but I wasn't going to go down without a fight. I needed a date for that gala, and I wanted to roll up with someone handsome, accomplished, and hopefully a full foot taller than Max. That little prick could eat shit.

"Nope. Not buying it."

"Oh, you sweet, dumb man. You don't get it. Most of your species are not as highly evolved as you are."

He stared at me, dumbstruck.

"I scare the shit out of most men. It's not a bad thing —in fact I take great pride in it—but it makes it really hard to date." I had been told I was "unapproachable" so many times. If one more prick told me to "smile more" I was going to move to an island and start a cat colony.

I smiled and sipped my wine. "Most guys are turned off by my height. And then those that aren't are intimidated by my career."

He nodded. "Some men are cowards."

"You know, I love watching a man's balls shrivel up when I tell him I'm a corporate lawyer. It is satisfying when people are exactly as shitty as you think they are."

Declan smiled. "I need to see this. I would love nothing more than to watch you destroy a bunch of weak, insecure men." He pinned me with an intense look, and I fought the urge to fan myself. A sexy man smoldering at me while also complimenting my ass-kicking skills. Be still my throbbing vagina!

Declan sat and thoughtfully sipped his beer. "I guess I can see that. You are intense, which I happen to appreciate in a woman. But I still think you are far away from resorting to dating apps."

I shifted in my seat, debating how much about my current predicament to share. Could I trust him? Would he think I was such a dumbass? But, at this point, who else could I talk to? I didn't have any friends and my mother certainly wasn't a confidante. I had to take what I could get.

"There is a bit of backstory."

He shifted in his chair. "Why am I not surprised? Lay it on me."

"So the reason I am currently on dating apps is because I need a date for an upcoming event."

"Okay."

"And it's more than just a wedding or a party."

"What kind of event? An inauguration?" He smirked and I enjoyed how his eyes crinkled in the corners.

"No. It's a ball. The annual Massachusetts Lawyers Association Charity Gala. It's a black-tie fundraiser held in late March that is basically a who's who of the legal elite.

It's the kind of thing I would normally try to get out of attending, but this year I am being given an award."

"Seriously? That's awesome."

"Not quite. The team I worked on is getting the award. We set up a clinic at a local homeless shelter helping people with their debt issues. A lot of people have been the victim of predatory lending and are struggling with illegal or unethical debts. It holds a lot of folks back."

"So you help them?"

"Yes. We help figure out what's going on. Call the lenders, flex our legal muscles a bit, and sometimes reduce and sometimes outright knock out their debts. You would be surprised how many shady people prey on the vulnerable. And some folks have been the victims of identity theft and don't even know how to fight it." Setting up the clinic, training other lawyers in predatory debt prevention, and helping clients was one of the most satisfying things I had done in my career. It had taken two years, but we were up and running at several Boston-area shelters and had secured some huge wins for our clients. We had truly improved people's lives.

"So you are not just a legal badass, you are a good person too. Noted." He took another sip of beer and gestured for me to go on.

"So I was recently fired from my law firm. And under normal circumstances, I wouldn't dream of going. But I have an axe to grind with a partner who set me up after I wouldn't sleep with him." I paused, embarrassed to have to be telling this story out loud.

He immediately got mad. "Did he take advantage of you?" I could see him growing more and more angry. Normally this would annoy me—I hated when men tried to protect me—but with Declan it felt good, made me feel safe.

"Not exactly. He just quietly torpedoed my career in retaliation."

"That bastard."

I watched Declan's face change as I told him my tale of woe. I could see the rage bubbling up inside him as I recounted working with Max and what had happened. I told him about his text messages, the creepy comments, and the time he grabbed my ass. Declan had no poker face, that was for sure. He picked up his beer glass, and it looked like he could smash it in his big, capable hands.

"So what's the plan, killer? I know you have a plan."

"I'm not sure yet. I am lying low and figuring things out. Taking some much needed time off in the process."

"I don't know you that well, but I know you are not one who gets knocked down and stays down. What can I do to help?"

I loved that he wanted to help me. I loved that he listened to my humiliating story and still called me killer. I had let myself and the rest of womankind down by not fighting harder for my job, for not going to HR the minute he propositioned me. I wasn't feeling like a killer. I wasn't feeling like my usual controlled and strategic self. I was feeling like a timid, pathetic mess.

I forced myself to look him in the eye. I was so embarrassed and humiliated, airing my shame in front of a quasi-stranger. "What I really need is a date for this gala. I can't hide away in shame. I did nothing wrong, and I am going to go there and hold my head up high and receive my award for the hard work I accomplished." I wasn't going to give Burns & Glenn the satisfaction of erasing my hard work. It would also be an invaluable networking opportunity since I needed to line up a new job.

"Fuck yes, you are."

"So will you be my date?"

"What? Me?"

"Come with me, pretend to be my boyfriend. I'll get you a tux. You will look great in a tux,"—I winked for effect—"and we will go to a fancy party."

He shifted in his seat, clearly uncomfortable. He sat silently for a moment, clearly formulating his answer in his head.

"Why would you want to take me? I'm a fisherman, not some fancy corporate type."

"Are you kidding me, Declan? You are the perfect date." I gestured to him. "You are tall and built and uncomfortably handsome."

He averted his gaze, and I detected a bit of a blush on his bearded face. It was really cute.

He waved his hand at me, embarrassed. "Objectifying me will get you nowhere, killer. I'll help you find someone more suitable."

I reached across the table and ignored the fizzle of electricity I felt when I touched his hand. "You are the only friend I have right now. And you are smart and interesting and tall. I just need someone to come as my date so I can hold my head up high and accept the award. I can't face it alone. I would be so proud to go with you."

He finally met my gaze and smiled. "Wow. You really know how to compliment a guy." He shrugged. "I'll do it. Because you are my friend and I want to see the assholes who screwed you over and underestimated you."

I beamed at him.

He stroked his beard. "I would be proud to be your fake trophy boyfriend for the night."

"Thank you, thank you, thank you!!" I jumped out of my chair and crushed him in a hug. He patted my arm gently, and I took the moment to discreetly enjoy his intoxicatingly manly smell.

"I owe you. Whatever you want. I am in your debt," I said. My mind was instantly filled with dirty thoughts. I meant what I said. I would do whatever he wanted. Maybe he wanted me to walk Ginger. Or maybe what he wanted involved nudity, and maybe some light spanking and hair pulling?

A girl could dream.

11

I WAS LYING ON THE COUCH IN FRONT OF THE fireplace devouring a regency romance from my aunt's collection when I heard a knock on the door. I shuffled over, hoping it wasn't a friendly neighborhood serial killer out for an evening stroll.

I peered through the door and saw Declan and Ginger standing there. Do I have enough time to go brush my hair and put on makeup? Probably not. Crap.

I opened the door. "Hi, guys." Ginger pushed past me and sniffed judgmentally around the living room, finally curling up on the floor in front of the electric fireplace. "What's up?"

"Can we come in?"

"Of course. Make yourself at home."

He walked through the door, removing his boots. I loved his manners. He didn't do these things out of obligation, but out of desire. He was so genuine compared to most men I knew. I gestured to the tiny floral couch. "Have a seat. Can I get you anything?"

"No, thank you. I just wanted to talk to you for a second. I'm sorry. It's late. I should have called." He looked stressed, and I wanted to hug him and smooth out those wrinkles in his brow. He paced a bit around the tiny room before settling on the couch. I scratched Ginger's ear and watched him for a minute. He was wearing his usual jeans and flannel shirt, and he looked good. He had rolled up his sleeves, revealing thick, ropey forearms. I had never stopped to consider forearms before. But Declan's were beautiful. Strong and capable, yet gentle, like the rest of him. I shook myself out of my daydream and tried to focus on the present.

I also caught his eyes traveling up the length of my body. I probably should have put on a bra under my sweatshirt and maybe something other than these flimsy sleep shorts before opening the door. I crossed my arms over my chest and gestured to the couch.

"Not a problem. It's nice to have company," I said, taking a spot at the other end and curling my knees up. He took up a lot of space, not just on the couch but in my tiny cottage, but I liked having him here.

"So I thought about our conversation last night at The Lighthouse."

My face fell. Oh no, oh no, oh no. I hope he's not having second thoughts. I want him to be my date so badly. "You don't want to go with me?"

He grabbed my hand. It felt so good. Warm and strong and large. "No. I want to go with you. But I have a favor to ask you in return."

Relief washed over my body. He was still holding my hand. "Anything." And I actually meant it. If he asked me to strip naked right now and roll around in the snow I would do it. If I was being honest, I would strip naked for any purpose he could imagine.

"So if I am going to be your fake boyfriend for your law gala, could you be my fake girlfriend for my brother's engagement party in a few weeks?"

Huh. Not what I was expecting. If I was being honest, I was kind of hoping he might want me to be his real girlfriend. But that wasn't possible. I was clearly not his type and he was not mine. Not at all. "Of course. But why do you need a fake date for a family event?"

Declan took a breath and rested his elbows on his knees. He faced the fire for a moment, composing his thoughts while staring at the flames. "So my mom has been riding me lately about being single. She is relentless. Trying to set me up, committing me to blind dates without asking my permission, and harassing me about joining dating sites." He ran his hands through his hair. He was clearly embarrassed.

I put my hand on his shoulder, and he looked up at me. I could see the firelight flickering in his blue eyes. He seemed on edge and twitchy, the total opposite of his usual intense, controlled energy.

I gave him a minute. "I love my parents. They are really awesome. And they have both gone through a lot this year. We almost lost my dad." He paused, staring at the fire. I kept my hand on his shoulder. "I love them so much, and I want to make them happy. But I can't suffer through more meddling in my personal life. It's bad enough I have to report up to my dad at the business I've been running for the past two years. I can't have my mom fixing me up with every random single woman she meets on the street."

"I get it," I said. "You don't want to disappoint them, but you also want to live your life. Trust me, I understand that more than you know." And it was true. Although Declan's family seemed completely different than my own, I could identify with the feeling of not being good enough. I understood what it felt like to disappoint your parents, to fall short.

"And I just want to live my life. I have a home and a

dog and a business. My father has been giving me shit about not being the 'settling down type' like my brothers. And I want to show him that I can be serious, even if it's only temporary."

He gave me an intense look and we sat, looking at one another for a minute. My heart rate sped up and I could feel my face flush. I didn't get flustered. I wasn't that type of girl. I took pride in my composure and control in any situation. But sitting on a couch with Declan Quinn was turning me into a swooning romance-novel heroine.

He continued, looking encouraged. "I'm happy. No one believes me, but I am. I like my life. And I am not going to waste my precious time on dating apps in some desperate attempt to get paired up."

He looked right at me. "No offense."

"None taken. I was desperate. I am not too proud to admit it."

He tipped his chin. "I respect that."

"But this is your family. We're really going to have to sell it."

"What, you don't think you can pretend to like me?" His grin was mischievous.

"No, no, not at all. I mean, I guess we have to do some research or something." What was it about this guy that knocked me off my game?

"We're already friends. And we already hang out. So we'll just do that more."

"But won't it be a surprise to your mom if you show up with a random girlfriend?"

"Yes. So we'll go out in town and be seen. The rumor mill will start up so fast we won't have to do much."

"It's not like I have that much to do at the moment."

"I like your can-do attitude."

I rolled my eyes at him. "So how do we do this?"

"While you are here in Havenport, we pretend to be

boyfriend and girlfriend, and when you leave, we break up."

I nodded, too confused and turned on to speak properly.

"You might have to do the heavy lifting. Everyone is going to be shocked I'm dating you," he added.

I punched his arm. "Bullshit."

He rubbed his arm dramatically, and I got up and started to pace. Not to brag, but negotiations were kind of my specialty. Sitting too close to him was messing with my hormones and I couldn't think properly.

My relationship history was peppered with one disaster after another. My romantic instincts were shit. So maybe a fake relationship was what I needed. At least we could set rules and conditions and actually follow them. It was like a beautifully drafted contract—no room for error, no gray area, just clear, concise instructions about what everyone was supposed to do. I was getting giddy just thinking about it.

Suddenly, I no longer felt powerless and confused. I was in charge. This is what I did, and I was pretty damn good at it.

I caught him eyeing my legs as I paced around the tiny living room. "Eyes up here, Quinn," I barked.

He sat up straight and looked me square in the eyes. "Yes, ma'am."

"I will agree to be your fake girlfriend, but we need rules, guidelines, a plan."

"Whatever you want."

"Actually, let me get my laptop. I can draft something up."

He grabbed my arm as I turned to head to the kitchen. "Slow down, killer. I don't think we need to put this in writing just yet. Talk to me."

He pulled me down to the tiny couch, and just like

that I was a nervous, quivering wreck again. Such was the power of Declan Quinn.

I sat up and smoothed my sweatshirt. "Let's just talk it through. We need to agree on a backstory, calendar the dates we've discussed, anticipate some of the potential pain points."

"What?"

"We can't just attempt a fake relationship willy-nilly. We have to pressure test it. Make sure it can hold up."

"How do we do that?"

"Practice dates, hanging out in public, a slow rollout."

"That works for me."

I stood up and resumed my pacing. "A fake relationship will work for both of us. Because I am going back to Boston and back to my career in a couple of months. And this way, we have an easy way to break things off and remain friends." It was actually genius. I could help him while I was here, and he would help me by being my date for the gala. I was a little mad I hadn't thought of it, actually.

"Boston's not that far away." He looked hopeful, and his blue eyes twinkled. Was he interested? Ha! Wouldn't that be nice. How was this guy still single? Clearly he must have some glaring flaws I haven't noticed, which boded well for the success of our fake relationship. If he was a closet narcissist or collected creepy dolls, I wouldn't be in danger of developing real feelings for him.

"But I will have to be totally focused. And there is no way I can do a long-distance relationship, even if that distance is an hour." He looked a little crestfallen. But it was the truth. If my career was going to recover from this, then it would take everything I had. I would have to work twice as hard to prove myself all over again. The thought made me nauseous, but I ignored it. "So that way, we can break up amicably, say it was bad timing or something.

And you can pretend to be devastated for a while to buy you some time from your mom."

He nodded, still watching me pace in front of the fire. "So from here on out, we're a couple?"

"Yes," I replied, still thinking through the variables.

"So we will do couple stuff."

I looked up and he was smoldering at me again. "Don't do that!"

He raised his eyebrows.

"That!" I said, pointing at his face. "No smoldering at me. Save that shit for your next fake girlfriend."

He laughed, a deep throaty laugh that made me want to go sit on his lap. Shit, I had to draw some clear boundaries on this relationship, and fast.

"Also," I said, avoiding his gaze. "No physical stuff. And definitely no sex."

He smirked at me, as if he found my crazy entertaining. "I respect your boundaries. But I'm here in case you get curious."

How dare he? "Curious?" I waved at him, manspreading on the tiny couch. "Unlikely."

He continued to smolder. If I had been wearing panties underneath these shorts, they would probably be dust on the floor by now. My legal poker face came in very handy in moments like these. "I could not be less curious, actually."

"I admire your ability to keep a straight face. You are a tough negotiator. But what if I drop and do some pushups?"

I felt my face falter but shook my head. Had he seen me staring at him last week? He must think I'm some pervy stalker who gets off on watching hot guys do pushups. It's the truth, of course, but I don't want him to know that.

I recovered and stood with my hands on my hips.

"This works. We will do a set number of fake dates and then go to the engagement party and the legal gala. As long as we follow the rules, this should work."

"We can continue to hang out as friends, right? Ginger has gotten attached to you." At that moment Ginger picked up her head and gave me a bored look.

"Of course," I said. I valued his friendship. He was one of the very few people I enjoyed hanging out with. "But there will be no hand-holding, kissing, or romantic hugging."

"What the hell is romantic hugging?" He smirked again and it was so sexy it made me wish he was just doing his normal smolder. "Are you afraid I'm going to give you a sexy hug and you won't be able to resist me?"

I rolled my eyes dramatically.

"And I don't agree to those rules," he continued. "We have to act like a normal couple. You don't know my brothers, but if we are going to convince everyone, then you have to act like you like me. So hand-holding, hugging, kissing, and general PDA are on the table."

"In public only."

"If you say so. And dancing. We'll have to dance together."

I made a face. I hated dancing.

"Do you know how to dance?" he asked.

"Not really. Why, do you?"

"I do, actually." That was a curveball. What other surprises did this hunky, tattooed dog dad have in store for me? "I'll have to teach you how to dance then."

"Fine." I hated dancing. Despised it. But the thought of being in Declan's arms while he led me around barking orders made me squeeze my thighs together. What was it about this guy that made me such a horn ball? "I'll put that in."

"In what?"

"The contract I'm drafting in my head right now."

"You are not writing a contract for our fake relationship."

"It's a mental contract right now."

"But what if you violate it? What if you fall in love with me and my man bun?"

"Not possible. But if I did, I would be in breach of contract. And you could sue me for damages."

"That certainly sounds romantic."

"I'm not trying to be romantic, Declan. I'm trying to be pragmatic. Rules are great. They help people color in the lines and understand expectations." And I knew I would need rules to keep my hands off of him.

"I'm all for agreeing on the terms, but this seems like overkill."

"Trust me. I am an expert in contracts. This will be watertight."

He laughed. "That sounds sexual."

I pinned him with a sharp look. "Focus. I'll draw something up for you to review. Do you know of anyone in town who is a notary?"

"We are not having our fake relationship contract notarized, killer."

12

ASTRID

"TRUST ME. THIS IS THE FASTEST AND MOST PAINLESS way to announce our relationship to the world," Declan declared as we walked down the street.

"Can't we just post on social media?"

"I don't have social media. I hate that shit."

I did not understand that at all. Stalking people on social media was one of my favorite pastimes. I never posted anything about myself, but I loved to troll Instagram and Facebook to get a glimpse of the lives of some of my old friends. And okay, a lot of my former enemies as well. There is a lot of ugliness at an all-girls boarding school. Sometimes, hate scrolling through someone's boring-ass life was very satisfying.

Declan pulled me into a shiny and retro-looking restaurant. The sign above the door read "Jackie's Diner & Newsstand" in one of those neon 1960s-style signs. It was charming and a bit kitschy.

Inside was a gleaming chrome countertop and also bright red vinyl booths. A gorgeous juke box in the corner was playing some Sinatra, and it felt as though I had stepped into a time machine. We grabbed a booth, and

Declan handed me a menu. I wasn't crazy about the early morning field trip but I was really hungry.

"This place is great," I told Declan.

"It's been here for generations. It used to be a newsstand with a lunch counter back in the day, but they converted the whole space into a restaurant. My parents ate here as kids. Things have changed a bit, but Jackie and Joe have done a really good job of maintaining the spirit of the place."

Within seconds of my ass hitting the seat, a smiling older lady rushed right over to our table with a coffeepot in one hand. She wore a baby-blue frilly apron and had a massive helmet of silver hair and frosted pink lipstick. She had a pair of rhinestone glasses hanging from a jeweled chain around her neck. Her whole look screamed "loving grandma" while her face yelled "don't cross me." I liked her immediately.

"Declan Quinn. It's been ages."

"Hi, Jackie. It's great to see you."

"And who is this lovely girl?" She put the coffeepot down and placed her glasses on her nose.

"Jackie, this is my girlfriend, Astrid."

She grabbed the tabletop to settle herself. "As I live and breathe, Declan Quinn. I never expected those words to come out of your mouth."

She leaned back toward the kitchen. "Joe. Joe. Get your ass out here. You need to meet Declan's girlfriend. She is real!"

Joe came ambling out of the kitchen to say hello. He was a kind-looking man, probably in his seventies, who wore a Mr. Rogers-style cardigan over his apron.

"It's a pleasure to meet you, miss. Now blink twice if this brute over here is holding you hostage."

Jackie hit Joe square in the chest with a menu. "Joe, don't make jokes. She is his girlfriend." She overenunciated the word, and I questioned if Joe was hard of hearing or if she was just used to him trying to ignore her.

He smiled again. "I am glad you are both here. You look hungry. Jackie, let's give the lovebirds a minute so they can order." He dragged his wife away while she continued to stare at me.

Declan leaned in closer and clasped my hand. "Sorry about that. Jackie and Joe are the backbone of the Havenport gossip scene. They are plugged in with everyone, especially the senior citizens. They are going to spread the news far and wide."

I felt mildly uncomfortable. I was not used to this kind of attention from anyone, not even my parents. People seemed to really care about Declan, and by some extension, me. It was unsettling.

"The food here is fantastic, by the way. What do you feel like?"

I opened the laminated menu and was overwhelmed by pages and pages of choices. Who knew there were so many options for breakfast? I know I shouldn't admit this out loud, but I really loved it when restaurants put photos of the food in their menus. It just helped me visualize the deliciousness. And right now I was staring at a massive pile of pancakes.

I flipped through trying to decide what to choose. Western omelette? Avocado toast? Steel-cut oatmeal with berries and cream? It was too much.

Most of the time I didn't eat breakfast. There just wasn't time, and it was easier to grab a protein bar at my desk. I couldn't remember the last time I had pancakes. They were calling to me.

"Earth to Astrid. Are you alright? If you don't like the food here we can just have coffee and go somewhere else."

I looked up at him. He was so sweet, and he really wanted to make sure I was comfortable. "No. Just the opposite. Everything looks so good, and I want to try it all."

"Then get whatever you want."

"I should get some eggs or something. But this photo of the pancakes looks incredible."

"I shouldn't say this. But those pancakes are life changing. My parents used to bring us here after hockey practice on Sunday mornings as kids, and the three of us would have pancake-eating competitions. We would eat until we made ourselves sick. They are that good."

I smiled. Before I knew it Jackie was back, refilling our coffee cups and whipping out her notepad.

"Astrid, dear, what can I get you?"

"Oh. I think I want the pancakes. But I have a question. It says here the house special is corned beef hash. What's that?"

Both Declan and Jackie looked at me quizzically. "You've never had corned beef hash before?"

"Nope. It looks great in the photo."

"It's basically salty meat with potatoes and onions."

I studied the menu. "Then we are definitely getting that. With eggs over easy."

"Would you like an English muffin? We make them in house," Jackie asked, pen poised at her notepad.

"I thought they were made in factories."

"Nope, homemade, kid."

This place was better than I thought. Good thing I promised Nora I would go to Krav Maga class with her tomorrow.

Declan smirked "and we'll share a stack of blueberry pancakes too." He winked at me and I blushed down to my toes.

"And two buttered English muffins!" I blurted, slightly embarrassed by my appetite.

Jackie smirked at us. "Coming right up. Let me go

take care of that table over there and I'll be back to chat." She patted Declan on the head, and I was shocked that any human being on earth could get away with that.

"Thank you for sharing," I said.

"It's a good idea. Like a real couple," he added, sipping his black coffee. I couldn't tell if he was disgusted by my appetite or impressed. I decided it didn't matter. One of the great things about a fake relationship was I didn't have to stress about all this little stuff.

Before I could even take another sip of coffee, Jackie came back and rested her hip on our table. "How did you two lovebirds meet?"

Declan and I looked at each other. I sat up straight. "We are neighbors. I am staying at my aunt's cottage across the street from Declan's house."

"Wait. You are Connie's niece?"

"Yes."

"Oh, sweetheart, what a small world. Now that I think of it I think she mentioned her niece was coming to stay."

Declan piped in. "And I took one look at her and invited her over for dinner."

Jackie looked shocked. "You invited her to your house for dinner?"

"Yes, ma'am. And I impressed her with my cooking."

"He sure did. I can't cook at all," I said, shrugging.

"Aww. Isn't that sweet?" she cooed.

We smiled at Jackie. That wasn't so bad. I think Declan was a little overcautious about the sweet old ladies in this town.

But then the real interrogation started.

"How long have you been together?"

"What do you do for work?"

"How long are you staying?"

"Is it serious?"

"Are you getting married?"

"Do you want kids?"

Her questions were coming so quickly we could barely get the words out to answer them. Jackie was relentless. I knew some two-thousand-dollar-an-hour litigators who could take a lesson from her.

Thankfully we were saved by Joe arriving with massive platters of food.

"This looks incredible!" I exclaimed.

Joe gave us a little bow. "Why, thank you, sweetheart."

Declan smiled at both of them kindly. "Jackie, take it easy on my girl." I felt a small shiver run through my body. Logically, I knew I wasn't really his girl, but part of me wanted to be. What would it be like to belong to a man like him? I had never wanted to belong to anyone. As a feminist I found the thought abhorrent, but the way Declan said it made me feel warm and cherished.

Jackie was undeterred. "Declan is a real catch, you know? His dearly departed grandmother was a very good friend of mine. And I look out for him and his brothers. At least Liam had the good sense to propose to Cecelia Leary. She is wonderful. Do you know her?"

Joe interjected, "Jackie, stop interrogating her. She's a nice girl."

Her eyes narrowed. "I hope so. Because this boy here"—she pinched Declan's cheek—"is one of the best. He is kind and helpful and loves his family. Don't let the long hair and tattoos fool you. He is no bad boy... he is the sweetest."

"Jackie, dear, let's let the lovebirds enjoy their breakfast. I'm sure they can answer your questions another time."

Jackie looked unhappy to be pulled away but took her coffeepot and left us in peace.

"That was intense."

"Did I pass the test? Can I stuff my face now?" I asked.

"Of course you can, killer."

———

"I'm impressed," Declan said, surveying the wreckage of our plates. "You are an excellent fake girlfriend. We totally convinced Jackie."

I raised my coffee cup to him in salute. "Thank you. You weren't bad yourself."

"It's funny, I feel less pressure since this is totally fake. Had you been my real girlfriend, I probably would have tripped over my words."

I forced a smile. I liked the clear nature of a fake relationship, but I couldn't help be just a tiny bit hurt that he clearly wasn't interested in anything real. Not that I had the right; I wasn't either. So I had to just grin and bear it.

"Regardless, Jackie can be intimidating."

"Oh, please. She is nothing compared to my mother," I said, taking the last bite of my English muffin.

"You've never mentioned her. What is she like?"

"My mom?" I took a huge sip of coffee to buy some time. "Justice Wentworth, as she is known, is a state Supreme Court Judge here in Massachusetts. She has been a judge since I was a kid, but she was elevated to the highest court by the Governor about five or six years ago.

"Wow. I had no idea."

"She's intense, kind of scary, and the smartest person in every room she enters."

"That must be a lot to live up to."

I snorted. "You have no idea."

"I really don't. Tell me more."

"There's not much else to tell. My mom has devoted her life to her career and public service. She did not spend a lot of time with me growing up. She tried her best, but it was just the two of us, and she worked really long hours." That was a bit of an understatement, but I found people didn't love to hear me complain about my absent mother.

"What about your dad?"

"My parents divorced when I was two. He remarried —wife number three—shortly after and now lives in Palm Beach with wife number four." My dad was a good person, but he was busy too. And I'm pretty sure my mom went out of her way to keep him away from me as a kid.

He nodded, clearly unsure what to say.

"My dad is great. I talk to him on the phone pretty frequently. He was a tax attorney for a long time and then became a tax professor. I have some half siblings from his first marriage, but we don't have much of a relationship."

"That's too bad."

"They pretty much hated me. He and my mom had an affair when they were at the same law firm. He left his wife and kids for her when she got pregnant with me." There it was. The secret family shame. I was the product of an office affair gone wrong, and not only did I wreck my mom's life, I also wrecked the lives of my half siblings. To say they had never forgiven me was an understatement.

"I'm sorry." He looked concerned, and I didn't want his pity.

"It's fine," I said, forcing a smile. "I don't love talking about my family."

He nodded. "Noted. Now finish your coffee like a good girl and we can go lie on the couch with Ginger and enjoy our food comas."

I smiled at him. I liked the way he cut off my self-pity at the knees. "Aww. You are so sweet. Can we watch TV?"

"Of course. What do you want to watch?"

What didn't I want to watch. I had essentially existed in a vacuum outside of popular culture for the last decade. I never knew what people were talking about, and it felt like I had missed out on all sorts of cool stuff. "I want to watch everything that's really good from the past few years."

"That's a tall order. Where do you want to start?"

"Have you ever heard of this show called *Game of Thrones*?" I asked. Hopefully he hadn't seen it already.

"Sure. I think you'll like it. The king sits on a throne forged from the swords of defeated enemies."

13

ASTRID

I HAD NEVER FELT LIKE THIS, SO EMPOWERED AND FIT and badass. Nora had talked me into going to a Krav Maga class with her, and since I had nothing better to do, I decided to go. I had a feeling I wouldn't be able to walk tomorrow, as every muscle in my body had been firing on all cylinders for the last hour, but my mind, my spirit... they were stoked.

I had never considered myself an athlete, but I played tennis in high school and college for fun and had enjoyed going to spin classes with friends back in law school. I liked exercise, I just didn't have a lot of time for it. So I thought I knew what to expect.

I'd done a fair amount of workout classes in my life, but nothing compared to this. It wasn't just martial arts— we were running and jumping and fighting and screaming. Yael, our instructor, taught us that Krav Maga was about saving your life and defending yourself. The workout was incredible, but what Yael taught us—how to be aware, be agile, and be ready—was unlike anything I'd ever done before. And I was hooked.

The punching, kicking, and blocking kept my mind

engaged and focused. I wasn't stressed, and I wasn't thinking about my career or my mother or anything else. I was solely focused on what I was doing, and I loved it.

I immediately found Yael and thanked her after class.

"You're welcome," she said in her Israeli-accented English. "You did well. When I saw you I thought you were one of those skinny girls who doesn't like to get her hands dirty. You impressed me."

"Thanks," I replied. I wasn't used to getting complimented on my physical prowess. "I can't wait to come back." She patted me on the back so hard it would probably leave a bruise and moved on to the other students.

This class was better than therapy. Not that I had given therapy much of an effort. Almost all my colleagues were in therapy—lawyers tended to be miserable people—but it was almost impossible to make time for. I regarded therapy as a luxury like yoga or baths that someone as busy and productive as myself couldn't possibly make time for.

It was a shame because my therapist, Dr. Martha, was actually pretty amazing. In our few sessions she managed to teach me that my billable hours did not measure my worth as a person. She pushed me to try and define my personal values and encouraged me to find validation and self-esteem beyond what I was able to accomplish professionally. Looking back, I really wished I had kept going.

Nora caught me on the way out, pulling me out of my own head. "I can't believe Yael said that to you! She served in the IDF for ten years. She probably knows how to kill a man with a rubber band and a glue stick."

I was flushed from the workout and the praise. "I am kind of in love with her." Yael was in her early forties and looked like a cross between Jillian Michaels and Gal

Gadot. She was effortlessly terrifying, and I wanted to learn all her secrets.

"Me too. She is my dream woman. Too bad she's married. But seriously, that is the highest compliment from her."

"I want to be her when I grow up."

"Take a number, lady. I've been obsessed with her for months. She moved here a few years ago. She's married to Rose Thompson, who grew up here. They have a couple of kids and live on the Thompson Farm. She's been a trainer here for a while but only recently opened this studio. I love her classes. She gives you an incredible workout and pumps you up to go out into the world and kick ass."

"Yes! It's empowerment with a side of cardio," I said, zipping up my coat.

"I want to fuck up this day."

"Me too. Let's kick Wednesday's ass."

Nora smiled at me. "I knew I liked you. Wanna grab some coffee?"

"Hell yeah, I do."

Nora led me to an adorable little place called High Tide. It was definitely different than the Starbucks on the first floor of my building, where I primarily procured my caffeine. It was kitschy and fun and a bit disjointed. Concert posters warred with floral wallpaper, and it was filled to the brim with mismatched tables and chairs.

I read through the chalkboard menu while Nora chatted with the tattooed, purple-haired proprietress. This place was awesome. Classical music played while people worked on laptops and moms chatted while bouncing their babies.

"You need to try a scone. They are incredible," Nora said, placing her order.

"Ooh. Can I have a blueberry?"

The punk barista handed me one on a delicate china

plate. "They are also award winning. First scone's on us. Are you new in town?"

I was taken aback a bit. I wasn't used to this kind of small-town hospitality. Nora patted my hand. "Say thank you to the nice lady, Astrid," she whispered, as if I were a child.

"Wow. Thanks." I tried to give her my most genuine smile. "I am new. I am visiting for a while. My aunt owns a cottage up on the north side of town, and I am staying there for a bit."

"Oh, you're Connie's niece! I have heard so much about you. Welcome. I'm Leah."

She gestured for me to sit down. Nora and I headed to a small table.

I bit into the scone. It was pure heaven. "I haven't had a scone like this since I was in London."

Nora smiled. "Told ya. These scones are famous in Havenport."

In that moment, sitting in the coffee shop with my new friend, enjoying caffeine and delicious baked goods and still on an endorphin high from the most fun workout of my life, I was happy. Just full-on happy. It was a good day. I couldn't remember the last time I felt like this— light and giddy and ready to face the world. Most of the time I felt like I was dragging around an invisible weight with me.

"Has Emily been to Krav class yet? She needs to try it."

"No, not yet. I keep nagging her. Let's both work on her. So do you want to go back?"

"Yup. I'll be there tomorrow. I don't have much going on, and this is the best I've felt in years."

"So what's going on with you and Declan? I heard you stared down Jackie at the diner last weekend." She gave me a pointed look.

Wow. News traveled fast in this town. I studied my

scone. I didn't want my face to give anything away. Nora was sharp, nosy, and missed nothing. And for some reason, my usual stoicism escaped me around her. There was something so genuine, so disarming about Nora that I couldn't help but spill my secrets.

I decided to keep it simple. "We're dating."

"Really?" She raised a perfectly shaped eyebrow.

I shoved some scone in my mouth and nodded.

"That's great. I'm not being rude, I swear, but Declan doesn't really date."

"He's dating me," I said with a small bit of defensiveness.

"I know. And I'm psyched for you. We all know he's a big softie underneath that broody, smoldering exterior. I'm glad you drilled down deep enough to find his soft center."

I smiled. I really liked Nora. "Me too."

"And I'm really glad you came into my store. Cece is so busy with Liam, I have been in need of some girl time."

"I hear you. I can't remember the last time I just hung out with a girlfriend. And those jeans are so comfortable."

"And your ass has never looked better."

I raised my coffee cup. "I'll drink to that."

I turned to Nora. "So what about you? Is there a special guy in your life?"

She shook her head, and her thick ponytail whipped around. "Nope. No one special."

"I don't believe you." Nora didn't seem like the type of woman who wanted for male attention.

"There isn't. Trust me. I wish I was getting some on the regular. Cece is insufferable, constantly going on and on about all the orgasms she is having. Makes me want to cut her sometimes."

I laughed. That would be super annoying.

She continued. "I date. When I feel like it. I also fuck when I feel like it. But it's been a slow year. I've been busy with my business, and I just haven't felt like making an effort with guys."

I nodded. "Trust me. I get it. I spent years working around the clock. I couldn't spare the time for a guy, especially if it meant I had to shower and put on makeup first. There just aren't enough hours in the day."

"Amen, sister."

We talked about Nora's business. She filled me in on her expansion plans, the new web portal she was planning, and about some of the challenges of retail. It was fascinating. I had spent years digging deep into clients' businesses, understanding everything about what they did, and I loved it. Hearing Nora's passion and vision was inspiring.

We talked about our families. Nora told me about her overbearing parents and her five older brothers, and I told her about my mom and being an only child. We laughed and joked, and it was so much fun to find a connection with another woman my age.

"So now that you are learning Krav Maga, are you going to go kick the ass of that guy who got you fired? Maybe a quick throat punch?"

There was a part of me that fantasized about that exact scenario. But violence was not the answer, at least for now. "No. I am going to get my justice. The truth will come out eventually. I'm just trying to lie low and recharge so I can go back with a vengeance." The firm was conducting an internal investigation into the failed merger. Once they learned I was not responsible for the mistake and that Max had framed me, I would either be offered my job back or they would give me a recommendation so I could find a new one. I could be patient if I had to.

"Good girl. They won't know what hit 'em."

I smiled. I forgot how nice it was to spend time with other women.

"But speaking of annoying friends who are having lots of sex." She eyed me warily. "You fought today with the intensity of a sexually frustrated woman. And you certainly don't look drunk on orgasms."

I felt myself wither under her stare. How could I throw her off the scent? If I couldn't keep Nora convinced for an hour, how could we hope to fool the entire town?

"Um… well… we haven't slept together yet," I said coolly, hoping that she wouldn't pry and we could just leave it at that.

"What? Not possible."

"Yes," I assured her. "We're taking it slow."

She almost spat out her coffee. "Bullshit. Declan Quinn is walking sex. The man sheds pheromones like skin cells. I have seen grown women walk into walls staring at his broody hotness. So what's really the deal?"

I didn't know what to say, since she wasn't wrong. I shrugged.

"Astrid, I'm your friend. Do not lie to me. Either you guys are sleeping together and it's so terrible you can't bear to tell me about it, or you aren't really dating. Or, you don't realize that you have a certified sex god as your boyfriend, and you need me to slap the shit out of you until you see sense."

I was fairly certain Nora would actually do that too. She didn't seem like the type of person who made idle threats. I didn't want to lie to her, but I couldn't betray Declan's confidence. I knew how sensitive he was about his family.

"I had a bad experience." It wasn't a lie. "And I need to go slow right now."

She put her hand over my hand. "If someone hurt you we can take care of him. My Nonna, she knows people."

I smiled. "Thank you. And remind me not to piss off your Nonna."

Nora snorted. "Good luck. Everything pisses her off."

"So we haven't had sex yet."

"I respect that. I don't understand it, but I respect your self-control. Your vibrator must be working overtime right now."

It was both inspiring and a little bit appalling how open Nora was about sex, especially in a busy coffee shop. I lowered my voice. "I don't have a vibrator."

She slammed her hand on the table, making the coffee cups wobble. "What? Why? How? Are you okay?"

I hadn't expected this response. It's not like I told her I dabble with street drugs or collect my own fingernail clippings or something. It was hardly weird to be vibratorless. Was it?

I shrugged.

"Shut the fuck up. How old are you?"

"Thirty-two."

"You made it to thirty-two years old and have never known the beautiful joy of a vibrator. We are fixing this right now."

Nora pulled out her phone and started furiously scrolling.

"What are you doing?" I whispered, fearing her response.

She raised one finger and I sat quietly.

"Hmmm," she said, not looking up from her phone. "What's your mailing address?"

I frowned at her.

"Either give it to me or I'm sending your present to Declan's house."

I looked around, trying to see if anyone had overheard our conversation. With my luck, Declan's mom would be standing there listening.

"Don't you dare." I whispered the address of the cottage and prayed she wasn't sending me sex toys.

She put her phone down, looking satisfied. "All set. You are my friend, and I will not allow you to have subpar orgasms any longer."

I stared at her. Did this woman just send me a vibrator?

"Trust me. Give this a try. Plus, a little battery-operated relief will keep you in control around Declan. You won't prematurely jump his bones if you are feeling satisfied. If you want to wait, you should be able to wait until you're ready."

I hated to admit it but she had a point. I respected a well-crafted argument and rock-solid logic. She also clearly cared about me, and that was a new feeling.

"Thanks," I said tentatively. "But I'm not a very sexual person."

She laughed. "Not possible. Orgasms are incredible and make life worth living. You need stress relief and you deserve the absolute best you can get. And you should not be depending on a man to deliver on that front."

I nodded, a bit dumbstruck by her.

"Plus. Taking charge of your own pleasure is a feminist act. You don't need a penis. You can take care of yourself."

She had a point. And it's not like I had been getting a lot of action recently. "Trust me, the guys I've been with have been underwhelming in that department."

"Don't worry. This will do the trick. At least until you are ready for Declan." She winked at me. "You will be good for him, I can tell."

"Thanks." I blushed slightly. Deep down I wanted to be good for him and knew I could be. But this was fake, not real. We were fake dating and eventually I'd have to go back to my old life. I couldn't help that I may have had a teeny crush on him. He was a both a certifiable sex god and unbelievably kind.

It's like she was reading my mind. "So what happens when you go back to Boston?"

I shrugged. "I don't know." We would break up. Of course we would. This wasn't even a real relationship. I shouldn't have agreed to this. The whole situation was extremely confusing. I liked clear goals and outcomes. This was already too messy for me.

I was going back to my firm. I was going back to my career. And, if for some reason that didn't work out, then I would start over at another firm. Once I did that there would be no time and no energy for a relationship, especially for someone like Declan. He was intense and generous and wonderful. He wouldn't want a girlfriend he saw once a month. He deserved someone who could give herself to him entirely.

"You are my friend, and I want you to have everything you want, okay? If that's Declan, great. If that's going back to that shithole law firm, that's great too. But don't forget about Havenport when you leave. We will all miss you."

We sat and chatted and ate and people watched. It was incredible. At this moment I regretted giving up on therapy. I wanted to reach out to Dr. Martha and beg her to help me. I wanted to tell her everything about Max and my cold dismissal from the firm, and Havenport, and Declan and my new friends. I wanted her to help me figure this all out. I was feeling so many things, and for the first time in my life, my path was unclear.

14

I MADE MY WAY BACK TO MY COTTAGE AFTER AN extremely awkward morning with Declan. I had gone over last night for dinner, and we had fallen asleep watching *Game of Thrones* on his couch. I woke up this morning snuggled up to him, drooling on his T-shirt. How mortifying. I was usually a very light sleeper, but after a few glasses of wine and a gigantic steak that I had shared with Ginger, I was out cold. It was nice, waking up in his muscular, tattooed arms. His body was warm and strong and I couldn't help but let my mind wander. What would it feel like to have him on top of me? Inside of me? Maybe the vibrator Nora sent me would get some use after all.

Before I could take a shower to rinse off a night of questionable decision-making, my phone rang. I knew this was coming. It was only a matter of days before she found out. I took a breath and answered.

"Hello."

"Astrid. What is going on?" Her tone was clipped and businesslike, with absolutely no empathy present.

"Hello, Mother. I am well. How are you?"

"Spare me the chit-chat, Astrid. Where are you? And

why aren't you at work?" My mother was all business, all the time. You didn't get as far as she had by making polite small talk.

"I am in Havenport, Mother. Aunt Connie is letting me stay at her rental cottage."

"Are you ill? Do you need a doctor? Because I can't imagine why you are at the beach when you should be at your office."

"Oh Mother, we both know that you know what is going on."

"I would like to hear it from my daughter. Do you have any idea how embarrassed I was? Hearing rumors about my own daughter? Scandalous."

"I think you are exaggerating."

"I was at the Women In The Law fundraising dinner last night and you were the talk of the table. I met some lovely young woman from Burns & Glenn. Charlotte something or other. She said you had been terminated for making some kind of catastrophic error. That can't be right. You don't make mistakes. I raised you to be careful and diligent."

Of course my mother takes my career failure personally. Of course she is thinking about how this makes her look instead of how it makes me feel. It was sadly typical of our relationship.

"Mother, I've had a very difficult few weeks. This has not been easy on me. I really can't argue with you right now." Dr. Martha had always been insistent that I draw boundaries with my mother. Now I remembered why it was so futile.

"But why? How did this happen? Did you lose focus? Did you bill fewer hours this year than last? Did you waste too much time on your pro bono project and neglect your clients?"

This was the most interest my mother had shown in

my life in a decade. Normally, she didn't care what I did, as long as I was winning awards and making her look good. Now, of all times, she decides she wants details? I knew this was a toxic relationship. I'd had enough therapy to know that. But I didn't know how to fix it or if it could be fixed. I decided to execute the nuclear option.

"No, Mom. If you must know they tried to fire me in retaliation for rejecting the sexual advances of a senior partner."

The gasp at the other end of the phone was no surprise. I could imagine her choking on her fancy tea in her chambers.

She was still silent.

"I politely turned down his advances on several occasions. And instead of acting like a gentleman, he kicked me off his cases and bad-mouthed me to the other partners. I spent six months doing grunt work to try and get back in their good graces, but you know as well as I do what happens once the rumors about your commitment start."

"How could this happen? Astrid, did you speak to HR?"

"I spoke to a few trusted people, and they told me that it would hurt my career more than it would hurt his to speak out. And at the time, I thought it was water under the bridge. I didn't know he was trying to get me fired."

"Men." I heard her exhale loudly. As difficult as my mother was, I could trust her hatred of the patriarchy, so at least we had that in common.

"So they fired you?"

"No. First that asshole gave me a terrible review and blamed me for a huge mistake that was made on a key merger."

"It's pretext. That's what it is."

"So when the managing partner sat me down to try

and fire me, I gently pushed back as these accusations were new to me. He then accused me of being too 'emotional.'"

"I am proud of you for standing up for yourself." Wow. I hadn't seen that coming. "But you need to make a plan. What are you doing to find a new position?"

"I can't do anything right now. They have to do an investigation. The firm is facing malpractice suits and clients are panicking."

"But surely they will give you a recommendation?"

"No. I refused to sign the liability waiver. So no severance and no recommendation."

"What? Astrid, what were you thinking? You need to get a new job as soon as possible. You know lawyers cannot have résumé gaps. It makes you look… flighty and unreliable."

"Mom, what they did was illegal. I have rights, and I'm not going to sign them away."

My mother let out a loud sigh. "Astrid, I am aware that you have rights. I have devoted my life to upholding those rights. But we both know that there are dire consequences for exercising those rights."

She wasn't wrong. If I sued a prior employer, no other law firm would ever touch me. I would be persona non grata in the legal community. Lawyers were expected to advocate on behalf of paying clients, but never for themselves.

"This is a terrible situation and one I wished you would never experience. But you've got to dust yourself off and find a new job. Keep working and keep succeeding. That's how you fight sexism."

"Mom, I disagree. Yes, if I do nothing and keep quiet then I save my own career. But what about all the other women? What about those who will come after me? I doubt I was the first woman Max Shapiro sexually harassed, and I won't be the last. If the firm is covering for him and creating a hostile work environment, then they should be held accountable."

My mom was quiet on the other end of the phone. She hated making a fuss. Despite being a judge, she would never recommend taking legal action. It would wreck my reputation as well as hers. "Astrid, I say this as both your mother and a woman who clawed her way to the top in a man's world. I admire your desire to fight the good fight, but it will hurt you personally. And you've worked so hard and have so much potential. At least consider signing the waiver and moving on with your life?"

I felt the fire within me extinguish slightly. My mother had a way of taking the wind out of my sails. "I will consider it, Mother."

"So what have you been doing?" she asked, changing topics. "Reading industry publications and journals? Taking continuing legal education courses?"

"No, Mother, I've been exercising and making friends and reading romance novels."

I could hear her eye roll through the phone. "You can use this time productively. Even if you insist on waiting this out."

I felt like a small child again, always falling short in her eyes. "I don't know that I can ever get back to where I was. I don't think I can rebuild what I lost." I didn't often make myself vulnerable to anyone, especially my mother, but I was feeling so lost.

"You know as a judge I can't call in favors or advocate on your behalf. But I can send you some firms that may be a good fit for your skill set. Starting over in a new firm will be tough, and you will have to prove yourself one hundred ten percent every day. But you will get back on the partner track. You are smart, motivated, and above all else, you are a Wentworth."

———

I sat on Emily's deck, clutching a hot mug of coffee as we watched her three kids run around the backyard with their dog. Emily, clad in pajamas, day-old eyeliner, and a pink pom-pom hat looked at me quizzically.

"What is going on with you?"

"I'm hungover and cranky."

She smiled at me. I hated her perkiness right now. "You come back here and land one of the most eligible bachelors in town and yet you are sitting here moping on my porch?"

I shivered. "It's like twenty degrees out. It's hard to be cheery in this cold."

Emily snorted. "You try keeping these little monsters locked up all day. Trust me, if they don't run around they will eventually turn on me."

"By the looks of it they've turned on each other. Is that Jacob hitting Ezra with a tree branch?"

"It's fine. He's the youngest so he's tough. Coco will break it up." I looked down at Coco, the twelve-year-old chocolate lab, as she sighed and trotted over to where the kids were attempting murder.

"So what's eating your ass, and not in the good way?" Emily never failed to thrill me with her dirty mind.

"I'm just frustrated about my firm."

"You mean your old firm?"

"Why are you being such a Debbie downer?"

"Because I think you need to face reality. You may not be going back to law firm life. Don't give me that sad puppy face. I didn't say you wouldn't go do something else awesome. Why aren't you sending out résumés?"

She was annoying me. I thought she was on my side. "Without a recommendation from Burns & Glenn or a reasonable explanation for why I was terminated, I have no shot at another job right now. Especially as the legal gossip is already spreading." I pushed my hands through my hair, frustrated and exhausted.

"So what are you going to do?"

"Max retaliated against me because I wouldn't sleep with him. He did this. He set me up. And I want his blood." It was the first time I had said it out loud, but it was the truth. I wanted to sue. I wanted to take down Max Shapiro and every person who enabled him to hurt me. And I wanted to force a reckoning in the legal profession. I wanted transparency so women would get a fair shot in the industry. But was I really capable of achieving all this? My own mother certainly didn't think so.

Emily put her arm around me and squeezed. "I love you, Astrid. And I want you to get justice. But prepare yourself. He is a powerful, rich, middle-aged white man, right?"

I nodded.

"So all the scales are tipped in his favor. It's not fair. But it's also not surprising," she said.

"I know that. But I just can't accept it." And that was the truth. The firm trained me. It was the best, and I was the best. I wanted that partnership. I deserved it. I had billed more hours, worked on more pitches, done more pro bono, and kissed more partners' and clients' asses than anyone in the building.

"Ultimately, it's your word against his."

"I know. And that's why I'm so angry."

She squeezed me tighter, and I rested my head on her shoulder.

"How much does your mom know?" she asked tentatively.

"She knows enough," I replied. "She called me this morning."

"That explains your mood. Let me guess, you got the 'I'm disappointed' speech?"

"Oh, you know it."

She laughed. "Remember when I got caught with peppermint schnapps at my junior prom? My mom called your mom to give me the lecture. I still remember it. I think I have PTSD."

"That's my mom. She does it to criminals all day. No one is better at expressing disappointment than Justice Wentworth."

"True. But Astrid, you are a grown-ass woman. You don't have to please your mom or your law firm or anyone else. Take care of Astrid."

"I'm trying."

"And why are you in such a rush to go back anyway? You have Declan now. You are making friends here."

"I know. I like it here, a lot actually. I loved coming here as a kid. It always felt safe and welcoming, you know? Which is why my first thought was to come here when everything happened. And Havenport has not let me down. It's been great. But I don't have a job."

Emily rolled her big blue eyes at me. "Oh please, Astrid, I know you don't need money." She wasn't wrong. I was lucky. My parents paid for my education so I had no debt. And Burns & Glenn had compensated me very generously for my labor.

"I can't retire at thirty-two, Emily."

"Taking a few months off is not retiring. Plus you have your dad's trust, right?"

"It technically became mine when I turned thirty. But I haven't touched it."

"So you have quite the safety net, sweetie. Most people would kill for a tenth of that."

I knew I was lucky, and it made me feel ungrateful. The truth was that I didn't have to worry about money at the moment. But I still wanted to earn and succeed on my own. Not because my mother was a judge and not because my father had made a few good investments in the nineties.

"So that's it? You're just going to leave? What about Declan?"

I shrugged and studied my cold feet. I really needed to buy some winter boots while I was here. I had never spent so much time outside in my life.

"Astrid. Don't be a dumbass. He is really into you. And I've known him for almost my entire life and he was a confirmed bachelor. He is not the dating type. He especially isn't the publicly dating and PDA type." She took a big gulp of coffee and pinned me with her best mom look. "And you obviously like him too, or you wouldn't be dating him."

"It's fake." Dammit. I shouldn't have said that.

She whipped her head around, dirty-blonde hair flying. "What now?"

Before I could respond, she put up her hand. "Wait, hold on." She stood up and walked to the edge of the deck. "Ezra, put that down. We do not throw rocks at birds." She turned back to me and continued, "I am actually worried he may be a sociopath. Hopefully the others will put me in a nice home with the good drugs so I don't have to watch the TV coverage."

I looked at the kids in the back of the yard. "Is Jacob riding his bike down the slide? Oh, shit. With no shoes and no helmet?"

Emily observed the situation and sat back down next to me. "He's fine. Don't judge me, Astrid. You have no idea. Every time I popped out one of these little shits I lost a little bit more of my mind. I am a shell of a woman these days." She shuddered, and I kept an eye on the kids.

"So hold on," Emily said. "Why are you fake dating

Declan? It's not like you couldn't get a real boyfriend in a hot minute. And Declan? I've seen women stand in line just to talk to him and experience his smolder up close."

That made me jealous. My eyes narrowed and I got antsy. "No, it's not like that. Please, please don't tell anyone. He would be devastated if anyone found out. And embarrassed. I can't believe I spilled. I keep secrets for a living."

"Oh sweetie," she said, patting my hand, "I am just that persuasive. And your secret is safe, especially because I don't think this will be fake for long. I give you a week before things get real and you forget this fake shit. But please explain to me why you need a fake boyfriend?"

"I have to go to that legal ball in March to accept an award."

"And you couldn't find a date on Tinder?"

I rolled my eyes at her. "First of all, I was not on Tinder. And second, online dating is not for me. I tried and I failed, okay? Declan is my friend and I have to go to the gala."

"Oh, right. Yes. You have to go. Fuck those fuckers." I imagined the swear jar in her house must be overflowing at this point.

"I was going to skip it. But I realized that made me look guilty and ashamed, and I'm neither of those things. I am going to show up with my head held high."

"And a smoking-hot date?"

"Precisely."

"Good call. He will absolutely intimidate everyone, and he is so attractive all the wives and gay men will be drooling over him."

I smiled. He really was that hot.

"Got it. So Declan can conveniently be your date. What about him? Why on earth does he need a fake girlfriend?"

"His mother."

Emily nodded. "Ah. I can see that. She is relentless. We're in the same meditation group and she seems all mellow and zen, but when it comes to her sons she is pretty fierce."

"I can imagine. I haven't met her, but I hear she's... intense."

Emily nodded. "Oh yes. So he's lying to his family. That seems weird. They are all so close."

"Listen, it's not my story to tell. He is sensitive about his family and falling short of their expectations. And given the situation I've gotten myself into, I can't exactly judge, now can I?"

"No, you're right."

"So I am just going to be the best fake girlfriend I can be. We are going to Liam and Cece's party next month and that will be the big test."

She smiled and nodded at me like I was one of her kids. "I don't understand why this is fake. Why not just date?"

"Because it's fake. That's what it is."

"You say that. But is it really fake in your head? In your heart? What about your lady bits, Astrid? Does your vagina think it's fake?"

I didn't know how to respond. Of course my vagina didn't think it was fake. My vagina had a mind of her own around Declan. Just thinking about him made me clench my thighs together.

Emily was still staring at me. "I don't know what I want. I like him. A lot."

"In a sexual way?"

Emily could be so dense sometimes. "Yes, in a sexual way. You have eyes. I don't need to tell you he is scorching hot."

"Yes, sweetie, I've been married ten years but even I could see his hotness from space."

"Yes. He is solar flare hot. And it's difficult not to rub up against him whenever I see him. Nora gave me a vibrator as a present, and it's getting some use."

Emily laughed. "Of course she did. Nora is the best. Also, why didn't you have a vibrator?"

"Stay focused, Emily."

"Astrid, he's interested. Look at you. And he's inviting you over and hanging out with you? He's into you. Just go for it."

"I can't. I'm the one who set the ground rules. I was the one who negotiated the terms. I can't be the one that breaks."

"Aaah. So you want him to make the first move?"

"Yes. No. No, I don't want anyone to make any moves." I stood up, getting frustrated. "If he makes a move, I will be powerless to resist and then things will get complicated."

Emily shook her head at me. "All the best stuff is complicated. Simple isn't fun, kid."

15

ASTRID

Declan had insisted that the Annual Havenport Christmas Tree Burn was the perfect venue for our first town event as a fake couple. It was the only town festival or event in January, and it was dark, outdoors, and freezing cold, so no one would be paying too much attention to us. He said we could try out our fake relationship and get a feel for how to sell it. So I bundled up and hoped for the best.

I had certainly never experienced anything like this before. There were hundreds of people out in a frozen corn field chanting and yelling while the firemen lit up a giant pile of Christmas trees approximately the size of a small apartment complex. The sun was starting to set, and everywhere I looked, bundled-up people ate, drank, and huddled near small campfires that were set up around the perimeter. Kids ran wild, playing games and throwing snowballs across the vast open land.

"So am I dressed okay?" I was wearing a giant red winter coat and a red hat with a pom-pom on it. My legs were encased in thick thermal leggings, and I had just bought the cutest knee-high winter snow boots.

"You look great. It's going to be really cold. Are you sure you're warm enough?"

"Yup. Got new boots, and a hat, and everything. I'm ready." I felt ready.

He drew me closer as we walked. "Are you really ready?" He gestured between us. "You know, to be my fake girlfriend?"

I gave him my best lawyer stare. "I was born ready. Are you having second thoughts?"

"About my gorgeous brilliant fake girlfriend? Absolutely not. I am ready to be the fake boyfriend of your dreams." He grabbed my hand and pulled me toward the action.

It was muddy, wet, and freezing cold but I was having a blast. After parking up on a hill in a muddy lot, Declan led me down to a large clearing away from the main fire area. It was beautiful. I ignored how my new boots were pinching my feet—they had looked so comfy and chic at the store—and focused on drinking in this experience. Booths and trucks flanked the median area, which was filled with picnic tables. In the middle, a man with a chainsaw was creating elaborate ice sculptures while people looked on and took photos. Local restaurants and stores manned booths, selling hot chocolate and yummy treats. We spotted the Binnacle Brewery tent and headed right over. I took a deep breath to steel myself. This would be our first test. Declan grabbed my gloved hand and squeezed. "Are you ready?"

I nodded.

He led me over to a large booth lit by string lights. In the front was a giant snowman dressed in Binnacle Brewing clothing and a pair of sunglasses. People were taking selfies in front of it and laughing. The whole vibe was fun and a bit silly. I felt more relaxed already.

Still holding my hand, Declan marched me around the

side of the booth where several people were busy taking orders and filling beers. A large bearded man who bore a striking resemblance to Declan immediately stepped out and greeted us. Damn, Nora wasn't lying—these Quinn boys were really good-looking.

"Dec, you're here!"

"I am." Declan pulled me close and wrapped his arm around my waist. "And this is Astrid."

"Wow. The famous Astrid. I'm thrilled to meet you."

I didn't know what to say to that. I smiled as Declan squeezed me closer. "It's a pleasure to meet you, Liam." I held out my gloved hand and he took it.

He pointed to the booth where a beautiful woman with wild curly hair was busy pouring beer. "That's my fiancée, Cece," he said. She looked up and waved at me. "And that," he said pointing to a serious-looking tall woman who was working the cash register, "is her sister, Maggie."

I gave them both a wave, not wanting to disturb them. The line was really long. Declan had mentioned how successful Liam's brewery was and I could see it. Even in the freezing cold, people were lining up for it.

"After our shift ends, we'll find you so you can be properly introduced. In the meantime, can I get you a beer, Astrid?"

I nodded, rubbing my hands together.

"Cece also convinced me to sell spiked hot chocolate if you want to warm up," Liam said. He was tall, dark, and handsome, just like Declan. But for two people who looked alike, they had vastly different energy. Liam was open, friendly, and gregarious, where Declan was subdued and closed off.

"I would love to try your famous beer first. Declan talks endlessly about how good it is."

Both men smiled at each other, and I felt like I had passed some sort of test. Liam looked giddy.

"I'll be right back with beers for both of you."

A few moments later, Liam handed us both beers and watched while I took a sip.

"This is great," I said, taking another big sip. "Hoppy and fruity and crisp." I smelled it. "Are these Centennial hops?" Liam's jaw dropped. Declan turned and stared at me.

I shrugged. "I know a little bit about beer. A couple of years ago I represented Night Walker when they were acquired by Anheuser-Busch."

"Sorry, what?" Liam looked gobsmacked.

"Astrid is a corporate attorney," Declan offered.

"I do mergers and acquisitions. And in the process, end up learning a lot about my clients and their businesses. I spent two years prepping financials and learning about Night Walker's business, and they gave me a lot of beer. So I learned to appreciate the good stuff."

Liam continued to look at me like I had three heads. "And this,"—I held up my almost empty plastic cup—"is really good stuff."

Liam leaned over, clasped Declan on the shoulder, and said, "Marry this woman." I flushed crimson. That was embarrassing and not what I was expecting. When I had been preparing to meet Declan's family, I expected a lot more formality and more doubt. Liam was so kind and welcoming and clearly bought us as a couple. He gave me a nod and went back to his booth where Cece and Maggie were busy selling beer to a long line of customers.

Declan was quiet so I stood there silently finishing my beer. I took a moment to admire how good he looked all bundled up in winter clothes. His Carhartt jacket barely concealed the thick muscular frame underneath, and his slouchy beanie highlighted his perfect bone structure. It was cold, probably around twenty degrees, but he looked perfectly comfortable, at ease in his body and his surroundings.

I bumped him with my hip. "You doing alright?"

He looked down at me. "Yup. So I think we convinced Liam." He threw an arm around my shoulders and crushed me to his chest. "So how about I get my girl something to eat? There is an incredible taco truck here."

I felt a fizzy feeling in my chest at being called his girl. I was giddy, and it wasn't the beer I had just drunk. Touching him and being with him just made me feel good.

As we walked toward the taco truck, with his arm around me, I let myself imagine, just for a moment, what it would be like if I really was his girl. What if this wasn't fake? I knew it was a dangerous game to play, but I couldn't help myself. My usual self-discipline seemed to desert me whenever Declan was around. It had been so long since I had been in a real relationship. And even then, it wasn't half as comforting and secure as my temporary fake relationship. Being here with Declan made me long for something real, something lasting. I guess that was yet another thing I would have to deal with in therapy. At this rate, I'd be a functional human being sometime in my midfifties.

I was studying the menu, internally debating between barbacoa and chicken Tinga when I felt Declan squeeze my hand. I looked up from my taco daze to see two older people approaching. A tiny, determined looking woman with a steel-gray bob was walking ahead of a tall, cheerful man walking with a cane. Declan turned and whispered to me, "It's go time."

Declan straightened up as the woman approached me. "Declan, sweetheart. I didn't expect to see you here." She didn't let him respond before walking right over to me and grabbing both my hands. She looked up at me. "This must be Astrid. I am so pleased to meet you, dear." She held up my arms as her gaze traveled up and down my body before meeting my eyes. I felt immediately self-conscious. I desperately wanted this woman to like me. I didn't know why, except that Declan loved his family. I wanted them to love me too, even if I was just his fake girlfriend.

"It's a pleasure to meet you, Mrs. Quinn. And this must be Captain Quinn." I tried to turn my attention to him, but she did not drop my arms. She stood, perfectly still, assessing me. Probably calculating how she could get rid of me since I clearly wasn't good enough for her son.

So I was doubly shocked when she pulled me into a tight hug. For such a tiny woman, she was deceptively strong. "Oh dear," she said, finally releasing me, "you are so lovely. And please call me Annie."

"Mom, don't overwhelm her. She just met Liam and he acted like a weirdo."

"It's just such a pleasant surprise to see you with such a"—she paused—"lovely and accomplished young woman." She beamed at me. She turned to her husband who was walking slowly toward us.

"Captain, get over here and meet Declan's girlfriend," she clucked.

The Captain ambled over slowly and held out his hand. "Please excuse my Annie, she is overly invested in our sons' love lives."

I shook his outstretched hand and liked him immediately. His jovial, casual nature was in direct contrast to the tightly coiled intensity of his wife. "We've been hearing all over town how brilliant and accomplished you are. It's a pleasure to finally meet you."

I smiled and felt a little defensive of Declan. "Oh, I'm sure that's just rumors. And speaking of brilliant and accomplished, Declan has been filling me in on your booming business and all his innovative ideas for the future."

The Captain coughed and looked at Declan, who beamed with pride. It felt good, bragging about my fake boyfriend. Was this what real relationships were like? Two people having each other's backs and taking on the world together? Because that sounded really good right about now.

Declan pulled me close, as if trying to shield me from their well-intentioned questions. The Quinns seemed like kind, helpful people who really loved their kids. It made me feel a bit jealous actually. I couldn't imagine my mother ever caring about whom I was dating, and she was definitely not a spontaneous hugger.

After we chatted with his parents for a bit, they excused themselves to find some of their friends. Mrs. Quinn specifically noted how excited she was for me to attend Liam and Cece's engagement party in February.

As soon as they were out of sight, Declan grabbed me by the shoulders. "I have never seen my mom like that in my life." He took off his hat and ran his hands through his hair. "And the way you told my dad I was brilliant? Thank you."

I smiled at him, feeling a warmth spread throughout my body.

"Wow. This is going to work, Astrid. It's going to work." His smile was so broad, so genuine it broke my heart a bit. Why couldn't his parents just accept him as he was? Why did he need a fake girlfriend to win their approval? And why was I so sad that we were succeeding at faking a relationship?

Pull yourself together. This is the plan. Stick with the plan. He doesn't want to be your real boyfriend, and the last thing you need is a distraction. This is a mutually beneficial arrangement to help you get your life back on track. "So did I earn a taco?" I gazed up at Declan and batted my eyelashes.

"Sweetheart, you earned a dozen tacos. Let's feed you."

My fake boyfriend certainly knew the way to my heart.

———

This was one of the most fun nights I'd had in years. The Christmas tree fire was incredible. Declan had introduced me to his other brother, Callum, and asked him to take a picture of us. We posed in front of the massive pile of trees before it was lit, and it was easily five times as tall as we were. We took a few pictures, including one where he was kissing the side of my head while I laughed. Logically, I knew I should post it on Instagram as evidence of our relationship, but part of me wanted to keep it private, a sweet reminder of this surprisingly fun evening.

"So you and Khal Drogo, huh?" Callum was studying us curiously. I stood up a little straighter, meeting his eye. I wasn't about to let his skepticism get under my skin. Callum was the complete opposite of Declan. He looked like a young congressman in his expensive wool coat and cashmere scarf.

I smiled. "I get that reference!" I realized after the fact that I sounded like a total dork.

Declan put his arm around me. "I've been catching Astrid up on all the TV and movies she's missed. We're currently watching *Game of Thrones*."

Callum seemed confused, so I tried to explain. "I haven't consumed much pop culture for the past ten years. I've been working nonstop and haven't made time to keep up with this stuff."

Declan put his arm around me. "I will happily educate you."

He wiggled his eyebrows at me, and I tried to suppress a giggle.

"How do you feel about superheroes, Astrid? My brother is obsessed," Callum teased.

Declan looked sheepish. "I read a lot of comics as a kid."

"I haven't seen any superhero movies."

"There are dozens of them."

"I'm only really interested in the ones with female heroes."

"Oh, that's easy, there are only like three of those."

"Shocker," I deadpanned.

We ended up watching the fire being lit with Callum and some of the other friends from town. Nora was there with Cece and Maggie, and Emily and Derek came over to say hi. Aunt Connie had taken their kids home, so they were craving some adult time. We all sat and drank beers and spiked hot chocolate. I didn't know Derek that well, but it turned out he was hilarious. He had us rolling with stories of his architecture clients, all delivered in his signature Texas twang. Emily and Derek were clearly obsessed with each other in a very affectionate, public way. Not my style at all, but I had to admit it was sweet. It warmed my heart to see them so happy together after a decade of marriage and three kids. Emily deserved all the good things.

I felt welcomed and accepted into this group of friends. Every few minutes Declan looked at me, and I felt warmth spread across my body. His intense gaze unnerved and excited me.

At one point, a strikingly attractive Asian man wandered over and was chatting with the group. He looked familiar, but in the dark it was hard to place him.

Suddenly, Callum was introducing me. Turns out I was standing in front of Lucas Kim. Tech genius-Forbes

30 under 30-MIT grad-reclusive billionaire Lucas Kim. I was starstruck.

"This is Declan's girlfriend, Astrid."

I shook his hand and stared at him.

"It's nice to meet you," he said as he smiled. I nodded mutely.

Declan, sensing my hysteria, chimed in. "Astrid is visiting Havenport for a while. She is an attorney, most recently at Burns & Glenn in Boston."

Lucas Kim smiled. "Wow. That's great. I have used them over the years for a variety of business. That is very impressive." I almost choked on my tongue. Lucas Kim thought I was impressive?

Get it together, Astrid. You're a Wentworth, for Christ's sake. "Thank you. I had the pleasure of working on some matters for you a few years back. The acquisition of ScansTic?"

"Wow." He gave me a dazzling smile. "You were on that team? Fantastic. That was a tricky one but it worked out beautifully for us. Charlie, my general counsel, isn't very forthcoming with praise, so let me just say thank you." For a billionaire genius he was one of the most genuine, friendly people I had ever met. He instantly put everyone at ease. Everyone except Nora, who was currently shooting eye daggers at him.

I blushed and I could feel Declan shift uncomfortably next to me. "Don't thank me, it was a big team and I just did my part. And don't be too hard on Charlie—he had a lot going on and put in some long hours with our team. He flew to meet us in Delaware for the bankruptcy hearing on one day's notice."

"I forgot about that. You're right. He is a good guy and certainly keeps my ass in line. What a small world, seeing you here in Havenport."

We chatted for a few more minutes about people we

knew in common and how I was liking Havenport. He made the rounds, talking to everyone, including Derek, who he seemed to be quite friendly with.

I turned to Declan who was standing with Callum. "How do you guys know Lucas Kim?"

Callum chuckled. "Luke? He plays basketball with us on Sunday mornings."

"He is a hell of a point guard," Declan mumbled.

"So you're friends with him?"

"Pretty much. He's always around town raising money and participating in events. He's a really good guy," Callum said.

Declan stood quietly sipping his beer. He seemed uneasy. I shifted in my boots, since I had developed a very painful blister on my right heel. I knew I should have broken these in.

After another hour, I was pleasantly buzzed, full of tacos, and cursing these damn cute boots. I should have bought the ugly ones. They probably lasted decades and felt like your feet were being spooned by fluffy clouds. Instead I went for the cute ones. And the cute ones always got you. Chewing your feet to shit and leaving you with lifelong scars.

Despite the freezing cold, it had been a really fun night. Declan was the perfect fake boyfriend—he bought me tasty things to eat, introduced me to people, and snuggled me into his broad warm chest when I started to get cold. The problem was that he was making me feel a lot of things. Things I shouldn't be feeling and definitely did not want to deal with at the moment. I was confused, happy, and more than a little bit turned on. I knew I couldn't act on it. My rules forbid it, and my brain knew it was bad. But my vagina, that sneaky bitch, kept urging me on, tingling at the smallest bit of contact.

16

DECLAN

I was restless. Out of sorts. Confused.

Tonight was a huge success. I introduced Astrid to my family, my friends, and half of the town, and everyone seemed to believe in our fake relationship. I should be elated right now. So why was I feeling so frustrated?

There was a part of me that felt ashamed. I was thirty-five years old, for God's sake. Old enough to know better than to fake a relationship and lie to the people I loved. But I felt trapped and defensive, and this situation presented a clean, easy way out. I had never been one to take the easy way out. My parents certainly never allowed it, and the navy beat those impulses out of me. So why now?

Astrid. She was truly unlike any woman I had ever met in my life. I was an introvert—being with people exhausted me and I looked forward to my solitude to recharge. But it wasn't like that with Astrid. If anything she energized me with her brains, her beauty, and her take-no-shit attitude.

It had been years since I had felt this way about a woman. My desire to be near her and learn more about her scared me. I didn't want to hurt her. I didn't want to get hurt. So her rules, which in typical Astrid fashion were very clear, succinct, and comprehensive, were a good thing. I wouldn't get any ideas. I already had a lot of ideas, but nothing I would act on.

Because there was no way a girl like Astrid would be interested in me. We had nothing in common. Her world was one of skyscrapers and multi-billion-dollar deals. She lived a completely different lifestyle than I did. There was no chance of a real relationship. She was committed to getting her career and her life back. And as her friend, I wanted to help her.

As Astrid and I hiked back to my truck, I got more and more angry with how she reacted to meeting Lucas Kim. She acted like he was a celebrity, which I guess he was. I never cared much about that stuff, and Luke was a really fun guy, but seeing her lose her cool over him? It punched me in the gut. Because it reaffirmed what I already knew. She was way out of my league. I would only bring her down. No matter how confused I felt at the moment, we would never be real. The raw jealousy pumped in my veins, and I was overcome with nervous energy.

Astrid lagged behind as I climbed the muddy hill up to the back parking lot. It was dark and late and cold, but I wanted to get in my truck and get home. I turned around to see what was taking her so long.

"Are you okay, slowpoke?"

"I'm fine."

"Because I want to get home before sunrise." Even though it was dark, I could see the fire in her eyes. She stopped walking and put her hands on her hips.

"What is your problem, Declan?"

"I don't have a problem. I just want to go home."

"Bullshit. We were having an amazing night and then

you started acting angry and weird the minute I began talking to Lucas Kim."

I strode over to where she stood, immobile in the snow and mud. "I don't know what you are talking about."

"Stop it, Declan."

"Listen. I get it. He's a handsome rich guy. Do you want to fake break up with me so you can go after him? It's fine. Just tell me the truth."

A scary calm settled over Astrid's features. Her mouth was a hard line, and her eyes bore through my skull, but she was controlled, impassive. "Declan Quinn, are you jealous? Because you have no reason to be. You are my fake boyfriend, so you don't get to be cranky if I am interested in someone."

I exhaled, not realizing I had been holding my breath. She was right. I was an asshole. She deserved someone like him. I couldn't compete with that.

She walked closer to me and put her hand on my chest. "But it doesn't matter because I do not want to date him. He seems like a cool guy who is very interesting to talk to, but I am not attracted to him. I am committed to you, my fake boyfriend, and no one could ever get between us." She moved closer until our bodies were almost touching.

She looked up at me with that cool, intense gaze, and I felt something in my chest loosen. Why was I getting jealous? I couldn't catch feelings for Astrid. I couldn't flip out every time she had a conversation with another man. "I'm sorry," I whispered, finally realized how idiotic I was being.

She tapped me on the chest. "Apology accepted. Can we go home now?"

"Yes," I replied, and offered her my arm.

"I'm sorry I am walking so slow, but these new boots have chewed up my feet and they are frozen and bloody right now." I looked down at her trendy snow boots and laughed. Yup, that sounded about right. Before I could talk myself out of it, I had slung her over my shoulder and was fireman carrying her up the hill to my truck. She put up a little bit of a fight, but I was much too distracted by the round supple ass in my line of sight. Goddamn, I loved these leggings. I wanted to spank this ass and bite it and… *stop, you perv*. She is a friend and you are helping her. Don't make it sexual. Too late. My dick had not gotten the message and was ready to party in my jeans.

When we reached my truck, I walked over to the passenger side door and let her down. She slid down the front of my body, and my skin caught fire beneath my winter layers. When her feet hit the ground, she leaned back against the door. I placed my arm on the door frame, caging her between me and the truck. I tried to will my heart to stop racing.

"Tonight went well," I said, attempting to be casual.

"Yes. I agree."

"You are the best fake girlfriend I've ever had."

"You are the only fake boyfriend I've ever had."

I smiled. She sighed and looked up at me. I couldn't read her. I had no idea what she was thinking. But my own brain was screaming "kiss her," and I could think of nothing else. I stared at her plump pink lips, trying to remember why this was such a bad idea. Her green eyes were hooded with lust, and she was breathing heavily. I wanted to fight it. This urge to take her, to claim her, to make her mine was overwhelming. And I knew I would have to fight it eventually. But at that moment, standing in a frozen corn field in the middle of January, I couldn't fight it. So I gave in.

I gently cupped her face and kissed her. I wanted to be gentle, I wanted to be careful, but one taste of her luscious mouth and I lost every shred of self-control I had.

For someone so cool, so impassive, Astrid kissed with fiery passion. What started out as sweet and gentle escalated very quickly. A small moan escaped from her lips as she pushed up on her toes and wrapped her arms around my neck. We were devouring one another, possessed by some strange passion. She tasted like beer and smelled like a campfire, and I was so turned on at that moment, I knew I could make some very bad decisions.

We kissed and kissed until she bit down hard on my bottom lip. A bolt of electricity surged through my body, and I pinned her up against the truck. She wrapped one long leg around my waist and I fumbled with her coat, trying to get my hands on her incredible body. Her hands were in my hair, and she pressed herself up against my aching cock while I contemplated stripping her naked in this field. She was soft and sexy and kissing the hell out of me. But I couldn't let this go further. We had an agreement, and I was nothing if not a man of my word. I gently put her down and broke away from the kiss.

She slumped up against the truck, panting. Gone was the frosty ice queen, and instead I was faced with a wild sex goddess with fire in her eyes. It felt good, knowing that I could make her breathless. Knowing that I could break down that controlled facade and make her go wild.

I took a step back to stop myself from making another mistake. "Astrid, I'm so sorry."

She looked dazed. "What?"

I ran my hands through my hair. At some point I had lost my hat, but I didn't care. "I shouldn't have kissed you."

"I'm pretty sure I enjoyed it," she replied, still catching her breath.

I smirked. "Pretty sure?"

"Why don't we do it again so I can be certain?" She

gave me a mischievous grin, and my dick ached even more.

"I shouldn't have done it. I don't want to violate the rules."

"Screw the rules. I'm sick of rules," she quipped, still smiling at me.

It would be so easy to just forget about it and do whatever I wanted right now. But I liked Astrid. She was my friend, and I knew she was hurting. I had to do what was right, as much as I hated it.

"Hop in. I'll drive you home."

Before the words even left my mouth, Astrid had transformed herself. Gone was the wild sex goddess, and the frosty professional was back. She nodded and hopped in the truck.

I wanted to be a good guy. I wanted to do the right thing. But the way she was acting, I felt like I messed everything up. I wanted her, that was clear. But I didn't want to hurt her or hurt our friendship. But I couldn't deny our explosive chemistry. That kiss completely rocked my world.

I knew we needed to forget this and go back to being friends. But how could I keep pretending this was fake when being with her felt so right?

17

DECLAN

It was Sunday morning. And instead of sleeping in or catching up on work, I was running with Callum. He had called me this morning and wouldn't take no for an answer, so I got dressed, jumped in my truck, and met him at our favorite spot on the pier.

"Is Liam coming?" I asked.

"Nope. Told me to fuck off. That Sunday mornings are for his lady."

I shook my head. "Bastard."

"I'm a little jealous though," he mused.

I kind of agreed but would never say it out loud. Liam had found his soulmate, and although I was definitely not looking for one, it did seem nice. Sunday morning spent snuggling, drinking coffee, and having sex sounded pretty amazing. Especially as I was standing on a pier in the middle of January freezing my balls off with my older brother.

Cal was engaging in some elaborate looking stretches.

"Are you training for a marathon or something?" I asked.

"Nope."

"Then what's with the fitness obsession?"

"What's wrong with taking care of my body? I say we go eight or nine today." He rubbed the back of his neck, his tell. And I wanted to dig further.

"Miles?" Ugh. I hated running. I did it because I wanted to stay fit and my dad's heart attack scared the shit out of me, but I tapped out at three or four most days.

"Come on, let's get going," he barked impatiently.

We ran through town up Water Street to the boatyards and commercial docks. We set an easy pace, and the town was so peaceful this early in the morning that it seemed like a good time to figure out what was going on with Callum. After a few miles we looped back around the hill toward downtown. I was already dreaming about a breakfast sandwich from the diner. Maybe two, given how brutal this run had been.

"So what's going on with you? You're dating Astrid?" He raised an eyebrow at me.

"Yup." The less I said the better. My brother knew me better than anyone on earth and just happened to be super brilliant. The odds were good he could sniff this one out if I slipped up.

"Care to elaborate?"

"Nope."

"It's just a surprise. You aren't the relationship type. At least you haven't been in a while."

"I know that. But I like her. I'm a thirty-five-year-old man. I am smart enough to know what to do when I like a woman."

"I know you are."

"Good."

"How about we go up by the hospital and then back downtown? It's only another mile or so. I'll buy you coffee?"

"Sure. But you are buying me eggs too."

"Deal."

———

It wasn't so bad. The town was so quiet and peaceful at this hour. We had looped up past the hospital all the way toward the highway and turned around. We ran by the old Thompson Farm and through the more rural side of town and then back downtown, where things were starting to wake up. Running was a lot more fun with someone else. Callum looked tired and in a better mood, so I knew it was time to strike.

"So," I asked, "are you going to tell me what's going on?"

He feigned surprise. "What do you mean?"

"Don't bullshit me, Cal. I know something is up with you and you are not alright. You are running yourself into the ground, literally, and haven't been yourself for weeks." I raised my eyebrows at him and sat silently waiting for him to answer.

He stared at me blankly, stretching his quad while holding on to the park bench. An outdoor yoga class was getting started on the pier, and there was a lot of chatter.

I took a step closer. "You are my brother and my best friend. We have always shared everything with each other. Also you have stubble. You hate my beard and constantly give me shit about it. If you are not shaving then something is up. You know I am a vault, man. I just want to help. "

Callum looked at me and let out a sigh. "Fine. Let me finish stretching."

After cooling down we sat on the bench in silence, looking out at the harbor. People were taking their small craft out, enjoying the warmer winter weather and the bright sunlight. I longed to be on the water. I spent most of my time in the office these days, and it was starting to get to me.

I gave him time. I didn't want to rush him. And so we sat. Silence didn't bother me. In fact, I reveled in it. It was nice hanging out with my big brother like this.

"Becca is engaged," he blurted out, disrupting our meditative silence. Oh shit. Becca was Callum's ex-wife. She was the love of his life who blindsided him by walking out one day and never coming back.

"What? Engaged?"

"Yup." His gaze was steely and focused on the horizon. "That's not even the worst part."

"And…" How much worse could this get?

"She is engaged to Patrick Richmond."

"You have got to be shitting me." Patrick was Callum's former best friend.

I put my arm around his shoulders. "I am so sorry, bro. That sucks. Those assholes deserve each other," I growled. I didn't get worked up about much, but someone hurting my family made me see red. I wanted to jump in the car and fucking rearrange that smug prick's face.

"Thanks, Dec." He turned to face me, and I saw how exhausted he looked. "It's been almost three years since the divorce and it still hurts." I didn't know the full details of Callum and Becca's divorce. As his brother, my job at the time was to get him drunk and make sure he showed up on time to his court dates. We were not in the habit of talking about feelings, so this conversation was already feeling strange.

He ran his fingers through his hair, and I noticed it had been a while since he'd had a trim. My older brother was always the cool, controlled one. He supported Liam when his first brewery went under, and he helped me figure my shit out after I got out of the navy. He was there for everyone. And part of me was proud that I could be there for him.

"So that's why you have been exercising like a demon?"

"I guess so. I need something to take my mind off this."

"Fair enough. I'm here if you need me. To talk, to drink, or to run. Got it?"

"Thanks, bro." He clapped me on the shoulder and offered a weak smile.

"Are you going to tell Mom and Dad?"

"Hell, no. Mom would probably go slash their tires. Or worse."

"Remember when she went to the psychic lady who used to set up a table in the town square and tried to put a curse on Becca?"

We both laughed. My mom was many things, but forgiving was not one of them. Becca had hurt her son and denied her grandbabies. My mom was still furious at her.

"Good call, the last thing we need is Mom getting arrested."

———

"So are we going to talk about Astrid?"

We had snagged a booth in the corner of the diner. It was busy, even though it was still early, and after two bacon, egg, and cheese sandwiches on homemade English muffins, I was feeling much better. The diner always made me feel better. It was a second home.

I sipped my third cup of coffee and tried to figure out how to avoid this conversation. "What is there to talk about?"

"I don't know. What is the deal? You seem anxious every time I bring her up."

I didn't know how to respond to his question. Was it because I was overwhelmed with anxiety about lying to my family? Or was it because I could not compartmentalize my feelings for her and knew things were already getting messy?

"I'm not trying to offend you. I am genuinely happy for you. It's been a long time since you found someone you liked enough to keep around for a while. It's a good thing," he said, gesturing Jackie for a coffee refill.

I was feeling defensive. "Let me guess, you think she's too good for me?" It wasn't shocking. I figured this would be the response of most people. But it kind of hurt to hear it come from my brother.

"No. Not at all."

"Bullshit."

"Maybe. But not for the reasons you think."

"Really?"

Callum pinned me with his big brother stare. "I don't care about her Ivy League degrees or her fancy job. You are one of the smartest people I know."

"No way." I hated when he did this. Tried to pretend I was as smart as he was. I knew it wasn't true, and I hated being lied to.

"You are, Dec. You are thoughtful and creative and humble. You are great. Don't put yourself down."

I knew there was a "but" coming. I waited for him to continue.

"But I worry about you. It takes a lot to get you out of your shell. And I am worried this girl will hurt you. She is clearly only here temporarily, and she comes from a very different world."

I debated how to respond. He was right. Of course he was. My brother was perceptive as well as smart, and nothing got by him, especially when it came to his family. Suddenly I was overwhelmed with the need to tell him the truth. He was my best friend, and I felt guilty lying to him.

"It's fake," I said, staring into my coffee mug.

"I don't follow."

"Our relationship. It's fake. We are friends who are faking."

"Why?" He looked totally confused.

"Because I want to get Mom off my back and show Dad I'm stable enough to run the company. It's starting to really grate on me. I feel like shit most days that I'm not like everyone else. That I'm not some super friendly charming guy like you who can find a girlfriend effortlessly. That I'm not the settling down type. I just want everyone to leave me alone for a bit, so Astrid is pretending to be my girlfriend while she's here."

"I want to talk more about why you feel the need to fake a relationship instead of having an honest conversation with our parents, but first, what about Astrid? Is she just a really nice person?"

I did not want to have that conversation with him right now. I had already made myself vulnerable. "It's not my story to tell, but she needs me too. I am going to be her date for some fancy law gala so she can network and find her next job."

"Ah. Is there someone she wants to make jealous?"

"No, why?"

"No reason. I can just see that you are perfect for that."

"Huh?" I grunted at him.

He punched me in the arm. "Dude, you are a tall, built veteran with long hair and tattoos. You will scare the shit out of whatever poindexter she used to date."

"I never thought about it like that."

"You are so clueless sometimes. I will never repeat this, but have some confidence, man. You are like an Irish Jason

Momoa. You walk in a room and most of the women stare at you." He gestured around the diner where there were definitely a few ladies checking me out. Including Nonna Riccio, Nora's eighty-year-old grandmother who sat at the counter fully made up in a fancy pink suit. I wasn't blind. I knew I got attention from women, but most of the time I didn't care. It made me feel like a piece of meat sometimes.

"Do you have a tux?" Callum asked.

"Nope."

"Okay, I got a guy."

"Of course you do."

"You will thank me when you look like James fucking Bond at this legal thing. If you are going to be her fake boyfriend then be the best goddamn fake boyfriend you can be."

Just the thought of wearing a tux made my skin itch. "I hate you right now, but you have a point." I sighed. "Fine. I'll go to your tux guy."

He smiled. I hated proving him right.

"But," I continued, "promise you won't tell anyone we're fake dating."

"Of course not. I'll keep your secret. I think you guys are lying to yourselves, but that's for you to figure out."

He wasn't wrong. Deep down I knew I was lying to myself, but it seemed preferable to confronting my complicated feelings. I couldn't tell him that sometimes it felt real. I couldn't admit that I was getting attached to her.

I hesitated. "And, it's complicated. And it doesn't help that Ginger is in love with her."

"Wow." He stroked his stubble and smiled at me. Asshole. He was clearly enjoying my anguish.

"And I kissed her, after the Christmas Tree Burn."

"Really?" He smirked that irritating smirk, and I hated myself for telling him all this. "How was it?"

Now I was pissed. I stood up. "Fucking magical. Is that what you want to hear? It was the hottest kiss of my life, and I can't stop thinking about it."

Callum pointed to my chair. "Sit down, Dec, and take a breath. We can figure this out."

"There's nothing I can do. I dug my grave on this. I'm going to hold up my end of the bargain because I'm a man of my word. And I'm not going to upset or confuse her with my feelings."

"But you have feelings?"

He was pissing me off. "Yes, Cal, and I haven't had feelings like this ever."

He laughed. That asshole actually laughed. "Oh shit. You are so screwed."

"Please don't remind me." I glared at him. As much as I appreciated him having my back, I also knew he was going to have a field day with this.

"Can we go back to the part where we never discuss feelings and just mess with each other all the time?"

"Yes, please," I replied. "This is more sharing than I've done in the past ten years, and I'm feeling faint." I fanned myself for dramatic effect.

He grinned at me. "What if we head over to the brewery after this and bust Liam's balls for a bit."

"It's a start."

18

ASTRID

I DIDN'T KNOW WHAT TO DO. DECLAN KISSED ME. And it wasn't just a kiss. He had owned me, body and soul, for a few sweet moments. A meteor could have hit the earth and I wouldn't have noticed.

The feel of his body was imprinted on me, and I couldn't shake the fluttering in my chest every time I thought about it.

I was in deep trouble.

First, he threw me over his shoulder and jogged up a steep hill like it was nothing. I was impressed by his strength but also a bit surprised by how much I liked being manhandled. I had never been with a big, dominant guy before, and it was a major turn-on. Declan was a man, a big strong man who was radiating pure sex and lust. Just the memory made me shiver.

But what did this mean? Did I screw everything up? I needed to talk to someone, someone who could help me figure this out. I grabbed my phone and texted Emily.

Astrid: SOS

Emily: You ok? Do you need bail money? Help burying a body?

Astrid: No. Need advice re: romantic shit

Emily: Give me 5 min.

A few minutes later my phone rang. "What happened? Are you okay?"

I let out the breath I was holding in. "Yes. I'm fine. Declan kissed me after the festival."

"And?"

"And it was amazing. It was intense and gentle and hot and rearranged some of my brain cells. Happy now?"

"Oooh."

"And now I'm confused and horny."

"Let me make sure I get it. You guys walked back to his truck."

"Actually he carried me back to the truck."

"Aw shit. That's hot."

"I know. It was incredible. And then he kissed me."

She squealed. "Aww, this is so romantic. I love it. A sweet first kiss!"

"No, it was a full blown make-out session with some light over-the-clothes petting, if we're getting technical."

She got serious. "Lady, when it comes to sexy times, technical details are always required."

"So what do I do?"

"What do you want to do?"

"I have no idea. I want to walk over to his house and rip his clothes off."

"Attagirl."

"But I also don't want to compromise what we have. This is the first time in my life I've had a real friend. Someone loyal and kind who isn't looking to stab me in the back or get ahead. You and Declan and Nora—you guys are all I have right now."

"I get it. This goes against every instinct I have, but I think you should just take a breath. Don't do anything. Just sit with this and you will figure it out."

Not what I was expecting from Emily at all.

She continued, "I hate myself for saying this. Usually I am all in favor of hot sex. And you know it would be hot." She had a point. I wasn't imagining our chemistry—it was intense.

"It would be scorching."

"So better to just take a breather. You've had a lot going on. Take some time for yourself and figure out what you want."

"That's really good advice."

"Thanks. I think I'm having an out of body experience. I think Cece is rubbing off on me with her whole responsible, sensible deal." She seemed confused by her own reasonableness. "Anyway, do you know what you need?"

I had no clue. "What?" I replied.

"A girls' night."

———

I was not one for socializing. Work was a convenient excuse but I just wasn't a social butterfly. Usually after an hour I wanted to be home with a book. I swear I wasn't a bitch. At least most of the time.

Sure, I had been called a bitch more times than I could count in my life. Some days I actually wore my bitch status as a badge of honor. But mostly I was just quiet and more introspective than the average person. I liked to think things through, roll them around in my brain before speaking. I also hated having to talk to dumb people. So that made it difficult to interact with a significant portion of the population. Luckily, in my law firm ivory tower, I mostly interacted with other lawyers. That's not to say some of them weren't total idiots—there were plenty of those—but it did make things a bit easier in my day-to-day life.

But outside the cutthroat halls of Burns & Glenn, people behaved pretty differently. It was perfectly acceptable to be rude at the firm. We were busy and no one had enough time. If you let an elevator door close in someone's face or took a phone call in the middle of a conversation, it was fine, because we were busy and we were the best. And being the best meant focusing on work above all else.

But I was learning more and more that the "real world" was very different than the legal world. And I liked it. I liked that people said hello to each other. I liked that people held open doors and took time to chat and help out. I was amazed when Declan described how friends and neighbors had jumped in to lend a hand after his father had a heart attack.

And, as for me, everyone here had embraced me openly. Nora had instantly befriended me and welcomed me into their circle. Emily had become a trusted confidante. And Declan... there were no words for what was happening there. So I was determined to go out with my new friends, have a great time, and temporarily forget about all the weirdness with Declan.

Nora texted me ahead of time to "look hot." I didn't know what that meant exactly, but I decided on a pair of the new jeans I got at her store and a green lacy camisole topped with a leather jacket.

I had never owned a leather jacket before. It was not the sort of thing a Wentworth wore. But when I saw this at Nora's store, I had to have it. It was buttery soft and a cognac-brown color. I wanted it. I loved it. I wanted to be the woman who wore this jacket. So I bought it. It was expensive, but it felt good. It felt like another step forward in figuring out who the hell I was and what the hell I was doing with my life.

Liam was our designated driver for the night, so he picked me up in his SUV with Cece and Nora and dropped us off at the bar. From the outside it looked like a dingy dive. It had a giant neon sign of a whale holding a martini glass. It was retro and kind of funny. Liam gave Cece a very enthusiastic kiss and promised to pick us back up whenever we wanted. He looked a lot like Declan—tall, dark hair, and blue eyes—but his personality was completely different. He was friendly and approachable and seemed to be head over heels in love with Cece. I felt a pang of jealousy.

As we entered, we were overwhelmed by the huge crowd. It was loud and quite packed for a Thursday night. I had never in my life gone to a bar during the week. It seemed irresponsible. In college and law school I was too busy studying and obsessing about my grades. The thought of being out late on a school night terrified my inner good girl. And going out period was impossible at the firm. I worked every night either at my desk or on my couch. There were not many opportunities for weeknight cocktails.

Nora led us to a large banquet style table in the back corner where two ridiculously attractive men were canoodling and sipping trendy cocktails with a woman I recognized as Cece's older sister, Maggie.

Nora shouted over the crowd, "Christian, Dante, meet my new friend, Astrid."

They both smiled, and I was blinded by perfectly straight white teeth. Dante, the shorter of the two, jumped up. "Oh my God, I am so happy to finally meet you. You are the sneaky bitch who got that hottie Declan Quinn to settle down."

He was Latino, in his early thirties, and wearing a very

trendy tweed vest and several leather cuff bracelets. I liked
his energy. "I would hardly call it settling down. We're just
dating." I shrugged and took a seat as Cece scooted into
the booth, air kissing both men.

"Wait, don't sit down, I want to look at you."

Dante appraised me head to toe. Normally this type of
thing would make me uncomfortable, but he seemed
kind. And if his skin, eyebrows, and clothes were any
indication, he was probably in a position to give me some
impeccable beauty tips.

"You. Are. Gorgeous!" He wrapped me into a huge
hug. I was several inches taller than he was, so he was
basically hugging my boobs. I gave him a halfhearted pat
on the back. What was up with all the spontaneous
hugging in this town?

"Christian, don't you think so?"

Christian appeared to be in his late thirties and far
more subdued than his husband. He looked up from his
phone. "Oh yes. She's a hottie. Love the jacket."

"She got it at my store," Nora piped in.

"It looks like it was custom made for you," Christian
remarked. "I've got a guy if you ever need another." I
nodded. Christian looked far too cosmopolitan for this
small town. He seemed to be the type of person who "had
a guy" for everything.

Dante, on the other hand, was positively manic. "Talk
to me about your eyebrow strategy," he asked, taking a
long drag of a fancy looking martini.

I looked at Maggie and Cece who were chatting with
Christian. "Um…I don't have one."

He patted my hand. "I can fix that. And what about
this hair?" He grabbed at my hair, and I felt a bit
defensive.

I scooted back. Truthfully, my hair was one of the last
things on my mind most days. It was blonde and straight

and hung a bit below my shoulders. Most days I had it up in a messy bun or a sleek ponytail for work. I never styled it, dyed it, or did anything fancy to it. It was just there.

"Don't worry. I can make it savage. To match the rest of you." He waved his hands around my body. "Fierce hair for a bad bitch."

Nora and Cece were giggling as Dante grilled me and asked intrusive questions about my grooming routines. Under normal circumstances I would be offended, but he was so open and friendly, and clearly knew his shit, that I didn't mind.

"Christian, sweetie, be a good big brother and go fetch us a round," Nora pleaded.

Christian sighed like an annoyed big brother. "Astrid, what are you drinking?" he asked politely.

"Whiskey neat, please."

He nodded at Nora. "I like this one."

"Christian and Dante are investors in the bar, so he can just jump back there and get us drinks whenever we want." Nora gestured to the massive crowd at the bar. The two bartenders looked fairly overwhelmed.

"That's cool," I added, finally sneaking into the open seat next to Cece, praying that my inspection was over.

Dante drained his glass. "Yup. When Christian and I moved back here from New York we decided we needed to spruce up this sad little town. So we've been investing in local businesses like this."

"Oh, so you're in finance?" Finally, something I could actually talk about.

Dante made a disgusted face while Nora snorted. "Oh no, honey. My handsome hubby over there is the Wall Street guy. I am a hair stylist. I own the Chelsea Salon. It's on Water Street right before the shipyard?" He asked like I should know exactly what he was talking about.

Cece piped in. "Dante has completely changed my

life. My hair used to be a disaster." Dante visibly shuddered. "But then he taught me how to care for my curls, and it's been life changing. He is a genius."

Dante bowed in gratitude.

"Sorry, I've only been here a few weeks and haven't explored," I explained.

Dante looked disappointed in me, and I made a mental note to step things up in the beauty department. I did have a lot of extra time on my hands. "I am going to give you my card and you will come see me. You are the perfect raw material. Like a slab of Carrara marble."

Christian arrived with a small tray of drinks that he began handing out.

"Is my husband trying to make you over, Astrid? I'm so sorry. He does this a lot."

I smiled and accepted my drink.

Dante rolled his eyes at Christian. "My husband is the brilliant businessman. I am the style in this relationship." That was abundantly clear.

"What brought you guys to Havenport?" I asked while taking a big swig of spicy whiskey.

"He was a big deal on Wall Street, but he missed his mama. Typical Italian boy. So we moved back here." He smiled at Christian.

Christian rolled his eyes. "Don't listen to him. He also missed his mama and wanted to come home. Typical Puerto Rican boy." They exchanged a look, and Dante snuggled up to his husband in the booth. They were adorable, and fun, and seemed to have impeccable style. Nora was damn lucky to have such a cool family. I can't imagine ever discussing my eyebrows with my mother. She probably wouldn't notice if I shaved them off.

The drinks and conversation flowed freely. Emily arrived late, as usual, and Nora made her take a tequila shot as penance. I discreetly texted Derek so he could be on alert in case things got out of hand. I was well into my third drink—Nora had switched everyone to Moscow Mules—when Lucas Kim appeared at our table. There was a collective intake of breath. He certainly had a presence.

"Dante," he exclaimed, giving him a bro hug, "just the man I need to see. I have a business trip next week and desperately need a trim."

I couldn't help but get a little bit excited. I would love to pick his brain. He was an MIT-educated genius who sold his first company at twenty years old. And I couldn't help but notice in the well-lit bar just how handsome he was.

But as much as I could appreciate what a fine specimen of man he was, he didn't excite me like Declan did. He didn't make my belly flip-flop and my heart race. I was a bit starstruck, but that's really it.

Dante gave Lucas a megawatt smile. "You know I will always make room in my schedule for you, Lucas. Text me tomorrow and I'll fit you in."

"Thanks. I won't let anyone else touch my hair."

"Good boy," Dante replied.

The minute Lucas was out of earshot Nora was spitting venom.

"I can't believe you," she hissed at Dante. "Traitor. We are blood now. I let you marry my favorite brother."

Dante rolled his eyes, and I got the sense this was not the first time they'd had this particular argument. "Nora, he is a wonderful customer who tips incredibly well. All the girls at the salon are in love with him, and he recommended a software update for our billing system that has completely changed the business. I love that guy."

Nora crossed her arms in a huff.

"You can hate him, but literally everyone else on planet earth loves him," Dante added.

Nora sat stonily in silence. I wished I knew the

backstory here. It must be a doozy for her to hate him that much. But as impressive as Lucas Kim was, I felt solidarity with my friend. She had offered to kick Max Shapiro's ass for me, so I put my arm around her and gave her a squeeze.

We chatted and drank, and I was finally feeling myself relax. My new friends were loyal and hilarious. I was feeling better than ever. Then, I felt a vibration in my pocket. I pulled out my phone and glanced at the screen.

It was a text from an "unknown" number that read, *Sign the fucking form, Astrid.*

My stomach dropped. Who was texting me? And how did this person know I hadn't signed the waiver? I felt cold and clammy and wanted to get out of here as quickly as possible.

Maggie, who seemed like the type of person who noticed everything, looked at me with concern. "Is everything alright?"

I nodded silently. "I'll get you a glass of water," she said kindly.

I sat and sipped my water while everyone chatted around me. What was I doing? Did I really think I could take on Max and the firm? Clearly he knew what I was up to.

"So," Christian said, tactfully changing the subject, "what should we nickname Astrid?"

I popped my head up. I was definitely feeling the cocktails. "Huh?"

"Christian and Dante give everyone nicknames," Emily explained. "It's what they do."

Nora perked up. "Christian started it as a kid. He used to call me Veruca Salt because I'm a spoiled daddy's girl who gets whatever she wants. It stuck, despite the fact that it's no longer applicable."

Christian coughed into his hand. "Not true."

Nora continued, "Cece is Tangled, because of her hair."

I nodded. Yet another movie I hadn't seen.

"And I'm Von Trapp," Emily added, smiling.

Christian must have sensed that I didn't get it. "From *The Sound of Music*? Emily is a hippie-dippie preschool teacher who loves to sing." That was the truth. I guess it did fit her well.

"And you..." Dante said, pointing at me with his glass, "You are definitely Elsa."

"Oh, hell no," Nora protested, "she is Furiosa."

"Oh yes. I love me some Charlize with one arm." Dante giggled. "Can I shave your head? You would look great with a buzz cut."

I could not even follow this conversation right now. "Um, no thank you?" I replied.

He nodded sagely. "You're right. Something slightly softer. I'll work on it."

"I'm feeling Elsa, guys," Emily added. Christian offered her a high five.

"You have a real Elsa vibe," he said. "Oh yes. Tortured ice queen with a rage problem? Yup, that's it. Are you Swedish?"

I shook my head. "Norwegian, actually."

"Close enough," he said. "I knew it. You have a real Viking princess look. I stand by Elsa."

"But Anna is really the hero of the story," Emily added.

"No way," Maggie protested. "Anna is just the the plucky little sister. Elsa has the powers."

I zoned out slightly during the Disney debate, which was actually getting heated. This was fun, but I started to feel a bit down. I loved my new friends, but I was jealous. They all knew who they were and what they wanted. I had no clue. I felt confused, frustrated, and really, really horny.

I wanted Declan, but I also wanted to go back to Burns &
Glenn. I knew I couldn't have both, and it sucked.

Nora sensed my unease. "What's up, Elsa? You can
share. You're among friends here."

I shrugged. "I'm just confused. Confused about
Declan, confused about my career, totally confused about
my life."

"We've all been there," Cece assured me. "When I
came back to Havenport last year I was a total mess. These
guys helped me figure my shit out."

Emily held up her glass. "I propose a toast. To figuring
your shit out and making awesome friends in the process."
I smiled.

"Hell, yeah!" everyone echoed.

After we toasted, Nora looked at me. "You know what
you need?"

I stared at her. A cab home? A new job? A personality
transplant so I won't be in my own head all the time?
Another vibrator because I was afraid I was going to wear
the one she gave me out with all the sexual frustration
Declan had caused me?

"Lizzo," she declared.

Everyone started nodding immediately. I had no clue
what she was talking about, and my mind was still
spinning from the text.

"We all need Lizzo," Emily said. "But Astrid really
needs her."

"What is Lizzo?" I asked.

Everyone looked at me in horror. You would think I
had just pulled out an AK-47 or told everyone that I saved
all my fingernail clippings.

"Sorry, guys, I don't have a lot of cultural references for
the past ten years. I worked so much there wasn't a lot of
time to keep up with pop culture. I need you guys to help
me catch up."

"Oh, no problem there, Elsa. We will change your life by introducing you to the amazingness of Lizzo," Nora said over the loud music.

"Christian, sweetie, can I have your phone, please?" Nora asked, batting her eyelashes at her brother.

Christian sighed and handed it to Nora, who turned to me and explained, "Christian can control the juke box from an app on his phone. Watch out, bitches, I'm programming a playlist."

Before I knew what was happening, Nora and Emily were dragging me to the back of the bar where there was a small dance floor. Cecelia begrudgingly joined us after Nora chastised her for texting Liam during girls' night.

The music was pumping and everyone was dancing. The lyrics were speaking to me and I found myself feeling strangely empowered.

All my friends screamed in unison, "Feeling good as hell."

The beat was catchy, and I was on my fourth drink so I was able to temporarily ignore my hatred of dancing. My new friends were having fun, and I didn't want to offend anyone.

Pretty soon I was cutting loose, grinding with Nora, and shaking my hair to the lyrics. Lizzo's advice about taking control of my life resonated, even through the bar noise and slight buzz of alcohol.

The girls were singing, and Dante joined us, twirling Cece around the dance floor. I was having so much fun, and I was overcome with emotion. These people were awesome. And they liked me. And I liked them. When was the last time that happened? I liked who I was around them. I was still me, but I was a relaxed, fun, and adventurous version of me. I would never admit it, but it seemed like Havenport was changing me.

NORA: ASTRID YOU ARE NOT WEARING A PANTSUIT TO the engagement party.

Astrid: Why not?

Nora: Because it's not a board meeting or a state funeral. When are you going to realize you are gorgeous and have a killer body? Please wear something cute. I'm begging you.

Astrid: I could wear a skirt suit instead...

Nora: Stop it. You're giving me a migraine.

Emily: Astrid you're hot. Please take a minute to enjoy it because before you know it you'll wake up with three kids and will pee a little bit every time you sneeze.

Nora: Emily TMI! We have talked about keeping a lid on your pelvic floor dysfunction.

Astrid: I don't have any cute clothes.

Cece: Um... we can fix that. Easily.

Nora: I obviously need to take control of this situation. New plan—everyone meet me at my store on Saturday morning. We will have goodies and cute outfits to try on.

Emily: I love a fashion show!

Maggie: I may have to bring my kids.

Nora: That's fine. I'll teach them how to make espresso. Give them a useful life skill.

Nora: Don't be late.

———

As much as I hated to admit it, girl time at Nora's store turned out to be a lot of fun. Things had been so strange with Declan since we kissed. It was good to kick back and take a break from obsessing about Declan.

When I arrived, the entire crew was already there, laughing and dancing. Dante had brought a manicurist from his salon who was doing nails, and he was styling everyone's hair. Christian had carried in multiple storage totes of tools and products and they'd set up a makeshift salon in the middle of the store.

Christian had appointed himself fashion police and was supervising us as we tried on different dresses. He was smart, intense, and kind of intimidating, which is why I liked him immediately.

I took a seat on one of the velvet couches, immersed in watching what was going on.

"Where did these come from?" Cece's older sister, Maggie, marveled, thumbing through gorgeous colorful dresses on a wheeled rack.

"I called in a favor," Christian said, feigning boredom. "Now strip down and try this one on."

Maggie looked horrified. "I can't wear that. I'm not nineteen."

Christian scrolled through his phone. "Blah blah, I'm tired of listening to you. Put it on your body."

"Mom. That one is amazing. You need to wear it," shouted her daughter, Ava. She was twelve and had a lot of opinions. True to form, Nora had taught her how to use the espresso machine, and she had been dutifully frothing milk for lattes for the last hour. She was a cute kid, precocious and sarcastic. She now sat on one of Nora's colorful velvet sofas with a book.

Maggie blanched. "I can't."

"You have the body for it," Emily pleaded.

"You mean I have no tits," Maggie replied, looking at the dress skeptically.

"You said it, not me," Christian added. "It's perfect. Just try it on already."

Maggie came out of the dressing room a few minutes later in a short puff-sleeved black dress with a dramatic deep V in the front. It hugged all her curves and highlighted her lean physique. She looked stunning. We all broke out in applause. I didn't know her well, but we seemed to have a lot in common, including our love of boring professional clothes. The last time I saw her she was wearing a shift dress and pearls, so this was a pretty big fashion risk for her.

Ava was jumping up and down. "Mom, you have to get it. You look hot."

Maggie turned and gave Christian a dirty look. "See. You're already teaching my impressionable daughter to be obsessed with clothes and appearances."

"I'm not, Mom. You know I am committed to being a scientist. Just because I can appreciate a nice dress for a special occasion does not mean I'm some superficial brat." Ava slumped back down on the sofa with her book.

Maggie admired herself in the three-way mirrors.

"I think you look great," I said.

"I have had a shit couple of months," she replied. "It might not hurt to remind myself that I used to be young and hot."

"Correction," Christian said, "you are young and hot."

He lowered his voice to an almost whisper, "Or at least hot."

She punched him playfully in the arm. "You got me."

I was helping myself to another scone when I heard Christian bark, "Elsa. You're next."

I spun around. I did not want to be in his fashion crosshairs right now. I was just an observer here.

I took a bite of scone and shook my head. I would just be polite and firm. I wasn't here for a makeover. I was here to hang out with my new friends.

"I'm not taking no for an answer. I found the perfect thing for you."

I gave him a weak smile. "Actually, I was going to wear one of my suits. I was thinking about my gray Theory skirt suit. It's really cute."

Nora shouted over from where she was getting her nails done, "Will you stop it with the suits? You're not Hillary Clinton, and even she knows when to leave the suits at home."

Christian looked at me with genuine pity. I realized that I seemed like a sad workaholic, which I was, but I didn't want my new friends to think I was that boring.

"Hey, Dante," he yelled over the chatter, "Elsa here wants to wear a sad business suit to the party."

Dante whipped around from where he was taming Cece's wild hair. "Are you crazy? You are going to this party as the date of one of the hottest bachelors in Havenport. You need to show the world what a smokeshow you are."

"Please don't ever use that word again," Nora begged.

Dante rolled his eyes and returned his attention to Cece's hair.

"Fine," I said. I thumbed through the rack. I could be adventurous. "How about this?" I asked, holding up a simple black shift with a side slit. "I could rock this."

Christian shook his head at me. "Nope. I have something special for you."

He held up a blue sparkly dress. Scratch that. I think it was a shirt.

"Um. No, thank you. I don't do sparkles." It was truly the last thing on earth I would ever wear. I was an Ivy League-educated lawyer, not a lounge singer in Vegas, thank you very much.

"Try it on."

I demurred. I didn't want to insult him or Nora, but I couldn't possibly wear that.

"Tough. Get your ass in there now!"

"Yes!" Emily yelled. She had already switched from coffee to champagne. "Try it on."

I sighed. It was pretty. But I studiously avoided flashy clothes. I had spent my entire life wanting to be taken seriously. And my mother had drilled into my head that sexy clothes, large jewelry, and heavy makeup would not achieve that goal.

Maggie, Ava, and Nora wandered over, curious to see my dress. I had never been one to succumb to peer pressure, but it seemed like a good time to start.

I stepped into the fuchsia dressing room and took off my jeans and T-shirt.

On the plus side, it had long sleeves. I loved sleeves. But it looked like it would barely cover my ass.

I got the glorified shirt over my head and walked out without looking in the mirror. Christian zipped me up and took a step back.

His jaw dropped. "Guys. Look at her."

Everyone stopped what they were doing and turned to look at me. I could feel my face burning.

"Turn around, Astrid," Nora shouted.

Dante agreed. "Look at yourself, Elsa."

I turned around to see how bad it was in the three-way mirror.

And… it wasn't bad? I looked like me. But a glam version of me. It was short, much shorter than anything I'd ever worn before. But the high neckline and long sleeves balanced it out.

It hugged my curves, and my legs looked miles long, even in bare feet.

I thought I would look trashy, but somehow I looked kind of chic.

I felt like a badass. Maybe this cool, sexy woman had always been inside me and I was just needing to let her out.

"This dress was made for you," Nora said, patting me on the shoulder.

"It's really short," I replied.

"No, it's normal length, you just have insanely long legs."

It had been so long since I had dressed up and taken the time to care about my appearance. I spent years dressing myself on autopilot—grabbing something clean from my closet and pulling my hair into a ponytail. I had no time to take care of myself, no time to shop or get my nails done or hang out with girlfriends. I wore black because it was easy and professional. It had been a long time since I put something on and felt pretty.

Dante came over and started playing with my hair. "So I'm thinking a high ponytail to show off her long neck and maybe some big statement earrings." He wasn't even talking to me as I stared at my reflection.

"Good call," Christian replied. "You have incredible style."

"Thanks, babe." Dante reached up on his tiptoes to peck Christian's cheek. Damn, they were really cute together. And they were both so generous to me, a virtual stranger. Forcing me out of my comfort zone and making me feel beautiful.

Emily came over and admired my dress. "This feels like the moment when Elsa lets her hair down and sings "Let it Go."

I still hadn't seen the movie, so I had no idea what she was talking about. She walked away belting out some song lyrics so I don't think she cared.

Staring at myself, I couldn't deny the dress worked. But the real question was, would I have enough courage to actually wear it?

———

A few hours later Declan and I arrived at the party. It was frigid outside, but the interior of the brewery was warm and welcoming. From the outside it looked like an old warehouse. The inside, however, was a completely different story.

Soft lighting highlighted the industrial feel, and large leather couches and chairs were clustered around a huge brick fireplace. The live-edge bar gleamed as bartenders filled drink orders. A band was setting up on a small stage in the corner.

"This place is amazing," I said, handing Declan my puffy coat. The brewery was industrial chic but homey. I could see why people loved hanging out here.

"Declan?" I repeated, turning around to see where he was.

He stood there staring at me. No, not staring, ogling me.

"What?" I asked, annoyed with him.

He tilted his head. "You. Your dress. You look…"

I raised an eyebrow.

He coughed and recovered his composure. "You look beautiful, Astrid."

I smiled. Was it wrong that I enjoyed having the power to make him speechless? "You clean up pretty well yourself." I smoothed the lapels on his charcoal suit and admired how good he looked. I had never pictured Declan in a suit before. It seemed totally antithetical to his personality, but it looked like it was made for him. He wore a crisp white shirt with no tie, and his beard was neatly trimmed. His hair was pulled back in its usual man bun, highlighting his strong jaw and full, sensual lips. Lips I was dying to kiss again.

After hanging up our coats, he offered me his arm. "Can I get you a drink?"

"Yes, please," I replied, looping my arm through his.

The party was in full swing, with people milling around everywhere. We found Cece and Liam by the bar. Cece looked luminous, and Liam could not take his eyes off her. They were so in love it radiated off them in waves. Every few minutes, Liam would brush a curl out of Cece's face or stealthily grab her ass when it seemed like no one was watching. They were purely and unabashedly in love, and I found myself feeling strangely sad. Not because I was jealous, but because I had never even considered that what they had found together could be possible for me. I had never stopped working long enough to picture what my life would be like with a soulmate. I just assumed I would stay single or marry another distracted lawyer someday. I didn't even consider this type of world-altering love.

To be fair, it's not like I had seen it many times. My parents could barely stand each other, and I didn't have many other relationship role models. Marriage always seemed to me like a practical choice you made after careful consideration and planning.

But with Liam and Cece, it was like they couldn't *not* be married to each other. They couldn't wait another minute to join their lives forever. And instead of being nauseated, it filled me with a warm, happy feeling.

Declan put his arm around my waist, and I rested my head on his shoulder. Was that kind of love even possible for me?

20

DECLAN

Astrid was clearly impressed by the brewery, and it filled me with pride. Although I would never, under any circumstances, say it out loud, I was really proud of my little brother. Liam had achieved so much, and was only able to do so by opening himself up to Cece. I supposed there was a lesson there, but I was studiously avoiding feelings and life lessons at the moment. I had to stay focused. Astrid was my fake girlfriend, and we were attending this event together. I was going to be an attentive and engaging fake boyfriend and that was it. I couldn't go breaking the rule again. Things had been awkward enough since the Christmas Tree Burn.

But that dress. Did she have to wear that dress? It felt like she was messing with me. First of all, it was the last thing I ever thought she would wear. Sparkly and short? Didn't seem like her, but seeing it on her body I couldn't imagine her in anything else. On anyone else it would be flashy, but on Astrid it was classy and subdued. She moved with such confidence and grace, it was such a turn-on.

"So they really fell in love while fighting about this place?"

"Pretty much," I said. "Once Liam realized how much smarter Cece was, he started listening to her, and they really took this place to the next level. Six months ago he thought he may have to close, and now business is booming, they are renovating and expanding, and we're starting a distribution company together."

She squeezed my arm. "That is so incredible. Cece is pretty awesome. I can see how she would be able to make all that happen."

"It just used to be so different. But Cece showed up with new ideas and she even got the whole town involved. She harnessed the power of all the locals—people donated their time, their expertise, and a ton of landscaping. Even on a shoestring budget, she managed to fix this place up quite a bit."

All of a sudden Astrid's body tensed, and she grabbed my hand. "There are so many people here. Think we can really convince them?" She looked nervous and I wanted to take her into my arms. Instead, I leaned over and kissed the top of her head. "We're gonna knock em dead, killer."

———

As the night wore on I realized I was having fun. And I had stayed way longer than the usual hour I gave myself at social functions. We drank and ate. Astrid and I even squared off on the vintage pinball machine. We chatted with my brothers, my parents, and a variety of people from town.

"Stop trying to lead," I said, trying to wrestle back control of this dance.

"You know I don't take orders," she pouted, unwilling to follow me. I thought about if that extended to the bedroom, and it was hot. *Imagine if she was as defiant in bed as she was out of it… Stop. Stop. Fake girlfriend. It's fake.* There had been several moments tonight when I had to keep reminding myself of just how fake this was, because things were starting to feel far too real.

We continued to attempt to dance, and I could feel her getting the hang of it. When she finally gave in to me, I felt the tension in her body disappear. As we danced to Stevie Wonder, I whispered in her ear. "See, sometimes it's fun to let someone else be in charge."

She gave me a sly smile that said thousands of filthy things. Or at least that's what I imagined. She may have been smiling because I had food in my teeth, hell if I knew.

I liked her way too much. I had spent most of my adult life focused on my job, my family, and self-preservation. I was not used to these runaway feelings, these urges that I had when it came to Astrid. I was a mess, and tonight was only making it worse.

I had to do something. I had to mentally put some distance between us. And I couldn't live with the awkwardness anymore. Especially because she felt so good in my arms.

I looked down at my shoes. I was such a coward. "I want to apologize."

She looked concerned. "For what?"

"For kissing you last weekend." I took a breath. I hated talking about this shit. "I don't want to mess up our friendship."

Her face was blank. I couldn't get a read on her. She was totally lawyering me right now. "Declan. I don't want to screw things up either."

I exhaled. "Okay."

"I mean," she said, playing with my hair at the base of my neck, "I liked it. But I know it can't happen again."

I nodded. This was not going the way I had planned. I thought talking about it would extinguish the heat between us, but now my collar was getting tight, and I had the urge to run out into the parking lot.

"I can't give you more, Declan."

"I understand." Actually, I didn't understand. I wanted to pick apart her lawyer logic and then kiss her senseless. But I knew that this was not a battle I could win. And I lacked the ability to verbalize any of the things I was feeling at the moment.

She nodded and rested her head on my shoulder while we swayed gently to the music. Meanwhile, I worked on ignoring my nausea and convincing myself that we could be just friends.

I was at the bar getting a beer when Callum slid right up next to me. "You know, Trent is going to start a betting pool on you guys next. The odds are that you're engaged in six months."

I turned slowly toward my brother, who was clearly really enjoying this.

I glared at him. "Fuck off, Cal," I replied through clenched teeth.

Callum smiled and looked over to where Astrid was chatting with some of her girlfriends. He shook his head. "You are in denial, man."

"And you are a prick, Fabio."

———

Of course Luke Kim was here, looking cover-model handsome as usual. He was out and about but seemed distracted by Nora. I couldn't blame him. Nora was pretty. She didn't hold a candle to my Astrid, of course, but any red-blooded man would be distracted by her.

My Astrid? My stupid brain was playing with me again. I couldn't go down this road. I couldn't get attached. I had already caught feelings, and I had to keep them from developing any further. I knew it would be hard when she left. I would lose a friend, a confidante, and a person who really got me. But if things developed into more? I would be lost.

"I didn't know you were from Havenport?" Astrid asked politely. I didn't like how she spoke to him, like he was royalty or something.

"I'm not. I grew up a few towns over. I used to come here as a kid and fell in love with it. I promised myself when I grew up and made it I would move here," he replied. Why are his teeth so straight and perfect? Bastard.

"That's so sweet."

"And now, after selling my company, I'm doing some work here and there but I'm mostly just taking a break and volunteering. I am on the board of the shelter in town. It really means a lot to me."

"That's fantastic," she replied.

"Actually," I said, jumping into the conversation, "Astrid does a lot of pro bono work. She is even getting an award in a few weeks." I was playing the part of proud boyfriend and it was surprisingly easy.

"That's fantastic," Luke replied. "Congrats. What kind of pro bono?"

I zoned out for a bit while Astrid told Luke all about her debt clinic. The brewery was packed. My parents were at the bar. I couldn't quite tell, but it looked like my mother was taking my father's beer away from him.

"That is fantastic. I can't believe I met you. I am actually trying to set up a legal clinic at the shelter," Luke said, grabbing his phone.

"Really?" Astrid seemed excited.

"There are a lot of legal hurdles for many of these families to deal with in order to get back on their feet. We have legal staff that help with the family law stuff, protective orders, divorce, child custody, that type of thing. But we're finding more and more that our residents need other legal assistance—housing, immigration, debt collection, bankruptcy, employment issues, government benefits."

"Yes. That makes a lot of sense. Legal problems don't exist in a vacuum. Usually people have several different things going on."

"Exactly," he exclaimed. "The local legal services organization is swamped, and we've tried to build partnerships with some outside law firms, but we need to put some kind of formal program in place. The shelter is not just housing. The crisis center assists tens of thousands of families all over the region each year. Organizations like this play a significant role in helping people, and I need to make the connection between our services and legal assistance."

He was so passionate, even I was impressed. I never had anything against Luke Kim. On the contrary, I thought he was a decent guy. But the fact that this tech billionaire was so devoted to women and children in crisis? It warmed my icy heart a bit. My parents had always given back to the community, but what was I doing?

"I'm not a brilliant lawyer like my girlfriend, but I'd love to get involved if I could. I don't suppose the shelter needs fish?" I joked.

He laughed. "Hey, your fish is amazing, man. But now that you mention it, we really need more local job placements. People want to work, they want good jobs, but it's hard to find some right now. I don't suppose you are hiring?"

I racked my brain. We ran a pretty lean operation, but

we were always in need of more bodies. "I could really use some admin help and a warehouse supervisor," I offered. I would talk to Callum about expanding payroll. We were up to our eyeballs in orders at the moment, and adding on some organized people would really help as we moved into the summer months.

Luke clapped me on the shoulder. "Good man! I will have my assistant call you on Monday and we can get some more details. Helping people find jobs is my favorite part of this gig."

I smiled at him. He really was a genuine, kind person.

"And Astrid," he said, turning to her, "I'd love to pick your brain about the legal stuff." He handed her a card. "Give me a call sometime."

Luke scampered off to go schmooze, and Astrid and I were left staring at each other.

"You should call him," I said gruffly, studying the contents of my empty beer stein.

She shoved me. "Don't be jealous, Declan."

"I'm not. He is a good guy and he is really committed to helping people."

"But I'm a corporate lawyer," she demurred.

I put my arm around her shoulders. "You are a brilliant, hard-working lawyer. I am pretty sure you can figure out all the stuff he was talking about."

She fussed with her hair. "Of course I could. I could set up a legal service delivery model for the shelter and get up to speed on the various types of law, or outsource to some local contacts, but that's not the point."

I waited, knowing there was more. Astrid was still working through her feelings, and I wanted to give her the space to do it.

She bristled. "I have to go back to Boston, back to a BigLaw firm. That's what I'm qualified to do. I've spent ten years working toward this one goal. I need to stay focused."

I gave her a tight smile. And that, right there, folks, was why I couldn't get attached to this girl. Because she didn't want this place. She didn't want me. She wanted to go back to her workaholic law firm life, and no matter how much I wanted to, I would not stand in her way.

21

ASTRID

I WAS FEELING BETTER. THE PARTY LAST NIGHT HAD been fun, and Declan and I seemed to get over the weirdness between us. I was worried that it would be awkward, but it wasn't. We had fun together, despite the lingering sexual tension. I enjoyed being around him. His quiet strength and his steady countenance calmed me. I didn't feel the need to fill silences with him. We enjoyed them together.

But I was still feeling uneasy. The memory of that kiss after the Christmas Tree Burn haunted me. I'd had more than a few sexy dreams about him since. He conveyed so much with his lips and his hands I couldn't help but want more. For someone who used to be able to go years without sex, I was now obsessed. I had never experienced this kind of want, this kind of physical longing before. I found myself staring at his lips or his big, strong hands without even realizing it.

But we both knew this was pretend. And the more time I spent with him, the more I appreciated his friendship. Despite his grumpy exterior and intimidating presence, he was a big softie who loved his dog and his home. I saw him go out of his way to help his brothers and his parents. He was truly one of the good ones, wrapped in a sexy, broody, tattooed package. And I knew I was lucky to have him in my life, even if he remained fully clothed at all times.

"What's this?" I asked.

Declan handed me a card and gestured to a large, strangely shaped wrapped gift next to the couch.

"You got me a Valentine?"

He shrugged and looked at his feet. I could tell he was uncomfortable. It was cute. He was so rugged and masculine that this hint of bashfulness was such a turn-on. As was his Binnacle Brewing T-shirt, which was hugging his chest and shoulders in all the right places.

I wondered if he had chest hair. I wanted to rip that shirt off and find out for myself. Focus, Astrid. Focus.

My approach to relationships had always been fairly cautious and boring. I had only slept with a few people, and it was usually after several dates and a lot of time spent figuring out if we were compatible. I had never felt this way with any of the guys I had dated or slept with. I never found myself daydreaming about a man's body or wanting to rip their clothes off. Declan inspired a curiosity in me that made me feel giddy and embarrassed.

"I feel terrible. I didn't get you anything." Was I supposed to get a Valentine's Day gift for my fake boyfriend? I had no idea. He was so thoughtful and kind. I was a shitty fake girlfriend. If we were really dating, I would just put out to distract him from my lack of a gift, but that was obviously not in the cards given the fake nature of our relationship. We had maintained our rules since the slipup at the Christmas Tree Burn, and I was not going to be the one to screw this up.

"I don't care. I just saw this and thought of you. Valentine's Day was just an excuse to give it to you."

I opened the card. It had roses on the front and was blank inside, and he had written his own message.

Happy Valentine's Day. Our relationship may be fake, but your beauty, smarts, and incredible ass are all real.

xoxo Declan

I looked up at him and felt a blush creep across my cheeks. I had never been given a Valentine as an adult. He wrote me a message, and it was so cute. And he thought I had a nice ass? I felt giddy and a little bit dizzy. I wanted to throw my arms around him and kiss the hell out of him again, but I had to keep my hormones under control. He was so kind and thoughtful. I couldn't ruin this all by sticking my tongue down his throat like a horny teenager.

What did this mean? I wanted to sit down with a notebook and analyze this like a tricky contractual provision. I loved riddles and solving complex problems, so it seemed natural to do a full due diligence on this Valentine. *Stop being crazy and open your present.*

"Open your gift."

I went to grab the gift, and it was insanely heavy. "What is this thing?"

I sat on the floor and began to unwrap the floral paper. My hands were shaking slightly. I didn't often receive gifts, so this felt special, significant somehow.

I tore all the paper away and stared. "What? Is this… a sledgehammer?" It was fancy looking, with a beautiful, polished wood handle. My name was engraved on the top in fancy script. It must have weighed at least ten pounds. I was really confused. What on earth did I need an admittedly very fancy sledgehammer for?

"Yup. I have a surprise for you. Grab your coat."

———

"What are we doing here?"

"You'll see."

Declan had driven us down through town to the headquarters of Quinn Fisheries. It was a massive shipyard with equipment and machinery everywhere. There was an enormous building with industrial garage doors on one side. I had never been to this part of town. It was much more commercial looking, and large fishing boats bobbed up and down in the water for what looked like miles. It was chilly, but bright and sunny, a brisk winter day and I was glad I'd worn my heavy coat.

He parked in front and grabbed my gift out of the back. He slung it over his shoulder and led me over to an area where there was debris and equipment lying around.

"Here, I made this for you." He gestured to a massive structure made of wooden shipping pallets. "We have had these and this other junk lying around. So I collected it all for you."

I stared at him. I wasn't sure what was going on. So there was a bunch of scrap wood and other stuff. Were we going to burn it?

He handed me a pair of safety glasses. "Here. To protect your eyes." I took them and put them on. They wrapped around the side of my face and reminded me of chemistry lab in high school.

We stood in silence. He was smiling at me, with his infuriatingly handsome face. Did he want me to sledgehammer? What would that accomplish? Surely we could put all this crap in one of the many dumpsters on the edge of the property?

He nodded toward the pile. "Get to work."

"So you just want me to what? Smash all this?"

He crossed his arms and smiled. "Yup."

"Why?"

"Because you can. Trust me, that is a great reason."

This was officially the strangest gift I had ever been given. But I was intrigued. I doubted I was strong enough to swing this thing, and while busting up old pallets and junk sounded like fun, I wasn't really connecting the dots.

"You can do it. Fuck it up, killer. Go nuts." I smiled. I secretly loved when he called me killer. I had never been the sugar and spice and everything nice type of girl. I wore my toughness like a badge of honor, and I appreciated that he recognized that.

Declan took a few steps back and put on the other pair of goggles. "Do you want a soundtrack?" He held up his phone.

I smirked. "Do you have any Lizzo?"

"For you, I've got everything."

He cued up the music, and I stared out at the tranquil ocean. There were docks with small boats and large ships, fishing nets, a large crane, and other machines I couldn't recognize. It was interesting, seeing this part of Declan, getting a taste of his world. It was so unlike the touristy downtown area of Havenport. This felt more authentic, more real, and I was happy that he brought me here. I appreciated seeing this side of him, this essential part of his life.

I looked at the wood. There was a ton of it. There was no way I could break all this up. I would give it a few tries and then let him have a turn. It seemed rude not to try.

I put both hands on the wooden handle of the sledgehammer and lifted it up, slamming it down on the wood. It was heavy, but easier than I thought.

Instantly the wood splintered with a satisfying crash.

Oooh. That was nice. Lizzo sang in the background, making me feel stronger and tougher than ever.

I raised it up higher, swinging it above my head and driving it down with my knees.

Yes. You're right, Lizzo. 100%.

It was fun.

Declan had music blasting from his phone and I was laughing.

I turned around to face him. "This is great!" I yelled.

He beamed at me and gave me a thumbs-up.

I swung again, harder, and broke through one whole pallet. I had no idea I was so strong.

Again and again I swung. My arms and shoulders were getting tired, and my heart was racing. Damn, this was an incredible workout. Wood splintered in every direction, and after a few tries I found a good rhythm. If I used my abs and legs to help drive it down, I was able to get even more power.

I reached a large metal tub of some kind. This could be harder. I put down the sledgehammer, did a quick stretch, and then picked it back up.

I swung it up, brought it down, and let out a primal scream. The sledgehammer hit the metal and crushed it, folding the tub in on itself. I dropped the sledgehammer and started jumping up and down, yelling.

Declan ran up to me. "Are you having fun?"

I grabbed him by the shoulder and kissed him quickly on the mouth. "So. Much. Fun." I was officially sweating. I peeled off my jacket and handed it to Declan and pushed up the sleeves on my sweatshirt.

I turned around and got back to work. Over and over I brought down the sledgehammer, destroying the wood, metal, and plastic that he had set up for me.

I yelled and screamed at the top of my lungs. And every time I swung, it was as though some of the tension inside me loosened. The knots of anxiety that had lived in my brain since childhood were slowly unraveling.

Declan was smiling and shouting words of encouragement. "Let it all out, Astrid. Get it all out."

"Fuck Burns & Glenn," I screamed as another blow

came down. Fuck those assholes who exploited my labor for six years and then turned on me. I gave them everything I had. I cancelled vacations, I let friendships wither and die, I suppressed every desire, every dream I'd ever had just so I could chase the brass ring of partnership.

"Fuck Max Shapiro." More crashing and destruction. He sexually harassed me and then tried to destroy my career? I brought the hammer down again, wishing it was his smug face.

"Fuck my mother and her stupid expectations." Slam.

"Fuck being a Wentworth and all the bullshit pressure." Slam.

"Fuck the patriarchy." Slam.

As I swung and swung, dozens of times, I felt the pressure lessen. That internal weight that I had been dragging along with me was getting lighter and lighter every time I swung the sledgehammer. It was as if this pile of junk represented all my anxieties and insecurities, and I was destroying them blow by blow. I yelled, I screamed, I cried, and it felt so good. I didn't even know what I was saying. I was yelling, mumbling, and sometimes screaming like a wild animal. Poor Declan probably thought I had officially lost my mind. But I didn't care. Something had shifted deep inside me, and there was no going back.

I was sweating and swearing and having the time of my life. The sizable pile that Declan had made me was reduced to rubble. I doubted I would be able to lift my arms tomorrow, but I didn't care. I felt good. I felt powerful. I felt like I could conquer the world.

I turned and saw Declan smiling at me. Thankfully, he was not running away from my crazy. I was panting and sweating and my eyes were teary. I dropped the sledgehammer, and he wrapped his arms around me. "I am so proud of you," he said, pulling me into a hug.

He felt strong and secure and safe. He accepted me as

I was and didn't ask me to change. He gave me this gift because he knew it would help me, it would heal me. He made me stronger and built me up. My entire life I had been surrounded by people who took from me. Took my time, my attention, my emotional energy. Everyone that had ever been close to me wanted something. Men who used me for sex or for professional connections. All those friends in college and law school that befriended me because of who my mother was.

But not Declan. Declan cared for me and gave me his friendship and support without asking for anything in return. I had wanted him for weeks, but at that moment, I could not live without him. My body burned for him. I craved him, and I couldn't pretend for another minute.

I grabbed his face and planted a passionate kiss on his mouth. He was stunned but quickly caught up, wrapping his strong arms around me and deepening the kiss.

"Declan," I panted as he kissed my neck. "Declan, take me home."

"Anything, killer. I will do anything you want."

He knew me better than I knew myself. He knew what would help me and heal me.

22

DECLAN

THE RIDE HOME WAS FRENZIED—WE COULDN'T KEEP our hands off each other. I desperately tried to keep my eyes on the road while Astrid kissed me and nibbled my earlobes.

Watching her fiery rage had turned me on. When I bought her the sledgehammer, I had never expected that she would use it like that. That she would let go of all that she had bottled up inside her. She was so strong, so fearless, that my admiration only grew deeper. Astrid was something special.

We kissed at stoplights and grabbed at each other like teenagers.

When I finally pulled in my driveway, she shucked her jacket and straddled me.

I had been dreaming about this moment. My seatbelt was still on but I didn't care. I had this incredible goddess on top of me, touching me, igniting me with her every touch.

My hands roamed down her shoulders, settling at her waist. I was consumed by her mouth, her hands, and her soft, warm body. I moved my mouth down her neck, softly searching for her secret spots while my hands settled onto her glorious ass. "Declan," she gasped as I tasted where her neck and shoulder met, and I was rewarded when she started to grind on my hard-as-steel cock. Her hands roamed up under my T-shirt, and I broke our kiss long enough to unbutton her jeans, revealing a scrap of lace under my fingertips. We were kissing and groping and grinding, and it was the single hottest moment of my life. My brain was short-circuiting and I needed to get control of the situation before I ended up embarrassing myself. I pulled back and looked at her. She was straddling me and looking wild and disheveled and unbearably hot. One thing was clear. She wanted me as much as I wanted her, and she was not hiding it.

"Astrid, we need to go inside."

She nodded, her eyes hooded with lust.

I carried her into the house, her jeans still unbuttoned, and we left a trail of clothes and boots in our wake. After sending Ginger outside, we made it to my bedroom.

I pushed her sweater up, kissing my way from her belly to her collarbones. She writhed and giggled as I held her down, savoring the sweet taste of her skin. Every inch of her was more beautiful than the last. I could die a happy man settled between her glorious breasts. I reached around to free them from their black lace cage and was rewarded with the most perfect pink nipples I had ever seen. Her breasts were larger than I expected, round and firm and the perfect handful. I sucked them greedily while she writhed underneath me, her hands tangled in my hair. I bit down, testing her reaction, and watched as her entire body shuddered with pleasure.

My killer likes it a bit rough. Noted.

While I was worshipping her breasts, she managed to get my T-shirt over my head. She pushed me back and drank me in. "You are so hot," she moaned while kissing and licking my chest. I knew this was going to be a power struggle. I knew she wouldn't just let me take control. And that made it even hotter. Astrid was not one to back down, ever. And I was up for the challenge.

Her fingers lingered on the waistband of my jeans while she stroked my cock outside its denim prison. She looked up at me with lust-filled eyes. "Please," she said, her lips swollen from our kisses. I would have given her anything in that moment. I allowed her to unzip my jeans and free my throbbing cock.

She gasped. That was an ego boost. And she immediately grasped it with her long, graceful fingers. After what felt like an hour, but was probably only an agonizing few seconds, she gently lowered her mouth down and licked the top with the flat of her tongue.

An electric shock shot through my body, and I knew I couldn't last long. She began working me with her hungry mouth, sucking and licking and gently tugging my balls. She was thorough and focused and clearly determined to make me lose my mind.

"You're killing me. You have to stop."

She looked up at me defiantly and shook her head. "Make me."

I almost finished right then and there. Her attitude and the look of pure lusty annoyance on her face nearly did me in. I knew I had to take control of this situation immediately. Luckily I was a lot bigger. I stepped back and pushed her up on the bed. She immediately snapped her legs shut. "I wasn't done," she pouted.

I ran my hands through my hair, trying to slow my racing heart. "You can suck my cock any time you want. Just please let me taste you first. I've been dreaming of this pussy."

She gave me one of her frosty ice queen looks and slowly, oh so slowly, opened her legs. I stood and watched her slowly surrender to me. I was going to drive her wild and have her screaming my name in no time.

She was lying back on my bed, naked except for a tiny pair of panties. She may have looked totally nonplussed, but I saw her chest heaving and I could practically feel her racing heartbeat. I was going to savor every minute of this.

I kissed my way up those glorious long legs, nipping at her inner thighs. She squirmed and giggled, and I held her down with my hands.

I stroked her over her panties, reveling in her wetness and the way her back arched off the bed. It was a relief to know that she was just as desperate as I was. I carefully lowered my mouth, teasing her before slowly pulling those panties down her strong legs. I wanted to rip them off, but I knew that I had to be patient with Astrid. I had to show her how much I wanted her by exercising restraint.

One lick and I was done for. She was slick and warm and sweet and so much better than I imagined. And I had done my fair share of imagining.

I got to work, trying to keep focused and bring my A game. I liked how sassy and defiant she was, but that only made me more determined to drive her wild. She thought she was in charge, but she was sorely mistaken.

I pushed her thighs down and took my time, licking, sucking, and using my large hands to make sure that every single part of her got my attention. In no time she was bucking off the bed, screaming and writhing while I held her in place.

"Please," she panted, her hips rising off the bed and her arms grasping at my shoulders. "Please, Declan, I need you. I need you now."

I slowly made my way up her perfect body, kissing and biting and taking my sweet time.

"What do you need?" I asked mischievously.

"I need you inside me."

"How badly?"

"So badly. Please… please."

Every word out of her mouth made me harder. I grabbed a condom from my nightstand and rolled it on, losing my jeans in the process.

I positioned myself at her opening and leaned down to capture her mouth in a passionate kiss.

"Stop stalling and fuck me already," she moaned.

"Yes, ma'am," I replied, thrusting into her and watching her eyes roll back in her head. Astrid was sweet, hot, tight perfection, and I thought I had died and gone to heaven.

"Oh my God. You're huge," she screamed so loud I'm sure the seals in the harbor could hear her.

I gave her a minute to adjust to my size and started to gently move. I could feel her nails digging into my back, and I loved it. She met my thrusts, moaning and panting. I needed to slow down, I needed this to last. I couldn't let this one get away from me. I slowed down, thrusting deep, and distracted myself by kissing and biting her neck. Soon, my patience was rewarded by her breathy moans. I could feel her climbing higher and higher.

"Harder, harder," she yelled as she began to spasm around me, her inner muscles clenching. Her face flushed and she threw her head back in ecstasy as she came undone. It was the most beautiful thing I had ever seen.

I was working at a furious pace now, and I was mesmerized by the way her breasts bounced with my every thrust. She continued to moan and whisper my name. "Keep going," I urged.

"I can't," she said breathlessly. "I'm a one and done type of girl."

That was not acceptable. I refused to believe her. "Oh, killer, you have so much to learn. Good thing I'm a good teacher." I gently lifted her up and kissed her passionately. "Now be a good girl and get on your hands and knees."

She shot me a saucy grin and slowly turned around, exposing her perfect round ass, and my vision blurred.

I caressed her hips and pulled her toward me. Slowly, I sank myself inside her, and this new angle felt impossibly tight. I knew I would have to work fast because I was already testing my limits and I wanted to watch her come apart again.

I slowly worked up a rhythm, and she began to writhe and moan.

Things were feeling good, too good actually. "Killer, this is incredible. You need to get focused because I don't know how much longer I can last."

"It's. Not. Possible," she grunted, meeting my frenzied thrusts.

"Bullshit. You are easily a two or three orgasms girl."

"Ha. I wish. Even you're not that good," she taunted.

I smacked her ass hard. "Challenge accepted."

I gently grabbed her blonde hair in one hand, bringing her even closer. And I used the other to gently snake around her waist to find her clit.

I picked up the pace, slamming into her with everything I had while gently rubbing her clit and pulling her hair. I could feel her climbing higher and higher, her body vibrating with pent-up need. I willed myself to keep going and was rewarded by her screams of pleasure. She took me over the edge with her, and I collapsed next to her on the bed, completely spent.

I couldn't see straight, and I wasn't sure my legs worked. I carefully got up to dispose of the condom and found my way back to bed. Astrid was flat on her back, chest heaving, hair disheveled with her glorious body on display. On her face was the widest, most genuine smile I had ever seen.

We fit together. We were right. We were made for each other. My heart was pounding and my head was spinning.

"That," I said, looking at her beautiful face, "was incredible. And you? Just… wow." I was babbling and incoherent and barely clinging to my sanity.

She sat up and studied me, her gaze traveling down my body and back up to my face. "Clearly you've never slept with a Type A overachiever before," she said smugly. She leaned down and gently kissed my cheek. "I don't settle for anything less than an A+ performance."

23

ASTRID

I COULDN'T STOP THINKING ABOUT DECLAN. THE WAY he felt on top of me, the deep sexy groans he made when he was inside me, the way his fingertips had left tiny bruises on my hips. I was getting all hot and bothered again.

To say it was the best sex of my life would be an understatement, because we shared so much more than just sex. Declan was the best everything of my life to date. The kissing, the foreplay, his incredible cock, the cuddling. The way he made me scrambled eggs and toast at one a.m. while we watched *Game of Thrones*. The entire experience was so above and beyond anything I had experienced before that to even refer to it as sex was unfair.

I couldn't even think straight. I had more orgasms in the last twelve hours with Declan than I had in the entirety of some of my previous relationships. He explored my body eagerly, learning what I liked and making sure to give me everything I needed and everything I didn't know I needed.

I could feel myself getting wet again just thinking about him. I would have to break out my new friend again. Nora wasn't wrong. I can't believe I lived this long without a vibrator. Now that I'd experienced it, I wanted to start handing them out to women on the street so that no woman would have to go without. Granted, it didn't come close to the orgasms Declan delivered, but it would at least take the edge off until I could see him tonight.

Just as I was about to reach for it my phone buzzed.

Emily: Leaving now. I'll pick you up in 10?

Oh shit. I'd forgotten about Monday breakfast. I promised everyone I would come. Ten minutes? That was not enough time to shower and make myself presentable. I looked in the mirror, and everything about my appearance screamed "just fucked." My hair was a mess, I had makeup smeared all over my face, and there was beard burn on my neck. I definitely had the post-orgasmic glow, and I couldn't wipe the shit-eating grin off my face.

Oh well. If anyone wouldn't care it was these ladies. I threw on some jeans and a hoodie and washed my face and brushed my teeth.

————

"I hereby call this meeting of the coven to order."

"Nora, we are not a coven," Cece said, while clearly texting Liam on her phone.

"I think we should be a squad. Like hashtag squadgoals."

"No, Emily. We discussed this. Squads are very 2017, and our connection is much deeper than some shallow Taylor Swift shit. Only witchcraft can fully bind and express our bond."

Maggie rolled her eyes. She was the odd one out in this group of friends. She seemed prim and proper and like she didn't have time for this shit. I liked her a lot.

"And welcome, Astrid. Thank you for finally taking me up on my offer."

Cece threw her arm around me. "We are so happy you're here."

"Thanks, guys," I said bashfully. The warm welcome made me slightly uncomfortable.

"So. First order of business. Astrid, there are a few ground rules. One, the coven is sacred. Everything we discuss is confidential and shared with total trust and no judgment."

I nodded.

"And second, sometimes during Monday breakfast we indulge in mimosas. If someone wants to make it Mimosa Monday there is no judgment here. And we never allow a coven member to drink alone."

I nodded again. This entire experience was going to be intense.

Emily raised her hand. "I move for Mimosa Monday. Derek has been traveling, and my kids are driving me crazy. They are being such little shits. I need a break and I'm exhausted and I hate my husband right now because he gets to sleep soundly in a hotel room and eat meals without people throwing food in his hair."

Maggie patted Emily on the back. "I have been there. I'm so sorry." Emily put her unwashed head on Maggie's shoulder. It was sweet how close everyone was. Maggie discreetly picked a Cheerio out of Emily's hair and patted her head.

"Ooh. I second the motion," Cece said. "I worked all weekend and need to relax."

I wasn't in the habit of breakfast drinking, but I didn't have to work. I didn't have clients depending on me and deliverables to get out the door. I didn't have to check the work of a bunch of junior associates who pulled an all-nighter finishing a memo. So I could indulge a little.

"Count me in," I said.

"I'm out," Maggie said with her face in her phone. "I'm on call today."

"Sadly, me too," Nora said. "I'm meeting some private equity suits this afternoon to talk about my business."

"Nora, that is so exciting. What kind of investment are we talking?" Maggie asked.

"Do you need help?" I asked tentatively. This was my area of expertise.

Nora smiled at me. "I may need to pick your brain after the meeting. They came to me. And I am desperate for some capital to ramp up my online business, so I figured I'd take a meeting."

I nodded. "If you have questions, go to the ladies' room and text me. I'll keep my phone on. I can pretty much guarantee you'll be the only woman in the room."

She reached across the booth and squeezed my hand. "Thanks, hon."

Jackie came over with coffee and took our drink order. I was starting to love this place. Aside from the food, the atmosphere was so homey and nice. Everyone waved to us when we came in, and several people came to the table to introduce themselves to me and say hello. The decor was vintage, but everything looked shiny and new. And the food was incredible.

"Astrid, you are famous. The brilliant beauty who tamed the beast," Cece gushed.

"I would hardly call Declan a beast," I replied, feeling a bit defensive.

"You have no idea what he was like before you entered the picture. Seriously. He was such a grumpy asshole. He used to pick on Liam all the time. Good-natured brother stuff, but still. His bad moods were relentless."

I knew she meant well, but I was a bit annoyed. Declan wasn't a bad guy, he was just an introvert who had a lot on his plate. I didn't want to be rude, but I wanted her to shut up already. I'm sure Liam wasn't perfect either.

Nora seemed to read me. "Astrid, you look a bit... tired?"

I couldn't hide the smile from my face. It felt unnatural. I wasn't a smiler. My resting bitch face was legendary. But I couldn't help it. Every single time I thought about Declan, which was approximately 47,000 times per minute, I smiled. I still couldn't believe I had jumped him. I was not usually one for initiating sex. But he did not seem to mind. In fact, he seemed to like my proactive approach.

Nora grabbed my mimosa. "I'm taking this away from you. You are sex drunk."

"I'm not sex drunk," I snapped, grabbing the glass and taking a big sip.

"It's cute that you think you can hide this from us." Emily patted my arm.

I took another swig of mimosa to keep from having to say anything.

"There is no judgment here," Cece said kindly. "I used to show up sex drunk too."

"She still does," Maggie quipped, furiously typing on her phone.

I exhaled. "Fine. I'm sex drunk. Happy?"

"I knew it."

Cece patted me on the shoulder. "Congrats. I am marrying a Quinn so I know what you're dealing with."

I laughed. I was smitten. I couldn't hide it from my friends so there was no way I could hide it from myself. Declan was awesome, and I had never experienced this type of connection in my life. I missed him already and I wanted more of him. I couldn't lie to myself and pretend this was a fake relationship anymore. My rules and plans and contractual provisions had gone out the window. I should be freaking out right now, but I felt great. Must be all the orgasms.

"What about you, Nora? You are the single gal here. What's happening in your love life?" Emily asked.

Nora sighed and dramatically sipped her coffee.

"Nothing. Nada. Zilch. I briefly dated a guy from Boston for a few weeks before the holidays. It was fun. Since then nothing."

"I find that hard to believe," Cece added.

"Believe it, ladies. I am single and loving it. Plus I've already hooked up with all the decent looking guys in this town, and the ones I haven't are either married to or dating you gals."

Maggie looked up from her phone. "Nora, there are a lot of guys out there. But I think you're just conveniently single right now because of one Lucas Kim."

Nora's fork clattered to the floor.

Cece patted Maggie's hand. "Don't go there."

Nora slowly looked up at Maggie, her face a mask of anger. "I despise Lucas Kim. And this is a place of trust, so I am not going to snap at you. But please, please do not imply that I have some kind of sexual attraction to that vile man."

Maggie was not intimidated by Nora's theatrics. "Nora, you don't hate him. You hate the feelings he inspires in your panties," she said drolly, taking a bite of omelette. Maggie was a stone-cold badass, and I prayed she would want to be my friend.

Emily and Cece exchanged looks.

Nora glared at Maggie, and I thought she would throw a punch. A tense moment passed and then Nora's face softened. "Oh Mags, you know me, I tend to have too many feelings. But I truly don't want to date anyone right now, and that includes Lucas Kim." I had no idea what had passed between them, but it was more complicated than I could comprehend. Nora's kindness toward Maggie was confusing, but then again I was new at female friendships.

Maggie smiled at Nora. "Hey, I get it. I don't know what's going to happen with Josh and me, but I promise you this. I will never, ever date again. Men are terrible." I didn't know Maggie well, but I could see that she was hurting. I knew she had two kids and was a nurse practitioner in town. I didn't know what had happened with her husband, but I sensed she wasn't the type to overshare.

"A-woman," Nora replied, raising her coffee mug.

I tended to agree with them, but at the moment I was too sex drunk on Declan Quinn to even appreciate a good feminist rant. I liked him and I liked being with him, and it all felt so natural, so easy. We complemented each other and had fun together, and he seemed to respect me and my career.

I certainly understood where Nora was coming from. Guys could really derail your life. Case in point was Max Shapiro. Nora definitely wasn't the type to put her needs aside for a guy, and I respected that. I guess I always put myself in the same category. It would be nice to have someone in my life, but I wasn't willing to compromise my goals for that.

And wasn't that what most women did? Compromise and bend and eventually break. My mom never compromised. And she focused on her goals with single-minded obsession. And she had been alone the entire time. And it's not like we had some amazing mother-daughter relationship. Her goals came at the expense of everything else. So maybe I was wrong. Maybe compromise didn't break you—what if it actually made you stronger?

"Emily, what's new with you?" I asked, hoping to turn

the conversation to her adorable kids and away from my sex life.

"The usual. Kids are insane. Derek is amazing, as always, but I'm super annoyed with him because every time he gets home from a trip, he keeps trying to make shower sex happen."

"You've got to be shitting me!" Nora exclaimed.

"I am so annoyed with him. We've been together for almost fifteen years. And during that time, I did not magically grow a foot in height. It is not logistically possible without a massive bathroom renovation or accidentally breaking his dick."

"I never understood shower sex," Maggie mused. "Seems like a waste of water."

"Yes," Emily agreed. "And honestly, sometimes the shower is the only place I get to be alone. My kids don't even let me pee in peace. Taking a shower after they've gone to bed and shaving my legs, or deep conditioning my hair, it's a luxury to me. I don't want a needy penis all up in my business when I'm having my alone time."

We all laughed. Emily was zany and loud, but smart and oh, so funny. I knew how much she loved Derek and her kids, but I could also see how the demands of three kids plus a husband who travels wore on her sometimes.

"Hm…" Cece mused. "I mostly just go down on Liam in the shower. It's faster and safer."

"Good call. Do you have any ideas how many times I've almost torn a ligament trying to contort myself in the shower for him?" I could only imagine. Emily was notoriously klutzy as a child and was known for being super accident-prone. My Aunt Connie joked the Havenport Hospital should have a wing named after her because she spent so much time there getting stitches and casts for her various injuries.

"The last thing I need is to have to explain to the ER doctor how I dislocated my shoulder."

Maggie chuckled. "As your health care provider, let me assure you that is not a conversation I want to have with you in a clinical setting."

Emily patted her hand. "Thanks, Maggie."

Nora took a sip of coffee. "Oh, Mags, have you treated any sex injuries?"

Maggie's eyes flashed, and I could tell she wanted to spill. "I can't tell you details."

"Yeah, yeah. Patient confidentiality. I know that. But give us something."

We all leaned forward.

Maggie played with the end of her ponytail. "STIs. So many STIs and so many antibiotic scripts written. Trust me, some of the people would be the ones you least expect."

We all laughed.

"But I've had a few minor sex injuries. Nothing super crazy." She thought for a minute. "Ooh. But when Josh was a resident doing his GI rotation, he did remove some weird objects from colons."

"Gross," Cece said. "So people stuck weird shit up their assholes?"

"So much weird shit. I think that's why he didn't go into that specialty," she mused.

"Good man. I also try to avoid butt stuff when I can."

"Don't we all, ladies?"

"Hey, don't knock it till you try it!"

"Oh, Emily," we all groaned.

————

After two mimosas, three cups of black coffee, and a massive plate of corned beef hash, I was relaxed, happy, and having a blast with my new friends. They were all so different, but they supported and loved each other fiercely. I felt proud that they had invited me into their circle.

"So what about you, Astrid?" Emily asked. "Do you want kids?"

I would normally not get into this line of questioning, but I had been buttered up with alcohol and delicious breakfast food and discussions of shower sex and butt stuff. "I do," I said, matter-of-factly. "But not for at least another five or six years."

Emily looked at me. "Sweetie you're almost thirty-three. If you want them, you should probably at least think about it before then."

"Oh," I said, "I froze my eggs when I was twenty-eight." I shrugged. It was expensive, and the hormones made me a bit crazy, but it was worth it not to have to stress about my dwindling fertility along with my billable hours.

"Why?" Cece asked.

"Everyone does it."

"Do they really?"

"Everyone in my world. All the women at my firm go to the same clinic. It's practically required." When we showed up as fresh law school grads they implied we would be working so hard for the next fifteen years that we would never have time to actually make a baby the old-fashioned way, so it was best to rely on science to help.

"A partner just had a healthy baby last year at forty-seven."

"Do you want to have a baby at forty-seven?"

"I'm thirty-three and I am so exhausted I can barely function. I can't imagine sleepless nights and potty training when I'm pushing fifty," Emily said. And she was clearly telling the truth, as her dark under-eye circles and messy hair did not lie.

I hadn't really thought about it before. I guess I just compartmentalized so well I never stopped to think about it. I did the responsible thing. I planned ahead so when the time came I could do it, even if I was super old. But part of me also figured the odds were not great that I would ever be a mother.

Why? Because there simply wasn't time in my life. Not for meeting a guy and building the requisite relationship necessary to procreate with someone. And frankly I didn't want to devote the time.

Maggie looked at me kindly. "It's worth it. I get it. I have a busy career too. And although my marriage is shit now, I have never regretted having my kids. I had my daughter really young, which completely destroyed my plan to go to medical school. But she is worth it. Being a mother changed me and transformed me and has enriched my life in so many unexpected ways."

She wiped a tear away from her cheek. Nora put her arms around her and squeezed. "We love you, sweetie."

"Thanks. I love you guys too," she said.

Cece leaned over to me. "Maggie and her husband have been separated for a few months."

I nodded. "I'm so sorry."

Maggie snapped back to her normal self. "Don't be. Life is too short to be in a bad marriage."

She forced herself to smile. "And seeing my sister so wildly and passionately in love made me realize that I deserve that too. So maybe someday I'll find it." Cece blushed, and I saw that sisterly bond in the way they looked at one another. I had spent most of my life yearning for a sibling. I figured that when I hit adulthood, being an only child wouldn't bother me anymore. If anything it was worse. Adult life was lonely and isolating and I wished I had siblings to share it with.

"I'll drink to that," Nora said.

We all raised our mimosas and coffee cups. "To wild passionate love."

Nora was not wrong. These ladies shared everything. And as the outsider, they were kind enough to just let me sit there and observe. I admired their friendship. Emily was my cousin, so I had known her my entire life, but these women saw a completely different side of her, and I was jealous. I was jealous of their friendship and the trust they had in one another. They supported and loved each other but they also laughed a lot. No one could take themselves too seriously with this crew.

How long had it been since I had a close, trusted friend? Maybe college? But I had let all my significant friendships wither and die because I had no time.

I had no one to blame but myself for my current predicament. I knew what I had signed up for. I saw my mom's life. I knew the toll it would take. But it wasn't until now, sitting at this diner with these sassy and funny women, that I started to truly understand what I had been missing out on. And it didn't feel good.

24

I couldn't stop thinking about Declan. I wanted to be with him all the time. My phone buzzed all day with his constant texts. At least he was thinking about me as much as I was thinking about him.

———

Declan: Why do you smell so good?
    Astrid: How can you smell me across the street?
    Declan: I remember everything about you, killer. Including how you smell.
    Declan: It's incredible. Is it perfume?
    Astrid: Nope. Just the blood of my enemies.

———

Declan: I can't stop thinking about you
    Astrid: Same. I am so sore.
    Declan: Did I hurt you?
    Astrid: Calm down. Only in a good way.

Declan: Don't worry I'll kiss it and make it better later.

Astrid: Promise?

Declan: Oh yes. I am having a shit day. When I get home I am going to pour myself a glass of whiskey and then lick it off your naked body. Then I want you to sit on my face and not get off until you've come at least three times.

Astrid: Wow. I don't know if I can wait that long.

Declan: You will wait.

Astrid: Or what?

Declan: I'll spank you.

———

I had been putting this call off for weeks. I needed to make it, but it was very hard to actually pick up the phone and dial. I needed to call Donna, my secretary at the firm. But just the thought of making contact with Burns & Glenn made me feel nauseated. Things were so good right now. I didn't want to spoil the wonderful things in my life with more law firm drama.

"Hello, Donna. How are you?"

"Oh Astrid, sweetie. I miss you so badly. Things are so weird here without you." Donna was the best. She had been assigned to me in my first year, when I shared her with multiple other associates. As I climbed the ladder, I insisted on working with her, and she became my personal secretary a few years ago. I could not function without her. She was professional, insanely organized, and a wonderful person who always had my back.

"I'm sure. Who are you working for now?"

Donna hesitated on the other end of the phone. "Charlotte Tobin-Meyer."

"Ugh." CTM was my nemesis. She even insisted on

going by her three initials, like she was Ruth Bader Ginsburg or something.

I laughed to myself. It was nice to know I wasn't the only person I knew with a nemesis. It was yet another thing Declan and I had in common. Something about my personality made it easy to make enemies. I should probably explore that in therapy someday.

I tried to hide the rage in my voice. Donna did not deserve my anger because she was assigned to work for the devil. That bitch had been competing with me for years—undermining me in front of partners, stabbing me in the back every chance she got, and generally being a horrific pain in my ass. One time, I think she tried to run me over in the parking garage. When I confronted her about it she said she had lost a contact. Bullshit. So it was not surprising she stole my secretary the minute I left the building. She probably thought she could get ahead with Donna by her side. The joke was on her. Donna would always be loyal to me. We'd been together for years and were like family. Donna had protected me and supported me every chance she got, and I'd done the same. Charlotte Tobin-Meyer couldn't even imagine what that kind of loyalty looked like.

"Thank you for the lovely holiday gift basket, Astrid dear. Paul loved the fancy pears." Paul was Donna's husband who had struggled with some health problems last year. I usually sent them all kinds of goodies during the holidays, but this year she asked me to keep it healthy.

"I'm glad he liked the fancy fruit." They were good people and deserved all the good things. So I felt bad asking Donna for a favor.

"So Donna, I don't want to put you on the spot."

"But you want to know what's really going on?"

"Yup. But not if you're uncomfortable."

"Hush. I will always tell you everything. You are like a

daughter to me." I beamed with pride at that statement. I didn't have many people looking out for me in this world, and if Donna was one of them I was honored to have her.

"Charlotte has moved in on all your old matters and is spending a lot of time with Max Shapiro. He is still as smarmy as ever." I never explicitly told Donna about what happened with Max, but she had suspicions which she didn't hide from me. She had actually warned me when we started working closely together about a year ago. If only I had paid more attention.

"And?"

"She is definitely moving in on your territory. The two of them pitched to Galaxy Fitness last week." I saw red. Galaxy Fitness had been my client for years. I had worked on multiple matters from them, and the Assistant General Counsel had been my classmate in law school. The thought of Charlotte working for them made me want to spit nails. I held my tongue and let Donna continue.

"And there have been a lot of meetings about what went wrong with the Sobmark merger."

"Any idea how it happened?" I asked, hoping against hope that my name would be cleared soon.

"Not sure. We have had a team of cybersecurity consultants in, and they are going through everything. Hopefully it will be worked out soon."

"Are people still saying I did it?"

"Astrid, we both know you didn't do it. I keep your schedule and your calendar and I know that you were in Los Angeles for a Galaxy Fitness meeting the day it happened."

"Oh, I know, Donna. I gave them all that information at my review and told them to check in with you to corroborate what I told them. Has the investigation team spoken to you?"

"No. Nothing. I can't help but think it's not a

coincidence they are not in a hurry to exonerate you. But, I was taking notes in a recent meeting and they said it may have been the Hong Kong team. So that might be good news for you."

Yes. I pumped my fist. We had a Boston team and a Hong Kong team working on the merger. We were both in and out of the virtual document room. It was definitely a possibility, and if attention was turned away from me, that would only ease my transition back.

"Thanks, Donna."

"Have you found a new job yet?"

"No, not yet. There are some extenuating circumstances." I trailed off, not willing to lie to Donna.

Donna was silent on the other end of the phone. It didn't seem like she was buying what I was selling.

"Anything else?" I asked. Donna was always well versed in firm gossip.

"People are still talking about you. Some people think you had a nervous breakdown. Others say you lost your touch and the partners turned on you."

Oh God. This was worse than I thought. Several people at the firm had had nervous breakdowns. It was practically a badge of honor and not a big deal. If you weren't in treatment for depression, anxiety, or alcoholism, it was expected that you soon would be. But not being able to cut it? To keep up with the work? That was truly horrible and would sink my reputation in the industry.

"Hold on, dear. I have to move to a more private space." I heard her walking through the office and then heard a door shut. "I also wanted to tell you something. So I heard some things. About Mr. Shapiro."

Oh shit. I was so embarrassed that Donna knew.

"There have been other associates."

I took a sharp breath. This was worse than I thought. It was bad enough I had received several more threatening texts, but there were others? I felt like I was going to throw up.

"Secretaries talk. And he was in the New York office for a while. And Lucy Smith—she supports the real estate group—she was there for a while as well. Apparently there have been a few. And all left under mysterious circumstances."

"Thank you for telling me." This was the last thing I wanted. It was bad enough that Max screwed me over, but to find out that others were involved as well? It made me sick.

"Do you remember an associate named Monica Sweeting?"

"Huh. I think so." Monica was an associate in the debt restructuring group. She was a few years ahead of me. I worked with her on a few deals when I was a junior, but didn't really know her.

"Apparently he was the reason she left."

"Oh." I was dumbstruck. All this time, I assumed it was just me.

"It's not your fault, dear. This place is a pressure cooker, and it's easy to be manipulated into staying silent."

"I feel worse that it wasn't just me. I can't believe there have been others."

"I'm sorry. But things are different now. Back when I was your age, women just had to shut up and deal with this stuff. You're different. You can fight back." I wasn't entirely sure what we were talking about anymore. How much did Donna know?

"It doesn't feel that way."

"I know. But Astrid, I've known you for years. You have a cool head and a big heart, and I know you will figure it out. He shouldn't get away with this."

I loved Donna. She knew just what to say to me. "It's just so frustrating," I vented. "They confiscated my laptop and company phone when I was fired. I have no evidence."

"Leave it to me, Astrid. Text me your mailing address on my personal phone. I may be able to help."

My heart soared. Donna was on the inside. If she had any information, it could help me make my case against Max and the firm.

"Anyway, the reason I was calling was to RSVP to the gala. I plan to be there."

"Oh good. I am so glad you are going to come. You deserve that award so much, Astrid."

"You do too, Donna." Donna had stayed with me late nights copying documents and proofreading our training materials. She was just as responsible for the success of the initiative as I was. As depressed as I was about this Max situation, I was proud of the work we had done.

"Oh, stop. I am always happy to support your brilliance."

"Thanks, Donna. That means a lot to me."

"So great. I will make sure you are confirmed for one of the firm's tables."

"And I will have a guest."

"Oh, really?"

"Yes. His name is Declan Quinn."

"Is he your boyfriend?"

I hesitated. "Yes. He is my boyfriend. I am so excited to bring him as my date."

"Oh, I am so happy for you. Where did you meet him?"

"I've been staying at my aunt's cottage up in Havenport. I met him here."

"I love Havenport. So lovely and so much history. I am glad you are having such a lovely break. It's about time you gave yourself some time to rest and relax."

"Yes. It's been nice actually. I've made some friends

here, and I'm reading and exercising. It's been a good change."

"I am so thrilled for you. That sounds like just what you need. Take all the time for yourself that you can. You deserve it."

I was taken aback by her comments. Donna was a kind, loyal person, but she was a professional to the core. She had worked at Burns & Glenn for over twenty years and knew what was expected of me. I guess I never stopped to think that maybe my burnout was visible to others. That maybe I was in worse shape than I thought?

"Can you do me one favor, sweetie?"

"Of course, Donna, anything."

"I want you to get the most beautiful gown you can find. Show up to that stupid party and look like a million bucks. Shove it in the faces of these self-important jerks who treated you badly."

My heart swelled. I didn't deserve her. "Oh, I will, Donna. Thank you for everything you do."

"And I want you to text me a photo of you and your handsome date."

"Will do."

———

I immediately pulled up her profile on LinkedIn. Monica Walsh née Sweeting had worked at Burns & Glenn for five years following her graduation from law school. She left abruptly in January, four years ago. She was now in private practice at a small firm in upstate New York. But there was a gap in her résumé. Over a year with nothing. That was strange. Usually associates went on to prestigious in-house counsel or government positions after leaving Burns & Glenn.

Looking at her professional headshot, I wanted to give

her a hug. I had no idea what had happened to her, but if it involved Max Shapiro then it couldn't have been good. I couldn't help but think how easy it was for him to prey on unsuspecting associates and lie to them. The environment of the firm—the constant paranoia and fear that you weren't good enough—made us sitting ducks. Looking back, he exploited my ambition, my desire to be the best, and my low self-esteem. We all wanted to get ahead, we didn't want to be left behind, and God forbid, fired. Burns & Glenn was the top of the profession, and there was a long way to fall if you couldn't keep up.

I wanted to reach out. To ask her what happened and offer my support. But that was awkward and weird. I debated for almost thirty minutes before sending her a direct message on LinkedIn.

Hello Monica. You may not remember me. I was the M&A associate who was part of your team on the PriCom deal a few years back. I really enjoyed working with you and wanted to connect regarding your career progression. I recently left Burns & Glenn and am weighing my options. I hope you are well.

I gave her my cell and my email address so that if she wanted to get in touch with me, she could. And if she didn't? Then I would just keep plugging along and try to get my job back.

I was feeling things. Real, painful, challenging things.

Work left me so busy I was just numb for years. I didn't have to think about things or feel things. Or deal with things. Productivity came before all else so I could just numb out in the pursuit of partnership. But now, I had to actually confront things. Things about myself and my family and my choices. And it sucked.

My stomach was churning. I felt angry and sad and frustrated. I was flooded with rage. I was angry at my parents, angry at myself, at the firm, at everything and everyone who had ever done me wrong.

But then my thoughts traveled to one person who had never done wrong by me. The person who only built me up and had never torn me down. The person who would have my back no matter what. He didn't care how many billable hours I'd logged or which awards I had won. He liked me for me.

I grabbed my phone and reread some of his dirty texts from this afternoon. And then I knew what I had to do.

25

ASTRID

I THREW MY SHOES ON AND HEADED ACROSS THE street to Declan's house. I was wearing sweats, and my hair was back in a ponytail. I didn't even care. I was a woman on a mission.

I had never considered myself a sexual person. On the contrary, I didn't usually understand why people were so obsessed with sex. I was no virgin, but I was not exactly experienced either. I'd had sex with a handful of boyfriends and it had been fine, or at least I thought it had been fine.

Turns out I had no idea what I was talking about.

Sex with Declan fried my synapses and reduced me to a quivering pile of hormones. Every time he touched me, I was consumed by my desire for him. I didn't get bored, think about my to-do list or anything else for that matter, because I was too busy screaming and moaning. Generally, my litmus test for good sex had always been whether or not I had an orgasm. If so, then it went in the "good" category. If I didn't, or the guy didn't even try, then it was in the "bad" category. I assumed if we both came it was a successful encounter. How sad I was. No wonder I didn't care about sex. I truly had no idea what I was missing.

I knocked on the door, and he opened right away. I looked up at him. He looked tired after a long day at work, but still oh so sexy.

"Are you okay?"

I pushed my way into his house and turned to him. I wanted him. I wanted him to distract me with his body. I wanted to get away from my old life and all the law firm bullshit. I knew I was safe in Declan's bed.

He walked back to the kitchen where he was putting away groceries. Ginger wandered over, and I gave her a scratch behind the ear.

My heart was pounding. I wanted to tell him. But what? I had no idea what I was feeling at the moment. I was angry and I was horny, but everything else? Total confusion. I had feelings. Lots of feelings. I wasn't one of those women who could cope with feelings. They confused me and distracted me from getting things done.

"I need you," I said softly.

He looked up at me with kind eyes. "What's wrong?"

I stared at him. "Nothing." I ripped off my sweater and let it drop to the floor.

He stared at me, confused.

I held up my phone. "Were you serious? About what you said? In your texts?"

He nodded.

I removed my tank top and stood in front of him in my bra. "So you really want me to sit on your face?" I smiled.

He walked over to me. "Yes."

"Good." I turned on my heel and headed toward his bedroom, shedding my clothes as I walked.

"Are you sure you're okay?" he asked as my bra hit him in the face.

I reclined on the bed in only my panties. "Never better." I nodded at him. "Take off your clothes." He quickly removed his T-shirt, and I was struck again by the sight of his body. I was already turned on, but watching him strip for me just made it so much better.

I had never seen a male specimen like Declan Quinn up close. Sure, I had seen hot guys in magazines and movies, but I had never had the pleasure of exploring a body like this one. I knew he was tall and strong, but I didn't know just how beautiful he was. His face was just one part of the perfect package. And don't even get me started on his actual package…

Declan's chest was broad, muscular, and peppered with a light dusting of dark hair. His shoulders and arms bulged with muscle and veins. He inched his jeans down his strong thighs, knowing it was torturing me. I was distracted by the size of his erection. It popped up above the waistband of his boxer briefs. I wanted so badly to take him into my mouth.

"Lie down," I instructed him.

He did. Grinning at me the entire time. I crawled up the length of his body, kissing and biting every inch of perfect manly flesh and pausing to gently kiss the tip of his rock-hard cock, which made him groan. I knelt over his face, holding onto the headboard. He wasted no time tasting me. Licking and sucking and using his strong hands to grab me and hold me still. I liked a man who got right to the point. He knew exactly what I needed.

I threw my head back and screamed. He grabbed my ass cheeks while his tongue went to work, hitting me in sensitive spots I didn't even know existed. By the time he slipped his fingers inside me, I felt like I was going to explode. I was thrashing and moaning and screaming. He didn't seem to mind. Every time I looked down I got more turned on by his sexy determination.

Declan was skilled with his tongue, there was no doubt about that. But it was the position, the power, the feeling of invincibility that had me teetering over the edge in minutes. He licked and swirled and I felt his fingers travel down the seam of my ass toward my back entrance. He lightly stroked it while sucking on my clit, and I started to shake. It was too much. Too much sensation. His tongue and lips and fingers and hands. He was stimulating every possible part of me, and I couldn't take it any longer.

He applied a bit of pressure, and I detonated like an atomic bomb, screaming and thrashing as a massive orgasm tore through me, lighting up every cell in my body. He didn't stop—just kept going as wave after wave hit me. I rode through it, feeling the build-up again. Before I knew it, he had slipped his finger inside, and I climbed even higher before orgasming again.

"Yes. Yes," I screamed. "More yes."

All the pent-up frustration, rage, and confusion inside me exploded as I screamed and begged and swore. It was as if I was levitating off the bed, and only Declan's skilled tongue and strong hands were keeping me grounded to earth.

When I rolled off him, I was spent. I looked over at his smiling face, wet with my arousal. "That was..." I trailed off.

"Did you really just have two in a row?" he asked in amazement.

"Yes, I did."

"I'm pretty happy with myself right now."

"You should be. But don't rest on your laurels. Now you need to fuck me."

"If you're sure."

"Oh, I'm really sure." I saw him reach over to the nightstand. Did I really want to take this step? I did. I wanted him and I wanted no barriers between us. "We can skip it if you want. I have an IUD. And I'm clean."

He looked at me in amazement.

"Are you clean, sailor?" I asked in what I hoped was a saucy way.

"As a whistle. Are you sure you're comfortable going without?" he asked tentatively.

"Yes," I replied, my heart pounding in my chest.

"Are you really alright?" He looked concerned.

"I'm angry and frustrated and pissed at the world." I was also feeling really confused about everything with Declan. I was falling for him. I knew it and I didn't know what to do with that. It took every ounce of willpower I had not to blurt it out in my post-orgasmic haze.

He nibbled my neck. "Do you just want my cock or do you want me?" For a split second, he looked vulnerable and this felt like a much bigger conversation. Declan was prickly on the outside, but it was at moments like this I could see the soft, kind heart beneath all that burly bluster.

"Both. I want both, Declan."

He rolled me over and slapped my ass quick. It stung, but also shot a bolt of electricity straight to my clit. He lifted me up onto my knees and placed my hands on the headboard. He kneeled behind me and gently thrust into me from behind, shallowly at first, then getting deeper and deeper while wrapping his arms around me. He played with my breasts as I savored the sensation of fullness.

In my post-orgasmic state, everything was heightened and I was overcome. Being stretched and filled and so possessed by him sent me into a state of near orgasm. I felt if he moved an inch, I would detonate again.

"You feel so amazing," he growled into my ear.

I moaned in response, unable to formulate words.

He started to move, slowly at first and then began to build up steam.

"I meant what I said earlier. I dream about this ass." He spanked me hard and then caressed the area gently.

"I could tell," I said. "You seemed to enjoy exploring earlier."

"I think we both enjoyed it, killer," he replied. I couldn't really argue with his logic. The angle was incredible, hitting me in all the right places. I was so spent from the earlier orgasms, his strong arms were probably the only things holding me up. But at this moment, I reveled in the punishing pace and the intensity of every stroke.

I wasn't usually very submissive. But submitting to Declan felt like the only choice. My body craved it. My mind craved it. I wanted to give him my body wholly and completely.

And since I had just sat on his face, it seemed like the right thing to do. And as he fell over the edge, bringing me with him, all I could think was that there was no way I could possibly avoid falling in love with this man.

26

DECLAN

ASTRID WAS NOTHING LIKE I HAD EVER EXPERIENCED in my life. She was a supernova.

I couldn't even remember what life was like before her because she made everything so much better. She was insatiable. For everything. Food, sex, conversation. She wanted to go for walks and listen to music and talk about literature. She had this beautiful, childlike enthusiasm for the simple things. And the simple things were so much more enjoyable with her.

She spent her time going to Krav Maga classes and hanging out with her girlfriends and was evolving right in front of my eyes. Her face had filled out and was no longer gaunt. Her body wasn't skinny; she was lean and strong. Everything about her was different, and I loved watching her transform into a better version of herself in front of my eyes.

Sometimes we talked, really talked, about our families and our lives and our choices. We talked about anything and everything. Childhood memories, dreams for the future. And sometimes we just enjoyed the silence together.

She asked me about my ideas and pushed me to talk to my father and make my case for the future of the business. She even pushed me to be more social, accepting invites from my brothers and her friends to hang out.

Liam and Cece had even come over one night for pizza and beer. I was not the dinner party hosting sort, but I could tell it meant a lot to Astrid, and we ended up having a great time.

I couldn't help but think ahead. And I was never that guy. But I thought about the future and I could see her in it. I didn't want a future without her.

She had shown me what a relationship could be. What true companionship and affection were. I felt like I had won the lottery. Like I should go out and tell everyone how awesome it is to have an incredible goddess for a girlfriend.

I didn't even care that this was supposed to be fake. It was real now, and that's all that mattered.

She owned me, body, mind, and soul, and there was nothing I wouldn't do for her.

———

As the days became weeks and the weeks became a month, she talked less and less about her career and her law firm. I knew she loved being a lawyer, but it was clear she had discovered a lot of other things she liked to do too.

She insisted on learning everything she could about the fishing business and had offered to help us review contracts for the beer distribution company as well.

"I brought Astrid along so she could take a look at these contracts," I said, walking into the brewery with my favorite girl. My brothers and I were up to our eyeballs in planning for the launch of our distribution company.

Turns out shipping and delivering beer was a lot more complicated than I had imagined.

"Thank God!" Callum exclaimed. "Our guy isn't returning our calls, and we need to start making decisions." He handed Astrid a stack of papers, and my eyes bulged out of my head. We couldn't ask her to read that entire pile.

Before I could object, she grabbed the stack like it was nothing and began to flip through the pages. Her eyes focused, and she had the sexiest look of determination on her face.

After a few minutes, she looked up. "These are shit. Who is your lawyer?"

Callum seemed taken aback by her bluntness. "A guy I've worked with a few times from Boston."

"Fire him," she said coolly.

"That's easier said than done. It's hard to find a good lawyer who is affordable and has the bandwidth to take us on."

"I agree with you. But this is rife with errors," she said, scrolling through a few pages, "and is missing some key provisions to protect you guys on the back end. It looks like someone googled 'contract' and printed the first thing they saw."

She gestured to me. "Declan, hand me my purse."

I passed her enormous purse over to her and she pulled out a notebook, highlighter, and some pens. She spread out on the top of the bar and got to work, crossing things out and jotting down notes.

"I'll have the master services agreement and the amendments worked out for you in an hour or so. We can talk through some of the provisions, and you may want to move some things around." She took a hair band off her wrist and twisted up her hair, exposing her gorgeous long neck, and I was overcome with lust.

My brothers both looked at me, impressed and a little bit scared. I shrugged. What could I say? My girl was brilliant and didn't suffer any bullshit. I felt a frisson of pride in my chest. This dynamic, savvy woman was with me. She was my girlfriend. I mean, technically fake girlfriend, but things had not been fake in the bedroom. To think that she would be with someone like me filled me with a deep sense of satisfaction.

"Liam, how about you grab us some beers while my lady works her magic."

————

"That was fun," Astrid said as we let ourselves back into my house. "You hang out with them every Tuesday night?"

I nodded. "It used to just be us three brothers, but the group has expanded a lot recently. They are a lot to take."

"Nah. I liked it," Astrid said. "I like getting to know your family. It helps me make sense of you."

We walked in, and Ginger lifted her head up off her dog bed. "Hi, Ginger," I said. She plopped back down, the dog equivalent of an eye roll.

"I actually think she might be a cat," Astrid whispered. I laughed.

I wrapped my arms around her and took a deep breath, breathing in her delicious scent.

"Hey," I said, cupping her face, "I don't want you to think I'm dating you for free legal advice."

"Awww. My legal advice is just one of the perks." She gave me a peck on the cheek.

"But not the best one." I squeezed her ass hard and she yelped.

"Seriously," I continued, "you are so sexy when you are in smart lawyer mode."

"You are lying. There is nothing sexy about me nerding out over a contract."

"Nope, super sexy." I pulled her in close and started kissing her neck.

"I've been thinking," she started, as I made my way down to her collarbone. "I think I may call Lucas Kim."

I paused, waiting for her to continue. "I have been thinking more and more about his idea for the Women's Shelter and I think I could probably help him out."

I exhaled. Did this mean she was thinking about staying? With me? Or in Havenport? I didn't want to get my hopes up.

"I think that's a great idea," I murmured into her hair. Could Astrid really stay here? With me? I had been bracing myself for her to go back to Boston. But what if she stayed?

She sighed and arched into me. I was addicted to touching her, and this light petting wasn't enough for me. She began to rub her ass up against me, and I felt my vision get blurry. Her need was as great as my own, and it made my heart soar.

I grabbed her by the waist and threw her over my shoulder.

"Declan, what are you doing?"

I smacked her once on the ass, hard. "I'm taking you to bed, beautiful, where I'm going to ravage you."

There was a pause, and I could hear her heavy breathing. "Then please proceed," she replied enthusiastically. I spanked her again for good measure and headed to my room.

I wanted her naked. All day every day. And I also wanted to talk to her. Because she was smart, insightful, and passionate despite the frosty exterior. We had fun together. And she brought out a side of me that was rarely seen. With her I was goofy and sweet and playful. All adjectives no one would ever use to describe me under pain of death. I wasn't a people person. But I was an Astrid person. She was meant for me. That was all there was to it. I never saw myself as the settling down type. I never believed that there was someone out there who would be compatible with me. But I was wrong. She was here—in my life and in my bed—and I was going to fight like hell to keep her.

27

ASTRID

Things had been great with Declan. We were in a pattern of cooking dinner, watching *Game of Thrones*, and then making love all night. I was tired and sore and had recently discovered the joy of an afternoon nap. Sometimes Ginger joined me, snuggling up with me on the tiny cottage couch watching the fire. I was content and happy and not as bored as I thought I'd be.

Winter was stretching on endlessly, but we were making our own fun. One night Declan brought home a two-thousand-piece puzzle and a bottle of whiskey. How did he know I loved puzzles? We stayed up most of the night, drank the entire bottle, and ended up making love on the living room floor in front of the fire.

My height came in handy. Declan was endlessly creative in bed. He was always coming up with hotter and dirtier ways to get me off. We realized that we could use my height to our advantage, making stand up sex, against the wall sex, and even shower sex much more fun. Days passed in a blur of sex, delicious meals, Krav Maga classes, and hanging out with my new girlfriends. I read books, took walks with Ginger, and drank endless cups of coffee.

Of course all good things come to an end.

I was tidying up the cottage in preparation for Declan to come over when my phone rang with an unknown New York number.

"Hello."

"Yes, hi. I am looking for Astrid Wentworth?" The voice on the other end was pleasant but sounded nervous.

"This is she."

"Hello, Astrid. This is Monica Sweeting Walsh calling." My heart dropped into my stomach. I had given up hope weeks ago that she would reach out. I knew what was coming, and it was the last thing I wanted to deal with right now.

"Thank you so much for reaching out, Monica."

"No, thank you. I'm sorry it took me so long to respond. Revisiting this chapter of my life is… difficult."

"I appreciate it," I replied, not sure where to begin. I can't come right out and ask, but I needed to know if she had the same experience I did. I didn't want to push this poor woman—I barely knew her—but my desire for justice outweighed these concerns.

"I suppose you want to know what happened when I left Burns & Glenn?"

"Yes."

"Five years ago I was assigned to work with Max Shapiro on a very tricky transaction. I was just a fourth year associate, and I was honored to be trusted with such important work. Max Shapiro was a really big deal in the New York office. So we worked together. He was tough but fair and a really good legal mentor. Then he made a move. I resisted a few times at first. But then he got more aggressive. Told me he would give me a bad review if I didn't. We ended up having an affair for a year. It was horrible. We had to keep everything a secret, and I felt so dirty. He told me he and his wife had separated and she had custody of his kids. That was a lie. They were very much married, and he would leave my apartment on Saturday mornings to go to his kids' soccer games."

"I'm so sorry."

"It was terrible. I was afraid to break things off with him, and I felt pressured to keep sleeping with him. I was only twenty-nine and didn't know how to navigate the power dynamics. I got really depressed and ended up developing a drinking problem. I was in a really low place. He systematically destroyed my self-esteem and lied to me constantly. I didn't trust myself anymore, and I was convinced that I would have no career if I stood up for myself."

My heart broke. I knew what that felt like. I knew what it was like to be impressionable and awestruck by the brilliant legal mind and drawn in to his web of bullshit lies.

"By the time I worked up the courage to break up with him, I was pretty much destroyed. He gave me a bad review, and suddenly no one wanted to work with me. The firm sat me down and told me I didn't have a future there, so I chose to quietly resign."

"Did you tell anyone about what he did to you?"

"Yes. I went to HR and then to my supervising partner. They said it was my word against his and since we had a consensual relationship there was nothing they could do. I was too depressed. I believed it was my fault. I was lucky to escape with some semblance of a career."

She took a deep breath. "But things have changed. I got help, got sober, and met my husband. We had a baby girl last year and I'm really doing well. I am at a small firm doing what I love. I have moved past Max Shapiro and his narcissistic bullshit."

"Good for you!" I said and I meant it. I was impressed. She had clearly rebuilt her life and it gave me some hope.

"So let me guess, something similar happened to you?"

Monica and I talked for over an hour. We traded law firm horror stories, and she told me all about her daughter and the work she was currently doing at her new firm. She was cool and easy to talk to.

I shared some things with her I hadn't told anyone. About how Max made me feel, about how much I hated myself after he touched me or said sexual things to me. She understood on a level that no one else in my life did. I told her about my refusal to sign the liability waiver and the threatening texts I'd received.

"They want you to just go quietly like I did," she said. "They want to just sweep this under the rug. But fuck them. And fuck him."

She was so right. It made me even angrier. The thought that the firm knew what he was up to and did nothing but shame and cast aside promising female attorneys? I wanted to punch something.

"I can't believe the firm is still enabling his bullshit all these years later. And it wasn't just me. Back then there were lots of rumors, including a paralegal that he groped at the Christmas party. She ended up quitting and was hushed up. Even though there were witnesses."

I had spent the entirety of the conversation wanting to ask something and talking myself out of it. I finally broke. "Why didn't you do anything?" I asked and instantly regretted it.

She sighed, and I immediately felt bad. I wasn't trying to shame this woman. I was just trying to make sense of what happened to me. "I should have. But at the time, I just wanted to get away from the situation. It had become toxic for me, and I wanted to put it behind me. And honestly, I worried that if I made a fuss, I could be blackballed. At least this way I left with my dignity intact and a good recommendation for my next job. My career recovered and I am happy with the choices I've made."

"I'm sorry I asked. You don't owe me an explanation."

"But I am kicking myself because if I had been braver, if I had been stronger, then you may have been spared this pain. And I am truly sorry, Astrid."

I started to cry. "Please don't apologize. It's not your fault. I should have spoken up. Kept records. But I was too scared." It was the truth and I hated myself for it. I didn't want to be scared and timid. I didn't want my future to be in the control of an aggressive sexual harasser.

"Don't beat yourself up. He didn't technically force me to do anything. But time and a lot of therapy have shown me that there is a big difference between forcing and free will, and what he did was coercive. He took advantage of the fact that he was my superior. That I wanted to impress him as a partner. He mentored me, took me under his wing, made sure I worked exclusively for him so I was isolated from other associates and partners. I didn't pursue him, but when he made a move, I felt like I couldn't say no. So I didn't." She was crying now too, and I wished we were in the same room so I could give her a hug.

The air left my lungs. The sexual advances, the touching, the thinly veiled threats. This was a pattern. This was abuse. And it was illegal. I had the power to stop this, and I knew what I had to do.

"I am so sorry if my asking questions has been upsetting for you. I am just trying to make sense of everything," I said, ungracefully wiping my tears and snot on my sleeve.

"Don't apologize. It's been years and like I said, I've gotten a lot of help. My husband knows all about it, and although he wants to kick Max's ass, he has been really supportive."

"It means a lot to me that you shared your story."

"Happy to help. So what are you going to do?"

"I don't know. I just want to move on with my life. Things have changed for me and I'm, I don't know, just better. Like life is easier and brighter and more fun outside of Burns & Glenn."

"Ha! Sister, I hear that!"

"But moving on and forgetting about everything will just let him get away with it. So as much as I don't want to, I am going to file a formal complaint with HR. Explain that he retaliated against me after I rejected several aggressive sexual advances and falsely accused me to get me fired." As an attorney, I knew that retaliation was against the law. "I'm not playing nice anymore."

"Do not let him get away with this!" Her enthusiasm made me feel stronger.

"And then I am going to go to the Equal Employment Opportunity Commission and file a lawsuit against him and the firm." I shuddered just thinking about it. Years of potential litigation and attorney's fees with no guarantee of success. But exercising the nuclear option seemed to be the only way to make sure no other woman went through this. "He can't go around destroying people's careers and their self-esteem. I don't want him to take advantage of another eager, impressionable woman who just wants to be a good lawyer."

"You are my hero, Astrid."

I blushed.

"And I have a daughter now. I hate to think her mom wasn't strong enough to stand up for herself. I think I want to file a complaint too."

"Don't beat yourself up, Monica. Things have changed so much in the past few years. And you are strong. Just talking to me proves it."

"They probably won't care because it was four years

ago, but fuck it. I'm going to lay it all out. Maybe all the evidence will catch up to him."

Together, we put a plan in place. We coordinated who we would reach out to in HR and brainstormed possible evidence we could present that would be persuasive. We also made a plan to reach out to some of the other women who had been rumored to have had run-ins with Max. Monica had a friend who was an employment lawyer, so she was going to contact her about filing a potential lawsuit.

Monica laughed. "This is going to ruffle a lot of feathers."

"I know." I felt excited, empowered, and ready to fight.

"Listen, Astrid, I am out of there. I have a career now that is solid and totally separate from Burns & Glenn. You have more to lose than I do. Are you sure you want to do this? Exercise the nuclear option?" I loved that she was worried about me. But if not me, then who would fight this fight? I didn't have kids or a mortgage. Hell, I had a trust fund from my dad. I could survive while the dust settled. If I couldn't practice law, I'd find something else to do.

"I have to do it. I have to fight," I replied. For so long I'd had no fight in me. I thought I wasn't good enough, smart enough, hardworking enough. I toiled away, late nights, weekends, I missed out on the entirety of my twenties, and my sacrifices were never acknowledged. Instead I was just told it wasn't enough and I should try harder.

But now I was older, smarter, and ready to battle. I wasn't going to let Max Shapiro hurt other women while he collected his millions from the firm. It was illegal and unethical, and he needed to be taken down. And I knew that I was just the woman for the job.

28

ASTRID

THE CONVERSATION WITH MONICA DRAINED ME. I wanted to go to bed for the next week, but I also wanted to see Declan and Ginger.

I walked over to his house, noting his car in the driveway, and knocked on the front door. I heard Ginger bark—she knew it was me and that made me feel amazing —and heard his footsteps.

He opened the door. "Come in."

The house smelled amazing. I was used to being spoiled by Declan's cooking, but the aroma of garlic and something herby filled the air and it made my stomach rumble. "What are you cooking?"

"Pasta with some fresh lobster." Oh my God, he was the perfect man. Why was he not married yet? Hot dude who cooks and loves his dog. I should put an ad in the paper. There would be women lined up from here to Canada.

I gave Ginger a pat and took off my boots. Declan walked closer.

"Astrid, you're shaking. Are you okay?"

"I wanted to tell you something. I just got off the

phone with a woman named Monica who I used to work with at Burns & Glenn."

I couldn't hold it in any longer. Tears poured out of my eyes. I couldn't control myself. Everything just came out of me. All the guilt and shame I had been carrying around. The dam broke.

Declan wrapped his strong arms around me and held me while I sobbed. He said nothing, but his presence soothed me.

I hiccupped. "It wasn't just me. There were others. At least one and maybe a couple more."

"Oh, Astrid." He stroked my hair and I clung to his chest.

"I let this happen to me. It's my fault."

Declan pulled back and tilted my chin up to look at him. "Don't say that. You did nothing wrong, Astrid. That place brainwashed you and mistreated you. You said no. You did the right thing."

"No, I didn't. I was more concerned about saving my job than protecting other women. I didn't think. Monica has a daughter. And now she wants to fight for her."

"That's great news."

"Yes. But why couldn't I fight? Why did I slink off in shame?"

"Because you are learning, you are evolving, and you are finding your fight."

I walked over to the couch and Declan sat next to me, his arm around my shoulders.

"We talked. She's a mom now and started crying when I told her what happened to me. We are going to file complaints against him with the firm. He retaliated against both of us. That's illegal. And we're going to contact some other women who may have been victimized. And then we are going to sue."

"I'm proud of you, killer." He looked deeply into my

eyes. "Astrid, you are one of the toughest, strongest people I've ever met. And maybe it took what happened to you for you to realize that. But with your strength, your grit, you can do anything. Truly anything."

"Thank you." And I meant it. Sitting here with him, I felt strong. I felt like I could do it.

"Is this going to hurt your chances of getting another law firm position?"

"In a fair world, it shouldn't. But this isn't a fair world. This is likely going to torpedo my career. At least for a few years. But I am willing to take my chances. If the firm has been covering up for his gross behavior for years, I don't want to work there anyway." All this time I thought it was just me. How could I be so naïve? But I was wiser now, and I wanted to make sure no other women would be taken advantage of.

Just having this conversation was making my blood pressure rise and my heart race. It was all coming back to me. The constant hopelessness. The fear and paranoia that everyone else was working harder and that I wasn't smart enough and dedicated enough to make it.

The firm is designed that way—to keep everyone working constantly. There is no praise, there is no achievement, just constant pressure and constant paranoia. I remember in my first year going to my first review, being very proud of myself for exceeding our annual billable hours requirement. The firm set a standard, and I had exceeded it. I expected a pat on the back.

Instead the partner doing my review sat me down and said I needed to do more. When I responded that I had exceeded the requirement, he said that was a floor not a ceiling and if my colleagues were working much harder it didn't really matter whether I exceeded it or not.

I was so confused. Why have a requirement if it was meaningless? What were we supposed to be working toward? Basically there was no safety. There was no feeling secure in your job. You had to stay hungry and keep your head on a swivel. No one was your friend.

Sitting here, wrapped in Declan's arms miles away from the office tower and all the firm bullshit, I felt safe. I felt protected. But talking to Monica brought it all back. I felt my shoulders hunch and my neck tighten.

What happened to me wasn't an isolated incident.

It happened at least one other time—one more woman who was screwed over with no recourse. And I knew in my bones there were others, and I was going to find them.

How could I have given that place my loyalty for so long? They tried to toss me out at the earliest convenience. Now that I was surrounded by people who actually cared about me, and I knew what true loyalty was, I felt gross. I wanted to run screaming into the freezing cold ocean just to get the stench of those greedy liars off me.

———

I loved it here. Declan's bedroom was beautiful. Large windows faced the ocean. The room was bare except for the huge queen bed. He had soft sheets and fluffy pillows, and everything about it just drew me in.

Lying in this bed with this gorgeous man was the highlight of my life.

I spent years of my life barely sleeping. Waking up every few hours in a panic, heart racing, pulse pounding in fear that I missed something. Or fearing that while I was sleeping someone else was working and passing me by.

But here, in this bed, with this man, I slept. Really slept. And I found that I loved it. Getting all snuggled up and just letting go. It had been more than two months since I'd been fired, but I had finally started to sleep through the night again, waking up rested and positive to start the day.

It didn't help that I usually woke up to a hot naked man who wanted to have his way with me—in bed, in the shower, on the couch, pretty much anywhere. We even made really good use of an ottoman in the cottage last week. I should probably get that steam cleaned before I move out.

Declan was insatiable. Every time I thought I was satisfied, he found a way to make me feel things I never thought possible.

We had spent the night watching TV, cuddling, and walking Ginger. It was perfect. Even more perfect when he gently stripped off my clothes and gave me multiple earth-shattering orgasms.

We were lying in bed, naked. He had lit the gas fireplace and the room was illuminated by the soft flames. He was spooning me, nuzzling my neck, and I felt boneless and content.

"I don't want this to be fake anymore," he gently whispered into my ear.

I turned around to face him. He was even more handsome with his wild-sex hair and bedroom eyes.

"Me neither," I replied, kissing him deeply.

"Astrid, this is real for me. So real. And I want it to be real for you too."

"It is." I cupped his face. "It is so real."

"I'm scared. I know it's not manly to say that. But I am feeling things. Real things. And I don't know what to do about it," he admitted sheepishly.

"First of all, feelings are fucking sexy. Second, I get it. I am confused as hell. But I want to be with you, and right now that's good enough for me."

He smiled at me. "I can live with that."

I settled in, snuggled into his broad chest. "Tell me something," he said.

"Whatever you want," I replied.

"Tell me a secret. Something real."

I thought about it, letting myself settle deeper into his strong warmth.

"So, don't tell anyone, but I secretly love kids."

"Um. Why is that a secret? It's not exactly strange to like kids." He sounded confused.

I sighed. "You don't understand. In my world it is. They would probably revoke my feminist card if I admitted to liking kids and wanting some of my own. In my world, kids are a liability. They hold you back, and more importantly, they make people take you less seriously." I wasn't lying. Everyone I knew who had kids had felt the impact on their careers. One of my old friends from the firm, Meghan, was told she was "obsessed" with her kids because she had photos of them in her office. At a review she was told it was hurting her career. Another friend was chastised by a female partner when she revealed she was pregnant with her second child. She was told one child was fine, but two was "out of hand."

Was this all just ugly sexism? Of course it was. But in a male-dominated profession it was part of the game. We all knew the rules. If you have kids, you pretend they don't exist until they go to a prestigious college and then you are allowed to brag about them. Leaving early or taking time off to care for said kids is sacrilege for both men and women.

Which is why my desire for kids was secret. I couldn't admit that I wanted some of my own. But Declan made me feel safe, made me feel cherished. I felt like I could share my real self with him. He shifted and looked me in the eyes.

"Do you want kids?" he asked.

I froze. This was meaningful on so many levels. I wasn't ready for this conversation. But there was no going back now. Intimacy was a tricky bitch. "I do. My knee-jerk reaction is to pretend I don't, and then maybe, you never know—but the reality is I do."

He studied me for a moment while I panicked. He was probably thinking about how quickly he could get me out of his house.

I couldn't stop the verbal diarrhea. "I was an only child. And my mother was, shall we say, distant. I didn't have the kind of hands-on parents that you did. So for me, I would love to have a child, or hopefully more than one, and kiss boo-boos and read bedtimes stories and take them trick or treating." And it was the truth. It was actually one of the things I spent much of my time talking to Dr. Martha about. She constantly reassured me that it was normal and healthy to want a family of my own and that I shouldn't be afraid to pursue it. My mind wandered. I wanted to be the mom who baked cookies, wore matching PJs on Christmas morning, and made a mess doing science experiments in the kitchen. I couldn't deny that those were things I wanted, and for the first time, I didn't want to deny it. I wanted to tell him the truth. I wanted this kind of intimacy. I wanted him to know me inside and out. I wanted to build a family—a happy, messy, fun family. I wanted to build a home filled with laughter and love.

"But it probably won't happen," I hedged.

"Why not? You're only thirty-two." He seemed so surprised.

"Because of my career, I don't have time to invest in finding a partner and building a family. And even if I did, I wouldn't have the time necessary to devote to them." I didn't say this part out loud, but I didn't want to be like my mother. If I was lucky enough to become a mother someday, I was going to do a damn better job than she did.

"Then get a new career." His face was serious.

"Ha. That's not even possible. I've only ever done this. I am only qualified to do this."

"I doubt that. You are an accomplished, brilliant woman with an otherworldly work ethic. You can do whatever you want."

"You say that because you don't understand my world. BigLaw is weird and has its own rules."

"Then screw BigLaw. Be Astrid. You don't have to be an associate or partner at Fuckface & Asshole anymore. Be who you want to be."

I looked at Declan's kind, handsome face and kissed him deeply. "You're right," I said. And for the first time in my life, I believed it. I didn't need Burns & Glenn. And let's face it, after I filed my lawsuit, I wouldn't be going to any BigLaw firm. And in that moment, I didn't care.

"Think about the future, Astrid. You can have whatever you want." On some level I knew that. I knew that I could pivot, career wise, find something new and be fine. But deep down I was scared. Scared that I wasn't enough. Scared that no matter how hard I tried or how hard I worked, I would fail the people who mattered the most.

29

ASTRID

It was game day. I had been psyching myself up all week for this, and I was terrified. I barely slept last night. At one point I just got up and sat on the couch and stared at the ocean for a few hours. Ginger came and sat beside me, quietly offering her support, which I appreciated.

It wasn't long after I crawled in bed with Declan that Nora showed up with coffee and dragged me out to Dante's salon. I kissed Declan goodbye. It must be so nice to be a man. He was planning a busy Saturday of exercise and hanging out with his dog. Even without hours of primping, I was sure he'd look amazing.

Normally, I tend toward conservative in all things hair and makeup. But Dante and Nora were too much to resist. In a few short hours I had every part of my body waxed, my finger- and toe-nails painted, my hair cut and colored, and professional makeup applied. I had never done anything like this before. Hours of primping always felt silly and like a waste of time. But we had a blast, sipping champagne while Dante told us the story about how he and Christian fell in love. I loved everyone at the salon and couldn't wait to go back.

Declan seemed to appreciate all the hard work when I returned.

"Look at you," he growled, wrapping his arms around me.

I touched my hair. "Dante talked me into it."

"Then I owe him a beer. You look incredible."

I kissed him deeply, lipstick be damned. He knew just what to say to make me feel so much better.

"I just have to grab my dress from the cottage," I told him, heading across the street to grab my stuff. When I got to the door I saw a small brown package on the welcome mat.

The label bore very familiar looking handwriting.

I grabbed it, closed the door behind me, and tore it open.

Inside was a padded envelope that contained a sim card and a thumb drive. A small Post-it was stuck to the outside.

Anne Greely, Margaret Simmons, and Liz Barkett
Give 'em hell.

Love,

Donna

My heart soared. Donna had come through. I knew this was the sim card from my company iPhone. And it would have all the evidence I needed to make my case. And these other three women? I hated the idea that there were more victims out there, but I was desperate to talk to them. To tell them what I was doing and hear their stories.

I packed everything back in the padded envelope and stashed it in my bedroom. Tomorrow I would get to work, but tonight, I had a gala to attend.

———

The drive to Boston was nerve-wracking. I was starting to panic. What was I thinking? I didn't want to face the Burns & Glenn people again. And what if Max was there?

Declan gently covered my hand with his. "Listen, there is no need to be nervous. We can walk out at any time. You don't owe these people anything."

I stared out the window, trying to breathe through my anxiety. I squeezed his hand.

"I mean it. We can turn around right now and go home. Or better yet, I'll take you somewhere really nice in the city tonight, anywhere you want."

His palm felt so steady, so resolute in my hand. "It's fine," I said softly. "I need to go. I need to show up. I need to show those assholes that I'm not afraid of them."

He turned and gave me a huge smile. "Then we will knock 'em dead, killer."

The Grand Bostonian Hotel was one of the oldest and the nicest in the city. I had rented us a room for the night to thank Declan for being my date. I figured that after I had my fill of boring legal people, I would want to tear off Declan's clothes and wouldn't be able to make it all the way back to Havenport.

Our room was gorgeous and came equipped with the champagne and ice bucket I had ordered. We hung up our fancy clothes, and Declan poured me a glass.

He raised his. "To you. You are amazing."

I blushed. "Hardly. To us," I said instead, not sure what it meant or what I wanted it to mean.

His eyes turned molten as he clinked my glass. "To us," he repeated softly, slowly easing the strap of my tank top off my shoulder and lightly kissing my collarbone. I leaned my head back and my fingers found his hair, tangling it between my fingers.

Soon I was straddling him as we furiously kissed, and I

tore his T-shirt over his head. His hands were everywhere, making me ache with want.

My anxiety was gone, replaced by pure lust as we shed our clothes and he carried me to the bed.

"Lie down," I said, my voice husky.

"You want to be on top?" He smirked.

"Yes."

"I'll give you whatever you need."

"What I need is you inside me. So follow orders," I snapped.

He leaned back with a filthy grin on his face. "Do your worst, killer."

I kissed my way slowly down his body, teasing and biting him as I made my way toward my ultimate destination. His hips bucked off the bed as I gently licked his cock, taking pains to go as slowly as possible.

He growled, "I can't take it."

I smiled. I loved the power I had over him. I loved how much he wanted me.

I straddled him and lined myself up. And then I carefully lowered myself onto his throbbing cock. Thanks to Yael, my legs were super strong now, and I needed it, because the sight of this naked god under my spell was making my thighs shake.

I felt every centimeter of his length, and I sank deeper and deeper, taking as much as I could. When I reached the base, I stopped and exhaled, holding his lusty gaze. I flattened my hands on his chest to steady me as I adjusted to his thickness. Then, I started to slowly rock.

Every cell in my body was on fire. My nerve endings sang with the exquisite fullness.

I had never experienced this before. I had never encountered this feeling. This total fulfillment, both physically and emotionally. Declan was giving me everything he had, and it was perfect. We were perfect together.

I rocked gently at first, gathering steam as I grinded myself on his pelvic bone and let the pleasure flutter through me. He used those large, rough hands to grab my ass and squeeze as I rode him.

He stared at me the entire time, his eyes hooded in lust, so focused on me.

I was not much of an exhibitionist. Most of the time, I didn't want to be seen. I was insecure about my body and my performance. My sexual partners in the past hadn't been this... intense. Sometimes it felt as if I wasn't really there.

But Declan was different. We were on the same wavelength, totally in sync as I rode him faster and faster. He leaned up and bit my nipples and I screamed. His hands were everywhere, on my neck, breasts, and ass. He started to rise up to meet my thrusts, and the deeper sensations totally put me over the edge.

I couldn't contain it anymore. "You are so beautiful," he grunted. I could tell he was trying to hold back, to wait for me, and it turned me on more.

I cried out as I continued to ride him, my perfectly styled hair flying everywhere and my breasts bouncing in all their medium-sized glory. I came apart and screamed as my orgasm ripped through me, tearing through every cell in my body.

Declan sat up as I rode the aftershocks, and stood as I wrapped my legs around his waist. He carried me effortlessly over to the wide windows that looked out at the Boston skyline. He pinned me to the wall, still thrusting, and kissed me deeply.

I clung to him as his thrusts accelerated, pressure building within me.

"You are mine," he growled into my neck.

"Yes. Yes," I cried. "I am yours."

I was completely helpless in his arms, as his thrusts grew wild, sending me to new heights. And then we crashed, together, over the edge. We stood, panting and sweaty, looking out at the view of the Boston skyline, and I knew something had shifted and things would never be the same.

30

DECLAN

The Grand Bostonian Hotel was the nicest place I had ever seen. The grand ballroom looked like it had been flown in from Versailles. Opulent draperies and ornate woodwork crowded every space. The walls were painted robin's egg blue to set off the arches and swirls in the wood. The ceilings had to be twenty feet high, and large crystal chandeliers hung at regular intervals throughout the vast room.

Our hotel room escapades had managed to help Astrid relax a bit, but now I was the nervous one. Could I do this? Blend in with this world?

Callum had worked his magic and gotten me the perfect tuxedo. I could have rented, but he insisted that if I was getting serious with Astrid that it was a wise purchase. It felt silly, decadent even, to buy a tuxedo. I was not that kind of guy, but it felt like an investment in my future and an investment in our relationship. And I was more than willing to make it.

I had my beard trimmed yesterday and was raring to go. My dad had even dropped off my grandfather's cufflinks for luck. As much as we were butting heads right now, I loved the gesture. Not that I would ever admit it. We basically exchanged grunts on the front porch, but it felt good to know my parents had my back with Astrid.

I was not prepared for the goddess who had returned to my house this afternoon. Astrid got out of the car in the same sweats she left in, but she was transformed. Her hair was shorter and choppier, showing off some of her gorgeous neck, and it was sexy as hell. Her eyes were all smoky and mysterious and her lips ruby red.

Now, everywhere I looked I saw middle-aged people in tuxedos and evening gowns sipping champagne. Uniformed waiters circulated with fancy silver trays of fussy-looking finger foods. A string quartet played softly but beautifully in the background.

It was glittery and fancy and so not my scene. My social anxiety was not great on a good day, but in a fancy ballroom filled with lawyers? It was at an all-time high.

On the bright side, all I had to do was take one look at my girl, and I knew I belonged. Astrid was beautiful, there was no denying that. But tonight she was so much more. She looked strong and powerful and regal. Her skin glowed and her muscles flexed, and I could tell she was ready for this. She looked like a warrior princess. And she was mine. At least for tonight.

I was proud of how far she had come. The first night she asked me to be her fake date, she seemed terrified of this event. Now, looking at her, I knew she was ready to crush this.

We turned some heads as we entered. It didn't help that Astrid was wearing a bright purple gown and my hair was longer than hers. I knew we were a striking couple, but in this crowd we really stood out.

We found our table number and headed over to one of the Burns & Glenn tables.

"Astrid," shrieked a mousy woman with a severe bob haircut. "I didn't expect you to be here."

Astrid glared at the woman and stood up a little straighter. "I wouldn't miss it, Charlotte. I am being honored with an award for my pro bono work on behalf of those less fortunate. Remind me why you are here since you weren't involved?" Her voice came cutting and I smirked. My girl was a savage.

This Charlotte person narrowed her eyes. "It's a big night for the firm, and as one of the most trusted senior associates, I was asked to represent us here tonight." The woman looked smugly at Astrid, and I felt her beady eyes travel up my entire body.

She grabbed the elbow of a balding man who had his face in his phone. "Have you met my husband, Dr. Keith Meyer? He is a gastroenterologist at Mass General."

Astrid shook his hand. "This is my boyfriend, Declan Quinn."

I wrapped my arm around her waist and squeezed tighter. I gave them both a firm handshake. Charlotte's eyes widened just a bit when I shook her hand. Good to know her poker face wasn't that good.

The two of them stood for a moment, glaring at each other. Reminded me a lot of whenever I had the great misfortune to be in the same room as Marcus Flint.

Since neither of them was willing to break this awkward staredown, I decided to step in. "Astrid, darling, can I get you a drink?"

"I'll head over with you, sweetie." She reached up and gave me a peck on the cheek. "Excuse us," she said to Charlotte and her husband.

As soon as we were out of earshot she leaned in. "I hate that woman."

"She is vile," I agreed.

She punched my shoulder. "Thank you! She is my

nemesis. She is always trying to undermine me to get ahead."

I laughed. "Then she is a demon hell spawn. We should fix her up with Marcus Flint when her doctor hubby dumps her."

Astrid raised an eyebrow at me. "I wouldn't even wish her on Marcus."

"Oh, please. I wish antibiotic-resistant chlamydia on him almost daily."

We giggled as we headed to one of several bars throughout the massive space. Lawyers sure did love their booze. Having multiple bars served dual purposes—it made it faster to get a drink and also helped people spread out within the massive space. I tried to take inventory of the event and the venue. I knew Cece and Liam would have questions. They were all about wedding planning right now.

Cocktails in hand, we found a spot and surveyed the room.

"See that group over there?" Astrid gestured to a raucous table of younger-looking folks. They seemed to be having a blast, but on the whole looked a bit shabbier and unkempt compared to the rest of the crowd.

"Those are the public defenders. They usually get pretty rowdy."

"And those tables up front,"—she gestured to where we had come from—"those are the BigLaw tables. All the largest law firms jockey for the first row of tables to show off their wealth and influence. Everyone will be wearing a Rolex and talking about their boats and planes. Most will be with their second or third wives, so watch out for flying hair extensions."

"What about the senior citizens back there?" I nodded toward the far side of the room.

"Oh, those are the federal judges. Mostly old white

guys still on their first wives. That table next to them are the state court judges. They will never mix or mingle. Federal outranks state, and judges are generally obsessed with rank."

I nodded, sipping my drink and taking in the scene. It was like a middle school cafeteria but with lots of money and influence.

"Oh shit," Astrid said, choking on her champagne.

I patted her back. "What?"

"Shit. It's my mother."

I scanned the room, which was useless as I had never seen the woman in my life.

"Oh no, she's spotted us. Stand up straight and look her in the eye. She can smell weakness."

"Astrid, I did not expect to see you here." Justice Wentworth was a tall, imposing woman in her sixties wearing a black gown and some serious jewels. Her hair was cut short, and she wore minimal makeup. Still, I could see the mother-daughter resemblance, as she was quite striking.

"Mother, I'm being given an award. Of course I had to show up. It's for such a good cause." Astrid's voice had changed. It was pinched and forced and high, totally unlike her normal speaking voice. Like she was trying to modulate every syllable to maintain control.

"And who is this?" she asked, unsubtly giving me a disappointed once-over.

"This is my boyfriend, Mother, Declan Quinn."

I offered my hand. "It's a pleasure to meet you, Justice Wentworth."

She shook it, returning my intensity. I was no stranger to hard-ass moms. My mom could hold her own with the best. But the justice was in a league of her own.

"I'm glad you decided to show. Best to keep calm and carry on in these situations."

Astrid stood next to me silently.

"I need to mingle. But it's good to see you looking so..."—she looked over Astrid, taking in her gown, her height, and her physique—"so healthy and rested."

It seemed like a compliment, but the way it was delivered made it sound like an insult. Astrid remained perfectly still, standing straight up at her full height, and gave her mother a frozen smile. "Great to see you, Mother."

She walked away briskly. Like Astrid, the justice moved with purpose and precision. It was maybe a minute-long interaction, but I could feel the tension radiating through Astrid's body. "Do you need me to take you back upstairs, killer?" I whispered in her ear.

She smiled at me and threw me a saucy wink. "Maybe."

———

We perused the silent auction items and sipped our drinks. Aside from the monkey suit, which I will admit looked pretty good, I was having a good time. Astrid couldn't keep her hands off me and needed me by her side constantly, which I didn't mind at all. I felt like we were in the giant ocean tank at the aquarium, and we were just sweet little fish being circled by dozens of species of sharks.

The MC announced it was time for dinner. We took our seats at one of the Burns & Glenn tables.

I pulled out Astrid's chair, and suddenly I heard a sharp, nasally voice behind me.

"What are you doing here?"

I turned around and came face to face with an older, wiry man. Astrid stood up and crossed her arms.

"Max."

His frown turned into a smile so quickly most would

have missed it. So this was the fucker who screwed over Astrid. What a joke.

His wife caught up to him and grabbed his arm. "Max, sweetie, is this our table?" she asked kindly. She seemed pleasant enough and gave us all a warm smile.

Astrid looked like she wanted to kick his ass. I would have offered to help but I knew my girl didn't need it. In fact, I could have offered to hold the phone so we could take a video and post it on YouTube, as a cautionary tale for perverts who try to coerce young women into sleeping with them.

Max's eyes were locked on Astrid, who strode forward, pulled herself up to her full height, and offered her hand to the confused woman at his side. "I'm Astrid Wentworth, a former associate at Burns & Glenn. You must be Mrs. Shapiro."

The woman shook her hand and smiled.

Max muttered "fired" under his breath. I coughed and gave him a stare. I watched him study me. His eyes traveled the length of my body, probably taking in my height, my muscle mass, and my face, which was currently saying "Get the fuck away from my woman." He wisely decided to deescalate the situation and grabbed his wife and quickly took a seat at another table.

Once we were seated and attention was diverted by announcing the winners of the silent auction, I turned to Astrid and searched her face for some clue as to how she was feeling.

She squeezed my hand.

Then she leaned in. "I wouldn't have been able to do this without you. Thanks for having my back."

A warm, blissful feeling spread through my chest. I lopped my arm around the back of her chair, laying clear claim to her, and sipped my whiskey. Although I could do without the monkey suit and the shitty company, I was having a good night.

I loved Astrid. I couldn't deny what I had known for a while. I would do anything for her. I wanted to protect her, but most of all I wanted to build her up so she could go out and fight for herself. Watching her masterfully work the room, head held high, was a beautiful thing. She knew her power, she knew her value, and she wasn't afraid to show it.

Dinner, speeches, more drinks, and an auction later, we were enjoying a dance when I felt a tap on my shoulder.

"May I cut in?" I turned around to find a dapper-looking man who looked to be in his eighties.

"Judge Forsythe!" Astrid exclaimed. "It is so good to see you. This is Declan, my boyfriend."

The judge enthusiastically shook my hand as Astrid explained to me, "Declan, I clerked for Judge Forsythe for a year after law school."

"Astrid, I'm thrilled you finally found someone who can keep up with you," he said, smiling at her.

I laughed. "I try, sir, but I'm only human."

He clapped me on the shoulder. "I like this one."

I left Astrid dancing with the judge and headed toward the bar, feeling pretty good.

As I grabbed my drink, I felt the air around me change. I turned and found Justice Wentworth standing next to me. That woman moved like a ninja.

"So are you and my daughter serious?"

I was unnerved by her presence. "Yes ma'am," I replied, taking a sip of whiskey.

"And how did you meet?" Her tone was not the least bit friendly. I could only imagine how terrifying she was in a courtroom.

"In Havenport. She is my neighbor."

"I see." She paused, studying my face. "And what do you do for work, Mr. Quinn?"

"I'm a fisherman. I joined the family business after serving in the navy."

She nodded and gestured to the ballroom. "You see, Mr. Quinn, this is our world. My daughter was born into it, and this is where she belongs."

I stood, sipping my drink, trying not to react to whatever she was trying to do.

"Her brilliance, her talents, they are appreciated here. She is not normal. She is not regular."

"I agree with you there. She is exceptional."

"Exactly. That's why she will not be happy in your seaside town doing whatever it is you people do there. She has an incredible mind that needs to be challenged."

I wasn't sure what to say to that. Astrid was brilliant, that was abundantly clear, but I didn't like the way she was disparaging my hometown, like it was some backwater filled with hicks.

"I admit you are very handsome, so I can see the appeal. But this is just a fling. She had to get this out of her system before buckling down and getting serious. This relationship cannot progress any further. You will bore her, and she will resent you."

I was struck by her casual cruelty. There were so many things to get angry about. But this woman would never see someone like me. She would never hear someone like me. My heart sank into my Italian leather shoes.

I stood up straight and looked her in the eye. "Thank you for your input. But I love your daughter."

"Then this will be even worse than I thought," she complained, draining the rest of her martini. She placed it on top of the wooden bar and took a deep breath.

"Let me tell you something about my daughter. She is a shark. She gets bored easily and needs constant challenge. She is not content; she is not grateful. She doesn't want to sit with a mug of tea and a good book. She needs to be accomplishing things. Moving forward, achieving her goals. It's just the way she is."

I sipped my whiskey, sad that Astrid had this total cow for a mother. She didn't understand one single thing about her daughter and truly had no clue. If anything, I felt bad for her. How could anyone be so self-centered and blinded by their wealth and privilege?

"I know she's had her issues and I thank you. Whatever you have been doing has worked. She looks sharper and more alive than I've seen her in years. I know that she is rested and ready for whatever challenges lie ahead. But it may be time for you to exit." As much as I hated her and knew that she was wrong about Astrid and about me, I could recognize a kernel of truth in her words. How many times had I suspected that Astrid would get bored with me? How many times had she made it abundantly clear that she couldn't wait to get out of Havenport and back to her legal career?

Before I could recover from the sting of that statement, Astrid was making her way over to me, smiling broadly. "Declan, please come dance with me," she begged. I looked at her beautiful face and couldn't say no, even though I wanted to throw up.

31

ASTRID

SO FAR THIS NIGHT WAS SHAPING UP TO BE BETTER than expected. First, Declan rocked my world up in the hotel room. And I mean Rocked. My. World. It was like he knew exactly what to do to get me out of my head for a little while so I could face this night head-on.

That was one of his strengths, helping me get out of my own head for a bit. He could tell when I was about to bubble over and knew just how to release the pressure. And he had found multiple ways to do it.

We walked in, arm in arm, like we owned the place and ended up having a decent time. Was it awkward? Yes. But not too painfully so. I found that Declan was incredible company and stayed close the entire night, fetching me drinks and complimenting me. I even saw him chatting amicably with my mother of all people while I danced with Judge Forsythe.

I spent a year clerking for the judge after graduating from law school. It was by far the best job I had ever had. I worked with him all day, accompanied him during trials and hearings, and researched points of law and drafted his judicial opinions. He ate lunch with me and the other clerks daily, filling us in with stories of a life well lived. We did important work, upholding the Constitution every day and treating everyone that came through our courtroom with deference and respect. He was old-school in the best way. We worked hard, but always took time to see the real-world consequences of our decisions. The judge didn't want to live in an ivory tower; he wanted to use his position to help people and believed our legal system functioned best when it worked equally for everyone.

I kept in touch with him and attended his clerks' Christmas party every year, but I hadn't spent time with him in years. He was older than I remember, but just as charming. Seeing him and his wife was a nice reminder that my legal career had been promising once. That there was a time when I truly believed in what I was doing. I wasn't just trying to bill twenty-five hours a day and resenting every minute of it. I used to view my career as an all-or-nothing proposition. Either I was a partner at Burns & Glenn or I was a failure who should do something else. Being here in this room with multiple generations of dedicated lawyers from all walks of life was a stark reminder that I was wrong. There were lots of ways to build a career and a life. And maybe it was time I started thinking that way.

My brain spun with ideas. I wanted to be with Declan, really be with him. And I wanted to live in Havenport. I had friends there, a life there, and I had discovered a lot about myself there. I loved it, just like I knew, deep down in my bones, that I loved Declan. I was bursting with love for him, and it took every ounce of self-control I had to keep the words from jumping out of my mouth. I wasn't this woman. I wasn't the overzealous type. I was cool and strategic, and I had to find the perfect moment to tell him.

It's funny, for someone that hates dancing, I had been

doing a lot of it lately. Between girls' nights with Nora at the Whale and practicing with Declan in his living room, I had danced more in the last three months than in the last ten years.

And I was realizing, more and more, that I didn't hate it. There was something so joyful and freeing about letting myself go. About losing all the inhibitions that I kept wrapped around myself like a protective shell and just being myself. It also didn't hurt to have such a handsome and capable partner.

Declan led me around the dance floor with ease and grace for a man of his size. He never took his eyes off me, and it felt like the most delicious kind of foreplay.

We were dancing slowly to "Moon River," and I was in his strong arms, dressed like a princess and successfully having faced Max Shapiro earlier. I was on top of the world.

"You are an incredible date," I said to him.

"Am I living up to your fake boyfriend fantasies?"

I leaned in and huskily whispered in his ear, "You are living up to all my fantasies, Declan. All of them."

He smiled, a big eye-crinkling smile, and then the next minute he spun me out and back. It had taken a while to trust him enough to lead me, but I was starting to get the hang of it.

"You are my fantasy, Astrid." His gaze was intense and unwavering.

I leaned in and kissed him gently. "I love you, Declan." Oh shit. It just came out. Dammit. I was supposed to be the cool one here.

He held my gaze as my heart beat so hard I could feel it in my toes. "I love you too." I resisted the urge to break into a happy dance and/or text Emily.

I smiled at him. "This is real. And I want this. I want real with you, Declan." There it was. What I really wanted, deep down in my bones. I had done it. I had let myself be vulnerable and had gone after what I really wanted.

He leaned in and whispered softly in my ear, "I will give you anything you want."

Then he kissed me. Gently, but insistently. He was tasting me but also marking me as his. I had never been interested in being possessed by a man, but with Declan it was different. I knew I belonged to him and he belonged to me, and it was crazy but also beautiful and just right.

The rest of the night passed by in a blur. We danced, drank champagne, and kissed. We sampled the teeny tiny trendy desserts and laughed. My mother kept her distance, obviously, since events like these were for networking, not spending time with your only daughter. And we generally had a good time. I chatted with a few former colleagues and some law school acquaintances, and overall it was pleasant.

I graciously accepted my award with my team from Burns & Glenn—including Max, that assface. The MC said really flattering things about our team and me in particular, and listed the statistics about the work we had done at the shelter. I was proud. I had done that. I had an idea and I executed it.

It made me think a bit about what Lucas Kim had said. Maybe I could scale this up? Build a bigger and better model? Help more people in a more fulsome way? I loved the law, and I loved solving problems. Could I pivot and use my powers for good?

It was worth thinking about. I had never seen myself as the do-gooder type, but I was beginning to feel a pull toward public service. Maybe it was my mother's influence or maybe it was Declan or Havenport, but spinning around this dance floor with the man I had fallen in love with, the world suddenly felt so big and so exciting. Brimming with possibilities. I had faced my fears. Not only had I shown up here with my head held high, but I had told Declan how I felt. I felt liberated. All the old anger and bile that lived within me was gone. I was ready for whatever came next.

––––––

I left Declan speaking to one of the partners about boats while I hit the ladies' room. Turns out he had a lot in common with the high-end lawyer crowd—they all loved boats and he was definitely an expert. I ended up chatting with a former colleague who had moved to the DA's office and got a bit turned around on the way back to the party.

I found myself in a long hallway which I thought led to the ballroom, but apparently led to some unused conference spaces. I was heading back to the ladies' room when I felt his presence.

"What do you want, Max?" I turned around and there he was, stalking me like prey.

"What the fuck do you think you're doing, Astrid? I am not going to tolerate your little games."

I glared at him. "Leave me alone, Max. You've done enough damage."

"Damage? Talk about damage. I know you filed a complaint against me. And I know you got that bitch Monica to file one too."

He grabbed me by the arm.

"Max, let go of me," I said calmly. I was not going to get into a screaming match with him.

"No," he slurred drunkenly. "You are a liar and a slut. You refused me and knew there would be consequences. You don't get to blame everything on me. How dare you?"

"Max, let go of me." I could feel my skin bruising. I pulled my arm out of his grasp, rubbed it, and tried to slowly back away. Before I could get very far, he grabbed me by the shoulders and slammed me into the wall.

"You like that, Astrid? You like being knocked around? Because if you try to fuck with me anymore, this will get a lot worse."

"Stop it, Max. Get off me." I tried to push him off, but he was strong.

"Is this what you like, Astrid? Is this what that overgrown orangutan does to you? What were you trying to accomplish, waltzing in here with that Neanderthal?"

His face was inches away from mine, and my eyes were watering from the smell of alcohol on his breath.

He shook my body, slamming the back of my head into the wall. I screamed.

"Shut the fuck up." My eyes filled with tears and my ears were ringing from the impact. He wrapped his right hand around my throat, and I started to hyperventilate. My head was spinning. I tried to use my free arm to push him back but he was too strong.

"You will withdraw your complaint. You will not sue the firm. Do you understand? I am not losing everything I worked for because some stuck-up whore can't keep her mouth shut."

I was panicking. Max was strong and had me pinned. My head hurt from where he slammed me into the wall, and I was feeling scared and disoriented. I could feel his hand slowly tightening on my throat, and I knew I had to do something. His beady eyes were fixed on me and filled me with dread.

And then, something took over. I could hear Yael's voice in my head. My muscle memory kicked in. Next thing I knew I was yelling "stomp" while slamming my Louboutin directly into the top of Max's foot. It got stuck in the leather of his shoe, and I twisted it as he screamed in agony. I managed to kick it off before he stumbled back. I knew I had the opening I needed. I stepped into my staggered stance and threw a punch with my right hand. It connected with his face, and I could feel the bones of his nose crunch with the impact. Fuck, that hurt. I think I broke my hand. He stumbled back farther, screaming at me.

"You cunt. You fucking bitch. I am going to fucking kill you."

I didn't even have to think. I knew what I had to do next. "Groin," I screamed at the top of my lungs, and my knee connected in the exact spot.

Max crumbled to the ground, a screaming, bloody mess. He was ranting and moaning. I collapsed, panting. The adrenaline flowing through my body made me shaky, but I knew I had to get out of there.

The next thing I knew several people had come over and were helping me up. I was dizzy and scared.

"Astrid. Astrid, what happened?" I felt Declan's strong arms wrap around me. "Oh my God, I couldn't find you." He gently cradled my body. My head pounded and my vision was blurry.

My heart was racing and I could barely speak. "I. Max. He attacked me. And then threatened me." Declan looked at Max, still on the floor, and I knew he would kill him if he had the chance.

"That bitch," Max yelled. "She attacked me. Call the police. Call 911. I need an ambulance." Several people had rushed to his side and were helping him with his injuries. "Arrest her. She attacked me unprovoked. She is a disgruntled former employee. Mentally unstable."

Declan was rubbing my arms while I shook. I had been scared. Really scared. I had no idea what Max was capable of. I shifted most of my weight so that Declan was supporting me. He kept rubbing my back and whispering that everything was going to be fine. That I was safe. "I won't let anyone hurt you, Astrid. I'm here. I'm here with you." He held me close as I sobbed into his pristine dress shirt.

My brain knew I was safe now, but my body didn't. I felt like I was running for my life. And it was so scary.

"You did the right thing," he kept repeating over and over, knowing exactly what I needed to hear. "You did the right thing, killer."

32

DECLAN

I WAS STILL TRYING TO UNDERSTAND WHAT HAD happened. The police had arrived, and I held Astrid close as she sobbed into my shirt. Her body was shaking like a leaf, and she could barely stand up. I didn't know the details, but I could put the evidence together.

That piece of shit Max Shapiro was on the floor screaming and crying to anyone who would listen that Astrid had attacked him. I didn't believe a word out of that weasel's mouth, but one thing was certain. She had done a number on him. His nose hadn't stopped bleeding, and I could already see two telltale bruises forming under his eyes. His shoe and foot were all messed up, and one of Astrid's sparkly shoes was lying on the floor beside him.

The police thankfully pushed back the crowd of onlookers and approached Astrid gently.

"Ma'am. I am going to ask you to come have a seat so we can ask you some questions."

She nodded.

As I helped her over to the chair, Max kept yelling, "Officer, arrest her. She assaulted me. I want to press charges."

Astrid glared at him as she stood up. "Shut up, Max. You are lucky I didn't do worse."

"You cunt. That's big talk coming from you. Now that your dumbass bodyguard is here, you think you can threaten me."

"It's not a threat, Max. It's a fucking promise." She stomped her foot. "And don't ever speak about my boyfriend again, you cocksucker."

"You are such a dumb cunt," he yelled back.

Astrid flew at him, fists flying. I grabbed her by the waist and hauled her back into me.

"Calm down, Astrid," I said into her hair as she tried to pull away from me.

The police officer tried to interject, putting his body between Astrid and Max, but she dodged around him and stood, hands on her hips, in front of Max's prone body.

"I will break your ugly-ass face again, Max. Don't ever put a hand on me or any other woman for that matter. We both know I can fuck you up, and I will happily do it again."

I grabbed her and picked her up, trying to get her out of this situation.

"Did you hear that, officer?" Max shouted. "She threatened me again. I am in fear of my life. I'd like to file a protective order."

Astrid growled. "Killer, you are making this worse," I pleaded with her.

She turned to the police officer, her face a mask of calm. "Officer, this man attacked me. I acted in self-defense." The police officer looked skeptically from Astrid to Max, who was still slumped on the floor, bloody and bruised. His wife had gotten him some ice in a towel that he was applying to his clearly broken nose. Served him right.

"This woman assaulted me! My foot! My nose! Arrest her at once."

"Now, now. We are going to bring you both down to the station and discuss this," the police officer said. He gestured to his fellow officer who was pushing the crowd back.

"I want to press charges. This was assault and battery," Max ranted. "She clearly has some kind of special training! She is a deranged ex-employee who thinks she's in love with me."

His wife gasped and glared at Astrid.

I put my arm around her waist, protectively. "I did no such thing, officer," Astrid explained. "I was headed to the ladies' room when that gentleman grabbed me, slammed me into the wall, and threatened me. I defended myself— successfully, I might add—against the attack. And I would like to press charges against him as well as secure a protective order."

Despite the best efforts of the police officers, a crowd had gathered. Astrid stood, tall and unwavering. She was not embarrassed—she was a total boss. Listening to what that prick had done to her made me want to bash his face in further, but even I could admit she had done a damn good job on her own.

She curled into my chest and I whispered in her ear, "Good job."

She smiled at me.

"Ma'am, we are going to have to take you both down to the station while we sort this out. There are witnesses, and we are going to ask the hotel for the security footage. But this is much easier if you cooperate."

"Wait a minute," I interrupted. "I don't see why you need to arrest her. She was just defending herself." Max could rot in jail for eternity, but Astrid did nothing wrong.

"That remains to be seen, sir, and based on the injuries

sustained by both parties, we need to investigate thoroughly."

I felt sick. My girl was getting arrested. For defending herself against assault? Astrid was right, the patriarchy was a motherfucker.

I looked through the assembled crowd, and I found a stern set of gray eyes boring holes through my skull. Justice Wentworth. She strode over and assessed the situation.

"What on earth did you do, Astrid?"

"Mother, I was attacked. I was terrified and I fought back."

She nodded. "Astrid, you know I can't be associated with this type of behavior. I am going to go home."

The police led Astrid away in handcuffs. I listened as they read her the Miranda rights. My heart clenched and I couldn't breathe. Logically, I knew she was in the right, but I couldn't bear to see them handle my woman like that.

The officers were nice enough to give me the address of the police station where I could meet them and Astrid once she was booked.

I went back to our table to grab my jacket and Astrid's purse and saw Judge Wentworth headed toward me.

"A person in my position can't be associated with this type of thing. I trust you can handle this?" she demanded, glaring at me with her arms crossed.

"Yes," I replied tersely. "If by situation, you mean bailing your daughter out of jail then yes, I can handle it."

She smiled and I hated her.

"She was assaulted and she is scared. And now she's being arrested," I continued, waiting for Astrid's mother to act like... well, act like a mother.

She shrugged. "It will all work itself out, I'm sure." She started to walk away and then turned back around. "You know, I can't help but think that this is your influence. Astrid has never behaved like this before," she said icily.

"She was attacked by a vindictive man who took advantage of her and got her fired. I think your anger is misplaced, ma'am."

"I understand the factual circumstances. But unfairness is not a reason to jeopardize your future. What happened tonight will have serious consequences. And I can't help but think that you led her down this path."

I was dumbstruck. Who was this woman and how could she live with herself? Her daughter was being arrested and she was just leaving? After her child had been physically assaulted? What kind of mother did that? My mother certainly wouldn't. The thought of my mother here made me chuckle. I could only imagine the verbal tongue-lashing these poor police officers would receive.

But now I had to focus. Astrid needed me. For months, I had struggled with my overwhelming desire to protect this woman. The irony, of course, is there was no one who needed my protection less. But I still wanted to give it to her. And in the one moment where she needed me, the one moment where I could have helped her, I wasn't there. It should have been me kicking that guy's ass. It should have been me being led away in handcuffs. The guilt I felt was crushing. But there wasn't time to dwell on it. I had to get my girl out of jail.

33

ASTRID

"What are you in for, Barbie?" the older looking woman asked, as I sat, wearing one shoe and a gorgeous dress, in a holding cell.

"I don't think she's Barbie," added the other. "I get more of an Elsa vibe from her."

Was I the only person on earth who hadn't seen that movie?

"I was attacked by my former boss, and I kicked his ass."

"Right on," the older one said. "Is that why you only have one shoe?"

"Yup. I stomped on his foot with the other, and it tore through his shoe and cut his foot open."

"Sweet. What else did you do?"

"I kneed him in the balls, and I think I broke his nose."

"Awesome." She reached out and high-fived me.

The younger one looked confused. "Wait, so you did all this in that fancy outfit?"

"Yup," I said. "We were at a black-tie gala actually. This dress is surprisingly comfortable."

They both laughed.

"Can you show me your moves?" the younger one asked.

"Sure," I replied.

———

By the time Declan bailed me out a few hours later, I had taught Yasmin and Roxanne some self-defense moves and had given them the email address of a law school colleague who did criminal defense work. I enjoyed getting to know these women and hearing about their lives. It made me feel even more certain that I wanted to focus my career on helping women. People who didn't live in a bubble of privilege and who could really use my help. More and more, I was realizing that maybe I could use my legal powers for good instead of evil.

I walked out of the holding area on one shoe and saw Declan, handsome as ever, with his brow furrowed. I ran into his arms, and he hugged me tight. "Are you okay?"

"I'm great," I replied, taking a deep breath full of his masculine scent. I felt safe and secure in his arms, and despite the fact that we were in public, I never wanted to let go.

"I spoke to the Lieutenant, and he said they will have a court order for the hotel security footage within a day or two and then will contact you for further questioning. He also said you should get a lawyer."

"I know," I replied.

He looked so worried. "And I just posted your bail. Sorry this took so long. They had to call in the bail bondsman and it's late."

"Don't worry. I'm fine. I was teaching the other detainees in my holding cell some Krav Maga moves."

He kissed the top of my head. "Of course you were."

I was exhausted but adrenalized. It would take a long time to process what had happened tonight, but I was grateful to have Declan by my side.

Declan, on the other hand, seemed weary and shaken. Was he embarrassed to have a potential felon for a girlfriend? Or had something happened after I was arrested? Did my mother say something to him?

I looked up into his big blue eyes. "Take me home."

We walked out to the car. Declan had thoughtfully checked us out of the hotel and packed up the car. It was like he knew that I would want to go home to Havenport. Huh. Home. It was weird to think about. I hadn't had a place that felt like home since childhood. And my mother's house was hardly homey. It was weird to think that a place I had lived for less than three months could be my home, but as I was learning, life was funny sometimes.

As we drove in silence, I replayed the evening's events over and over in my head. I was not ashamed of what I had done. Yes, I could have just kneed Max in the balls, but fucking up his foot and breaking his nose were really satisfying. That asshole put his hands on me and went too far. And if he did it to me, odds were that he had done it to someone else at some point or would do it again. Maybe that asshole would think twice before hurting or threatening another woman. That alone would be worth the criminal record. I was not ashamed. But these events did not happen in a vacuum. They impacted Declan as well.

"I'm sorry," I said to him as we cruised up the highway on our way back to Havenport.

"Why are you sorry? I'm sorry," he said, gripping the steering wheel so tightly I thought it might rip off the dashboard.

"Wait, what? I'm sorry I got arrested. I'm sorry I acted

like a WWE wrestler. I'm sure you are embarrassed by my antics." I shrugged and slumped down farther in the seat.

"Astrid, stop," he shouted. I was taken aback by his anger. "I am not embarrassed. Are you kidding? I feel ashamed that I wasn't there to protect you. You are my woman and you needed me and I wasn't there. The asshole tried to hurt you, Astrid. You have bruises on your neck, for fuck's sake. And I failed you."

"How could you think that? I just went to the ladies' room. There was no way to know that I would be in danger. You were there when I needed you. And you're here now."

He ran a hand through his hair. "I failed you."

Now I was getting frustrated. It had been a long night, and this was the last thing I needed. "Stop that shit, Declan. You have done nothing but build me up and help me realize my own strength since the day we met. I had the strength to do what I did tonight because of you. Because you helped me find my inner badass and let her out."

"You should be thanking Yael for teaching you those moves," he said.

"And trust me, I will. But you, Declan, you have made me so happy and made me feel so many things. I hate feelings. Truly. But with you, I want to experience things. I want to try things and I want to be the woman you think I can be." I was crying now, the enormity of tonight overwhelming me.

Declan grasped my hand. "I really am proud of you, killer. You really messed him up. I just wish that hadn't happened to you."

I nodded. "Me too." But since it did happen, I wish I had done worse. I stopped once he was on the ground and not a threat anymore. I should have kept at it and put him in the hospital. Maybe that way he would learn his lesson.

I knew I would eventually have to deal with the trauma of being attacked, but for now I was just angry.

"I love you, Astrid. And I want to protect you from everything on earth. I want to wrap you in my arms and make sure nothing bad ever happens to you again."

"I love you too, Declan. But you can't do that. It's not how life works. But I will tell you this, there is nowhere I would rather be than in your arms."

34

ASTRID

I woke up Monday morning after a solid twelve hours of sleep in Declan's bed with Ginger curled up by my side. Declan and I had spent all of Sunday curled up on the couch watching Netflix. He held me when I cried, made me delicious food, and never left my side. I was still bruised and shaken, but I was feeling much better.

I rolled over and saw a note next to the bed. *"Had to go to work. Coffee is in the kitchen and my mom dropped off some banana bread for you on the counter. Call me if you need anything at all. I'll see you tonight. Love, Declan"*

I sighed and stretched out in the luxurious bed and looked out at the ocean. Today was a new day. The drama of the weekend was over, and for better or worse, this was a new world.

I had no job. I had no future. And I didn't even care. I had Declan, I had my friends, and I had closure. Fuck Max Shapiro and fuck Burns & Glenn. That bridge was burned. And I was going to dance on its ashes.

I checked my phone. The girls were all texting about Monday breakfast. I had considered skipping, but I had nothing to be ashamed of. I couldn't lie around all day waiting for the Boston Police Department to call me and apologize for arresting me, right? Plus, my friends would probably want to hear about the gala and see some photos of my dress.

We had a mimosa toast at Monday breakfast to my kicking ass as I told them all about the ball, how incredible Declan looked in his tux, and the incident with Max. It wasn't easy to talk about, but they were so kind and supportive, unlike my mother, who watched me get arrested and didn't even bother to call me. These women had my back, and I loved them for it.

The next few days passed in a pleasant blur. I took walks with Ginger, played with Emily's kids, and went to Krav Maga class with Nora. At my insistence, she did not brag to Yael about the incident with Max. Sharing with my friends was one thing, but blasting this news out to the entire Havenport community when I hadn't processed what happened was quite another. I even called Dr. Martha, my former therapist, and set up an appointment with her for the next week. If I was going to move on with my life, process what had happened, and open myself up to what was next, I knew I would need her support. I was feeling ready. Ready for my future, ready for the next chapter.

I spent every single night with Declan. We cooked, made love, and sat by the fire reading together. Wrapped up in his arms I felt safe, I felt loved, I felt cherished. And I knew that this was where I wanted to be forever.

———

A few days later, I was walking Ginger when my phone rang.

"Hello."

"Astrid Wentworth? This is Maria calling from Burns & Glenn. I have John Waterson on the line for you."

The next thing I knew I heard a click.

"Astrid," he said jovially, "how are you?"

Considering the last time I had spoken to this man he had told me not to get so emotional, I wasn't sure how to respond.

"Fine," I said coolly.

"Great. Astrid, there is no easy way to say this. We are very sorry about what happened at the gala. The entire firm is embarrassed by the way that Shapiro behaved."

"Thank you," I replied. I didn't understand. Law firms don't usually admit mistakes, they just gaslight you into thinking they were right all along.

"And moreover, we regret the mistake we made. The firm leadership put a lot of trust into Max Shapiro and didn't fully vet the accusations made against him by you and other personnel."

"That's obvious. I trust you've seen the formal complaints filed by myself and Monica Walsh?"

"Yes. We had an emergency partners' meeting yesterday, and we are launching a full investigation. I wanted to thank you personally for coming forward."

I stood in stony silence. We had filed our complaints weeks ago. How could he so casually dismiss the evidence we provided? He didn't care until the partner in question was arrested for assault and battery.

"As you know," he continued, "reputation is everything here. And I'm deeply sorry yours was impacted by Max Shapiro's actions."

"Thank you."

"And I want to assure you, Max has been placed on indefinite leave from the firm without pay during the pendency of this investigation. He will not be returning."

I didn't care. They deserved each other. I said my

piece, I filed my complaint, and offered up the texts, emails, and photos on my phone as evidence. I did my part, and now it was time to move on with my life.

"And I want you to know we have cooperated thoroughly with the Boston Police Department, and I expect the charges against you will be dropped by the end of the week. So we would like you to return to the firm. Preferably at your earliest convenience but we are also willing to give you a few weeks given the recent incident."

"What?" I was gobsmacked. How was this possible? The Boston Police Department was going to drop the charges against me? Max had been removed from the firm? And they wanted me back at my old job ASAP? This was insane.

"We have had several clients ask for you, Astrid. You have a bright future here. And I know that you have been missed."

That was horseshit. No one had noticed I was gone. I knew that for a fact. When someone left, the vultures circled to claim their clients, their office, and their secretary. I even saw people pillage a former colleague's office and steal their legal journals.

I remembered reading an article about climbing Mt. Everest. About how hikers had to pass by the dead bodies of those who didn't make it on the way up. The atmosphere preserved the bodies, and the altitude made it dangerous to remove them. So hikers literally stepped over the dead and dying on their way to the summit to achieve their goal. That's what it was like at Burns & Glenn. Stepping over the bodies of your fallen colleagues on the way up. It was every man or woman for themselves. There was no room for compassion, no room for collaboration—only dominance. You could never stop watching your back because someone would take your spot in a heartbeat.

The minute I was gone, Charlotte pounced and took

my clients, my secretary, and my place at the firm. It was the way it was there—kill or be killed. What was once totally commonplace and normal for me was now repulsive. The last place I wanted to be was back in that office tower.

My heart sank into my shoes. The thought of going back filled me with such dread. A few short months ago this was my dream come true, but now I couldn't help but shake the nightmare of returning to my office, to my apartment, to a lifestyle devoid of anything but relentless, thankless work. And if I came back I certainly couldn't pursue a lawsuit. Yes, they fired Max, but what were they doing to prevent sexual harassment and discrimination? Were the people who covered for him being held accountable? How could I advocate for other vulnerable women if I picked back up where I left off?

"I have a call in five minutes. But you can arrange everything with my secretary. HR will do the rest. Welcome back, Astrid."

"Wait," I said.

There was stony silence on the other end of the line. "I need to process this information and decide if I want to come back," I explained.

His tone shifted, annoyance taking over. "If? Astrid, this firm hired you and trained you and built you into the lawyer you are today. This is the best place for you. I understand the past few months have been difficult and the events of this weekend were deeply traumatic. In fact, we have an in-house crisis counselor. I will have my secretary set you up with her."

He clearly wasn't getting it. "I will consider your offer," I said curtly, "and be in touch when I decide if I would like to return."

I hung up, feeling emotionally exhausted and angry. I had been having such a good day.

I had always prided myself on being the coolest person in the room. I was taught that there was power in control, in silence. I trained myself to be calm at all times and never cause a fuss.

But I couldn't deny that there was fire inside me. Fury, rage, anger. I had been suppressing it for decades. I convinced myself I was a quiet, subdued person, but I wasn't. I was just Astrid. And sometimes I was loud and sometimes I was quiet. I could do both. I was a full person now, one who swore and danced and had glorious orgasms.

Could I even fit in that world anymore?

I had grown. I had expanded so much since coming to Havenport. I had found my fight, and I couldn't give it up.

35

DECLAN

THE SEED OF DOUBT THAT HAD BEEN PLANTED BY
Astrid's mother had taken root in my mind and grown and
flowered over the past couple of weeks. I loved Astrid—I
knew that with total certainty. And I know she thought
she loved me too. But I could see the push-pull within her.
I could see the hold her career still had over her, and I
didn't want to stand in her way.

Unfortunately, the incident at the gala could
completely destroy her career, leaving her with nothing.
She wouldn't rebound from a felony conviction, that was
for sure. And right now, it was her word against that
asshole's. I wish I had been there. Everything would have
been different. She could lose everything and it would be
my fault. The more I thought about it, the more I believed
Justice Wentworth was right. I had led her down that
path. I didn't fit into her world and trying to force it
would only result in more problems and more heartbreak.

We were having fun and she was an incredible woman,
but the more comfortable we got, the more I grew
convinced that this was truly temporary. That someone
like her and someone like me could never make it work.

We came from different worlds. And I knew, deep down, that she wanted to return to hers. I could buy all the tuxedos and fancy shoes in the world, but I would never fit into her life. I couldn't. She had said it herself many times.

We had fallen into a comfortable rhythm these last few weeks. We spent every night together, but I felt further and further away from her every day. I couldn't shake the feeling that this relationship was dead in the water. I knew how hard things had been on her. And her mother was clearly not a great source of support. I wanted to be there for her and protect her. But the more I thought about it, the more I knew that keeping her wouldn't be supporting and protecting her. It would be selfish.

So I was not surprised when she burst into my house a few days later, flushed from the cold and vibrating with excitement.

"You will never guess who called me today."

I looked at her, rosy cheeks and plump lips stretched into a huge smile. This is how I wanted to remember her. Excited, full of hope and promise.

"Detective Connelly."

"And?" My heart skipped a beat.

"They are dropping the charges against me. They obtained the security footage from the hotel and will not be pursuing it further. But they are amending the charges against Max Shapiro to include strangulation and aggravated assault."

I ran to her and gathered her in my arms. "Astrid, that is incredible news." I spun her around and kissed her hungrily. I was so relieved. The thought of Astrid having a criminal record, or God forbid, going to jail over this horrific situation made me sick. This was such a relief. I held her and looked into her beautiful eyes.

"Why are you crying?" I asked gently.

"Because I'm so happy," she replied. She buried her face in my neck and inhaled.

"I hope that fucker goes to jail. And gets fired," I whispered into her hair.

She pulled back and looked me in the eye. "He was fired last week."

"How do you know that?"

She looked sheepish and took a step back, breaking our contact. "John Waterson, the Managing partner at Burns & Glenn, called me yesterday. Told me that they were cooperating with the BPD and that Max had been placed on leave pending an investigation. He is as good as gone."

"Why didn't you tell me?"

"I don't know." She looked at her feet. It was Astrid's tell. I held my breath, knowing what was coming next.

"He asked me to come back to the firm."

I exhaled. Yup. I knew it. This was what I had been expecting, and I was prepared.

I forced myself to sound cheerful. "That's great news, Astrid." I shoved my hands in my pockets to keep from reaching out to her again. I wanted to touch her so badly, but I knew I couldn't.

She walked over to the kitchen and poured herself a glass of water. I steeled myself for what was coming next.

"When do you start?" I asked.

"I haven't said yes," she replied, looking confused.

I walked over and stood at the opposite side of the kitchen island, bracing for impact. "But we both know you will."

"I don't know what I'm going to say," she said, crossing her arms.

"Yes, you do." I hated myself for doing this. Pushing her. But I knew I had to. What could I offer her? She had told me herself that she could not focus on her career and have a long-distance boyfriend as well. I didn't want her to give up her dreams for me.

"Don't put words in my mouth and thoughts in my head, Declan. I'm trying to figure everything out right now."

"There's nothing to figure out. You have to go back. You have such a bright future ahead of you." It was the truth. Astrid was brilliant and dedicated and could change the world.

And she deserved to be with someone like that, a man at her level. Someone who could give her the life she deserved. I was tied to this town and this region. Hell, I was tied to the ocean. She had a future filled with things I could only imagine or watch in a movie.

We had a good thing. She was incredible, and I could never feel this away about another woman. But I had to do the right thing. My parents taught me to be honorable and selfless, and this felt like a moment where I had to heed those lessons and make them proud. Deep down, I knew I was being more cowardly than honorable, but I brushed that aside. Yes, I was an asshole. And yes, I was mansplaining her life to her. But I knew what was coming. I could see the future, and it seemed better to do this now.

She smacked the countertop, and I saw her nostrils flare. Astrid was like a charging bull when she got mad. I was glad the sledgehammer wasn't around. "Declan, I don't want to go back. I want to be here with you."

I was desperate for these words, desperate for reassurance. But I knew it wasn't enough. "It would be selfish of me to keep you here," I pleaded. "We both know you are too smart and too ambitious for this town and this life."

She stood perfectly still, staring at me with complete confusion. I had to make her understand.

"Look around," I said. "This is who I am. I am a

fisherman. My life is the ocean and my boats and my company. This house, which I built myself, and Ginger. This is the entirety of my existence." It was true. I couldn't offer her much. Havenport was great, but it wasn't Boston or New York, or any other big city brimming with opportunities. "And if I thought I would be good for you I would give it all up. I would cut my hair and shave and try to be the corporate man of your dreams. But we both know that there is nothing I could do that wouldn't hold you back. You need your focus. You need to give yourself to these opportunities. You are getting the second chance you wanted. And you're doing it on your terms."

"I don't think I want a second chance with them." She looked at me with her chilly intensity. Her voice was calm and measured.

I knew I was digging my own grave. "You took on the firm and the boys' club and you won. That asshole is gone because of you. You didn't just slink away in shame. You stood up for yourself and the women who came before you and the others who will come after you. You earned this chance."

Her spine was straight, and her gaze was steely. "Declan, I have no idea what I want to do right now. I am confused and still processing everything that has happened. I came over here to share my exciting news with you, not to receive a lecture about my future." She took a breath and continued. "I don't think I want to go back. I want to be here, in Havenport, with you."

As she grew calmer and more controlled, I felt my blood pressure going up. Why wasn't she getting this? Why was she making everything so difficult?

"What about Lucas Kim?" she asked calmly. "I told you I wanted to explore my options working with him."

"What about him, Astrid?" The calmer she got the more unreasonable I became. "The engagement party was weeks ago. Have you called him? Have you made any moves to further the next stage of your career? No. Because we both know you've been waiting. We both know what you really want."

At this point I was too far gone. I was angry, scared, and frustrated, and fully taking it out on her. "If you wanted me, this place, something new, you would be pursuing it. Because if I know one thing about you, Astrid, it's that you go after what you want. You are tenacious. So if you wanted this, if you wanted me, it would be clear. There would be no confusion."

"That's not fair. I have been through a lot, and I've had the threat of a felony conviction hanging over my head for the past few weeks. I didn't know if I would be disbarred, for Christ's sake. I'm so sorry I didn't work out a new ten-year plan to your satisfaction." Her voice was so icy, so controlled, it cut through me like a knife.

I didn't want her hanging around because of me and then hating me because I kept her from everything she wanted. I knew I loved her. But I also knew I had to step aside.

She walked toward me, and I knew if she touched me I'd be done for. All my self-control would crumble and I'd beg her to stay here forever. "Declan, I love you," she said softly.

I put up my hand. "I am so grateful to have met you, Astrid. What we had was crazy and explosive and intense. We should part as friends and enjoy what we had."

"Had?" Her face turned stony. "Past tense? So this is already over? I don't get a say at all?"

I knew I was messing this up and hurting her. But I didn't know how to make her see sense here. She had to know that this wouldn't last long term. And a clean break now and an amicable parting would prevent so much heartbreak later. I didn't want to hurt her more than I had to.

"So you have nothing to say?" She put a hand on her hip and I began to sweat. She was an incredible interrogator. If I wasn't so terrified and angry I'd be turned on. "Don't pull this noble martyr bullshit with me, Declan Quinn. You can't tell me what to do."

"I'm not telling you. I'm just stepping aside so you don't have to feel bad about doing what you want to do."

"You have no idea what I want."

"Really? Then tell me. You want a life here? In a small town with me, a dumb fisherman? It's been fun for you— watching TV and playing with my dog—I get that. But it's not forever. This was a vacation for you. A break from reality. It wasn't real."

"How dare you? This has been more real than anything I've ever experienced."

"You don't get it. We are done. I'm not going to trap you here so you can be bored and miserable. You will resent me and hate me and hate this town. Go back to the city. Go back to your law firm. You are an incredible woman, and you can achieve incredible things. I will not be the one to hold you back."

Her eyes flashed with fury. "This is insane. You realize you are being a total dick right now. Whether or not I go back is my decision and has no bearing on my relationship with you. I love you and I want to be with you regardless of where I work."

"You said yourself you couldn't do both. You couldn't climb the ladder and be with me."

"That was then. This is now. Everything has changed, Declan. My relationship with my career, my relationship with you, even my relationship with myself. Everything is different now and I am just trying to figure it out. I don't know where I'm going or what I'm doing, but I want to be with you."

My heart was aching and my brain was spinning. I would give anything to say yes and hold her in my arms and tell her everything was going to be amazing. But I knew it wasn't the truth. And Astrid deserved better.

Her icy facade began to crumble as tears ran down her cheeks. "Support me. Let's work through everything as a team. Don't decide what's best for me and then dismiss me like I mean nothing to you."

I looked at her teary face and felt my heart crack open in my chest. "I can't do that, Astrid."

36

DECLAN

THE MINUTE ASTRID LEFT MY HOUSE I REGRETTED IT, and days later, I was still disgusted with myself. How had I spoken to her like that? How could I have pushed her away?

And I wasn't the only one. Ginger was confused and kept pacing around looking out the picture window toward Astrid's cottage. "It's no use, Ginger," I told her. "She moved out last weekend." Emily had come by with her SUV and helped her get all her stuff. We briefly made eye contact through the window, and Emily flipped me the bird. Guess I deserved it.

So she was gone. And everything sucked. But at least I knew she was back where she belonged. As much as I knew she was hurt, I hoped that it would be temporary and she would be busy and back to kicking ass in no time. I had even reached out a few times via text, as a friend, but she hadn't responded. She probably blocked my number. It was for the best. I bet she was doing great.

And me? I was not exactly killing it. I wanted to be at peace with my actions, but I wasn't. Doubt crept in, inch by inch, until I was drowning in it. I regretted everything about what had happened and was currently wallowing in my loneliness.

To say I missed Astrid was an understatement. I ached for her. I missed her presence, her conversation, her sense of humor. Astrid's beauty was just part of her appeal. I fell for her attitude. She was self-assured and aloof, and it was clear she did not give a shit about what anyone thought about her. She was cool and impassive, and I desperately wanted to know what she was thinking at all times. She could sit silently and observe everything. If I didn't know better, I would have sworn she was a spy. Nothing escaped her meticulous attention to detail. I found myself replaying conversations we had, memories we shared, over and over again.

I was resigned to being miserable and feeling sorry for myself. I worked and lay on my couch drinking scotch, because it reminded me of Astrid. Rare, earthy, and an acquired taste. Fuck, I missed her.

Thankfully, everyone left me alone—except for my brothers, who insisted I show up in person to our Tuesday night meeting at the brewery. It was the last place I wanted to go, but I was committed to launching our business, and if I didn't they would probably try to show up at my house.

I walked through the door, a few minutes early for our six p.m. meeting, hoping to keep a low profile. Unfortunately that was impossible for the Quinn brothers. "Cal, look who decided to show up?" Liam shouted over the taps.

Callum turned around and took one look at me and winced. I knew I was not my best, but he wasn't exactly helping.

"Where's Ginger?" Liam asked. "I bought her some cookies from that fancy dog bakery downtown." Poor Liam had been trying to win Ginger over for years, and she wasn't having it. No amount of fancy cookies would change that.

"She didn't want to come," I replied, taking a seat at the bar. "She hates me."

"Dude, she's a dog. She doesn't hate you."

I looked Cal dead in the eye. "She peed in my shoes last night. I went to put them on this morning and got a big surprise."

"Maybe it was a mistake. Maybe she had to go?" Liam offered.

"If you really think that then you don't know my dog." I knew Ginger. We had been through a lot together. And she was mad at me. I knew why. I was mad at myself. I deserved to have my shoes peed in.

"Fair enough."

Liam slid a beer across the bar to me. "So are you going to tell us what happened?"

I took a big sip. Liam's beer was annoyingly good. "Isn't this a business meeting?" I growled. "Let's work."

Cal clapped me on the back. "I would love to work. But we're not going to get anything done with you in your current state."

"What are you talking about? I'm fine."

They exchanged a look. "Declan, you are not fine. You look like shit."

I rolled my eyes. My brothers loved to pick on my appearance. They were just jealous I was the tallest and had the best hair.

"No," Cal said, jumping in. "You look worse than shit. You look like shit that died of dysentery." Liam laughed and I glared at Callum.

"Wait, what? Don't try to be funny, Fabio. We all know your job is to look pretty," I growled.

I went back to staring at my beer. I wished it was whiskey, but it would do for now.

"Dec, we're not talking business until you tell us what is going on. The whole town knows Astrid left and went back to Boston."

"Yup."

"And?"

"Did you have anything to do with that?"

"Yes."

"Care to elaborate?"

"No."

"Oh good. You're chatty today," Liam mused.

"Just tell us already so we can get on with our lives. We care about you. If you're not okay, we're here for you," Callum said.

"Astrid left. She went back to Boston. Back to her law firm. Back to her old life."

"And she dumped you?" Cal's face was sympathetic. He really was such a good big brother.

"Not exactly."

"Then what happened?"

"I sort of broke up with her?" I mumbled into my beer.

I stared at their shocked faces.

"I had to. It was the right thing to do," I explained.

"I'm not following. You let a goddess who actually wanted to be with you walk away? Willingly? You deserve to be alone, dude." Liam grabbed a rag and started wiping down the bar.

He wasn't wrong. "Yup. I do. Can we stop talking about this now?"

They shook their heads.

My stupid brothers weren't going to let me get away so easily. "Guys. We come from different worlds." She told me many times that she couldn't be in a relationship and climb the ladder at her firm. She was so talented and ambitious. I didn't want to hold her back. "I knew that she would get bored with me, and with Havenport, and resent me. I couldn't live with that. I want good things for her."

"So this was altruistic?" Callum's face was skeptical.

I shrugged.

"Bullshit," Liam muttered. "I call bullshit."

"I already feel terrible enough. I've tried texting her a few times, just to show that I still want to be friends. And she hasn't responded. I'm afraid to go anywhere in town. I half expect to wake up and find that Nora and Cece slashed my tires."

"That is something they would do," Liam said wistfully.

"I know."

"So you don't love her?"

"Of course I love her."

"Are you sure? Because generally you don't push people you love away."

"I'm so fucked up that I do." And wasn't that the truth? I was a mess. "I love her. But I know I can't keep her. She has to go out and do her thing, and I can't hold her back. I'm not enough. This town is not enough for her."

"How do you know that? Did she tell you that?"

"No. She didn't have to. I knew it. We had an amazing couple of months together and that's it. That's all I get." I drained my beer and wanted to be back on my couch, wallowing alone, with only Ginger to judge me.

Liam poured me a refill and paused for a minute. "You need to stop gushing about your feelings and do something," he said.

There was nothing I could do. I knew that. "Astrid said feelings are sexy," I muttered to myself, smiling at the memory.

"Yes," Callum said. "To women. We are not women."

"You should be talking to your woman about your

feelings. Not us. If you told her how you feel you probably wouldn't have screwed things up so badly," Liam said. "That's kind of the point. In a relationship you talk about your feelings with each other. Not random third parties." He was so smug I would punch him if I had the energy.

"So you are the relationship specialist now?" I quipped.

He shrugged. "I'm engaged."

I smirked. "It's not legal yet. The poor girl might come to her senses eventually." He threw a bar rag at me. I wished Ginger was here. She would have growled at him. Then I remembered that even my fucking dog hated me at the moment and sank further into my depression.

Cal clapped me on the shoulder. "You need to apologize, beg for forgiveness, and pray that she takes you back."

"Yup," Liam seconded. "Not only would that end this life crisis, but it would get you out of our hair, which would be excellent."

"Why can't you guys just let me wallow in peace?" I griped.

"Because we're your brothers. And we don't do that. Plus, this is supposed to be a business meeting. Not that we can conduct business with you looking... like that." He gestured at me with his beer stein.

"I've been working a lot," I snapped. "Paul and his wife had a baby. I gave him a few weeks off. So I'm Captaining his boat right now."

"Wait, if you are out on the water all day, who's doing all the other work?"

"I am, after hours. I just hit the office once we come back to port. I moved some meetings around and am basically handling everything at night."

"That's stupid. You can't safely Captain and run a crew if you aren't sleeping."

"Or eating."

"Or showering."

"Dec, you gotta get it together. Remember when I pushed Cece away? I was a mess."

I snorted. "That's generous. You were a basket case."

"Fine. But you two yelled at me until I got my head out of my ass and groveled. I got so lucky that she took me back. Trust me. I will never screw up that badly again." He shuddered and I believed him. Cece was amazing and had generously forgiven him after he acted like a total asshole. The great thing about my brother was that he was smart enough not to make the same mistake twice.

"But there is nothing I can do. She has to go back to her career in Boston. It would have never worked out between us."

"What did she say?"

"She didn't say anything."

"I'm not following."

"I told her that she should go back to the firm and that we had to break up because I would only hold her back. That she should go forward and kick ass and do great things with her life."

"So you told her what to do?" Cal looked exasperated.

"Dude… never tell a woman what to do. EVER," Liam shouted.

"Are you crazy?" Cal said, running his hand through his hair. "You're lucky she let you live."

I just sat there and took it, knowing that they were right. I had overreacted and projected my issues all over Astrid. I didn't even stop to listen to what she wanted.

"So, let me get this straight. You told the woman you're in love with, who had been violently assaulted weeks before, that you were breaking up with her for her own good and gave her no say in the matter?"

I nodded. Hearing it out loud made me feel even shittier.

I held my hands up in surrender. "It's for the best, guys."

"How? Did you ask her what she thought? What she wanted? She told you she loved you. And you decided for her that she can't be a lawyer and be in a relationship with you?" Callum was so logical and loved being right. I could tell he was enjoying rubbing salt all over my wounds.

"I take it back," Liam said. "You can't grovel, you can't apologize. You're not coming back from that."

"Thanks a lot, asshole."

"Stop," Callum said. We both looked at him as he paced around the bar. "It's not over. Declan screwed up, but he can fix it. We are Quinns. We don't give up when things get hard."

I tried to protest but he silenced me with a look.

"Our ancestors were starving to death and got on a boat in the hopes of a better life. We come from hearty stock, boys. We just have to put our heads together and figure something out."

"She hasn't returned any of my texts. I've tried to apologize. I've tried to reach out."

"Let me see if I can get some intel out of Cece," Liam said hopefully. "I can find out if she went back to her firm and if you have any shot at getting her back."

"Good thinking," Cal said, pointing at Liam. "I'll ask around. There has got to be some info floating around. Emily is family—she will know something. And I see Derek at the gym all the time. We will figure this out."

"But," Callum continued, gesturing at me, "you need to get it together. And in the meantime, you need to make peace with Dad. You need to realize that you are good enough. You deserve good things. You should take over the business and you should get Astrid back. But sitting here being depressed isn't going to accomplish anything."

He wasn't wrong. But I didn't want to give myself any false hope. I had a good life. I always believed that I had everything I needed. I couldn't let my heart hope for more.

But was it enough, having my business, my home, and my dog? It wasn't a bad life, that was for sure. But could I do better? Could I get out of my comfort zone and stretch myself? Reach for a brighter, messier, future filled with love and fun and family? I wanted to. But part of me wanted to just stay in my comfy rut and live here forever.

37

ASTRID

I STARTED TO BRIEFLY HYPERVENTILATE WHEN I walked through security up to the elevator banks. I wasn't officially back yet. I was here to meet with HR and discuss my return to work.

Still, I was dressed in one of my trusty black suits, which was feeling a bit snug. I had definitely packed on some muscle from all the Krav Maga and eating I had done in Havenport. I'd enjoy my strength while it lasted, since I'm sure I'd be back to skipping meals and pulling all-nighters in no time.

I got on the elevator with a litigation partner I recognized. She was typing furiously on her iPhone and didn't even look up when I walked in. I pressed the button and stood in the back, observing her hunched posture and flying fingers. There was a time I felt compelled to check my phone every minute of the day. Now it was in my purse, and my fingers didn't itch to email anymore. It was a weird sensation, but a welcome one.

The HR meeting took a few hours. They had a lot of questions about Max Shapiro and my work for him on the failed merger. Several people, including John Waterson, came in to say hello and welcome me back. Just being back in this building was making me twitchy.

"Can you excuse me? I need to use the ladies' room," I asked brightly, desperate to get out of the room.

After vomiting in the bathroom, I decided to call it a day and head home. I was supposed to give HR my return date by the end of the week, but I didn't think I could do it. Being in the building made me physically ill. I saw all the associates peering out their office doors to get a look at me, the disgraced former associate who got welcomed back after being assaulted by a partner. I didn't want their whispers, and I didn't want their pity. All I wanted was to get out of there as quickly as possible.

I couldn't go back. I knew it in my bones. But saying goodbye to a huge part of my life was daunting. This was all I had ever known. But I couldn't deny how much better I felt physically and emotionally since leaving that highrise. I couldn't deny that I had expanded my horizons and learned more about myself. I couldn't deny that I had fallen in love.

I had spent decades doing exactly what I was supposed to, being the perfect daughter, student, employee. But it was time to start being myself. I convinced myself I was quiet and subdued, cool and calm at all times—but that was just an act. I had finally begun to let my rage out and it felt good. I liked bright clothes and loud music and delicious food. I was passionate and emotional. Not some ice queen who never got upset, no matter how poorly she was treated.

But those days were over. I was a new person, and I couldn't go back to my old life. Just like my suits, it didn't really fit anymore. I could still force it on myself, but it wasn't right and I knew it.

———

"Open up, Astrid. We know you're in there." The familiar voice roused me off my couch.

It was nine a.m. on a Monday morning. What was Nora doing here?

I padded over to the door of my apartment and looked out my peep hole. I saw Nora and Emily. How did they find me?

I opened the door and Nora barged in.

"Thanks a lot for not responding to our texts!"

Emily was right behind her, holding Jacob, and Maggie and Cece were in the rear holding grocery bags.

"What is happening?" I asked, rubbing the sleep out of my eyes.

"You didn't show up to Monday breakfast last week. So we are bringing Monday breakfast to you. We never leave a coven member behind," Nora explained slowly.

Emily gave me a half hug. "And Jacob has an ear infection so he couldn't go to preschool today. But don't worry. I brought an iPad." At the mention of his favorite electronic, Jacob lifted his head off his mom's shoulder. "iPad?" She handed him her massive purse and told him to sit down.

"You guys didn't have to come all the way out here," I insisted.

Maggie walked slowly around my apartment. "Judging by the condition of this place, I think we did," she said kindly.

Emily gave me a pitying look. "If I didn't know better, I'd think my kids had been here." Her eyes traveled from the pile of dirty dishes and take-out containers in the sink to the laundry strewn all over the place.

I'll admit, my apartment was not in the best condition. But to be fair, I barely lived here and I was going through some things right now.

"I thought there was no judgment at Monday breakfast?" I snapped back.

Nora threw an arm around my shoulder. "Of course not, babe. We're not judging. We've all had our moments. But we're here now. And we've got your back."

It warmed my heart to know these women drove over an hour in rush hour traffic to see me, even if I was a tad bit embarrassed at my current state.

Cece was unpacking groceries. "Nora, you're leader. What are we doing first?"

"Cecelia darling, you know I prefer the term 'high priestess' but you're right. Troops, first thing is we are getting this one in the shower. Cece, you're on brunch duty. Emily, you are bartending. And Maggie, you are on cleanup."

"Already on it," Maggie shouted, her arms full of dirty laundry. Emily had told me she was a compulsive clean freak, but she hadn't been here two minutes and she was already tidying up.

"You," Nora said, gesturing to me. "When was the last time you showered?"

I shrugged. It was Monday, so maybe Friday? But I wasn't sure. The last week had been a total blur. Rather than admit that out loud, I decided to just head straight to the bathroom.

I turned on the harsh fluorescent lights and stared at myself in the mirror. I looked terrible. My skin was sallow, and I had dark circles under my eyes. My hair was limp and greasy and I had the beginnings of a massive breakout on my jawline. It had been eight days since I last saw Declan, and I was suffering. I missed him. I missed Ginger. I missed my little cottage.

I hated this apartment. I hated this city. I hated everything.

I took a long, scalding hot shower, washing my hair

twice for good measure and shaving my legs. I walked into
my bedroom to find a new outfit spread on my bed,
clearly courtesy of Nora. I pulled on the buttery soft
joggers and T-shirt and padded out to the living room.

Jacob was curled up on my couch wearing headphones
and watching some neon-colored cartoon on his iPad.
Maggie had made significant cleaning progress and was
now vacuuming, Emily was pouring mimosas into plastic
champagne flutes she must have brought with her, and
Cece was flipping golden slices of French toast on my
stove.

I was overcome with affection for this group of wild,
loyal women. They hadn't known me long but embraced
me as one of their own. They weren't perfect and neither
was I, but together, we were unstoppable. I got choked up.

"You okay, sweetie?" Nora asked, carrying a trash bag.

I nodded. "Thank you. For everything."

"Like it or not, you are one of us, Elsa. So get used
to it."

I smiled at her.

"Now I have to get back to your closet."

"What?"

"I'm cleaning it out for you. So much drab black and
lots of sad undergarments." She proceeded to head back
into my room with the half full trash bag. I didn't even
want to ask.

———

As nice as it was to have the coven show up for me in my
time of need, we were definitely squeezed in my tiny
apartment. Cece had outdone herself cooking brunch, and
we all took seats on the couch and on the floor
surrounding the oversized coffee table.

Cece made me a plate piled high with French toast

and crispy bacon. "I think this might be the first meal ever cooked from scratch in this apartment," I told her appreciatively.

She patted my head. "Speaking of this apartment. Do you moonlight as a serial killer? This place is creepy as fuck."

"Is there a secret room with a wall covered in photos and bits of string?" Emily added.

I laughed for the first time in weeks. "Stop, guys. I'll admit it's a bit…sterile."

"You barely have furniture," Nora said, gesturing around the room with her slice of bacon.

"I cleaned out your fridge," Maggie said solemnly. "Scary."

"You didn't have to do that," I said.

"Yes, I did. It was for the best." She shook her head and downed her mimosa.

After putting away an impressive amount of bacon and our second bottle of champagne, I worked up the courage to ask. "So I love you guys, and I appreciate all the help. But what are you doing here?"

"We are here to support you, to love you, and hopefully to drag you back to Havenport," Emily said in her singsong voice.

I loved them. But they didn't get it. "Guys, I can't go back. I appreciate everything you've done and what you are trying to do. But I can't ever go back after what happened with Declan."

"Tell us what happened. We'll be the judges," Maggie said.

"He sent me away. Basically broke up with me and said it was for my own good." I started to tear up.

Nora's face was bright red. "Are you shitting me? He told you what was good for you? That is some mansplainy bullshit right there."

She looked at Jacob. "Sorry," she whispered to Emily.

"Don't worry. Those are noise cancelling headphones. You can let it rip," Emily replied.

Cece poured herself some more mimosa. "I don't get it. He is clearly in love with you."

"He's not." I scoffed. It hurt, but it was the truth.

"Yes he is. He def is. I have inside info," she said.

"Oooh." Nora shoved Cece. "Spill, girl."

"Liam says he's miserable. Totally miserable and can't function. He and Callum staged an intervention, and he's just moping around depressed about losing Astrid."

That pissed me off. He didn't get to mope around being sad. He pushed me away. "Then why did he tell me to come back here and go back to my law firm?"

"You can't go back to your firm!" Emily shouted. "After what they did to you? You should be suing their asses into next year."

"I know. Trust me. It's complicated. I went last Thursday just to fill out some paperwork and I got sick. I threw up in a trash can. It was terrible. I don't want that life anymore." I took another sip of mimosa. "You have all shown me there is so much more out there for me. And Declan"—I sighed—"Declan taught me a lot too."

Nora wrapped her arms around me in a tight hug. I dried my tears. "Everything is shit right now, guys. My career is effectively over, and I'm not even that upset about it. I think the love of my life doesn't want me. And I can't even manage to shower regularly. I'm a mess." Tears rolled freely down my cheeks as I took in the sympathetic faces around me.

"Hey," Maggie said gently. "There is nothing wrong with being a mess. We are all messes in our own ways. It's part of the human condition. You just have to get up every day and try your best."

"Yeah," Cecelia said. "Liam and I are fighting. He

wants to get married yesterday, and I want to take my time and plan a wedding. It feels like we're not on the same page about anything right now, and it's making me nervous to be married to him."

"And I don't think Josh and I are going to reconcile," Maggie said softly.

Nora reached out and grabbed her hand. "I'm so sorry, Mags."

Maggie gently wiped the tears from her eyes. "I'll be fine."

"And I spend every waking moment of my life feeling like I'm failing and I'm a terrible mother," Emily said. She gestured to her four-year-old. "I think that iPad is going to be fused into his hands. It's the only way to keep him quiet sometimes."

"You're not a bad mom," Cece said.

"And me?" Nora said. "I'm perpetually single and will die alone."

I smiled. I loved these women. They really got me. "Okay, okay," I said. "I get it now, we all have our shit."

"Which is why we have the coven. We call each other out. We don't allow self-pity or any negative self-talk," Emily said.

"Ha. I told you the coven was going to catch on," Nora shouted. Emily shrugged.

"Astrid, you are a beautiful, brilliant queen who is going to go out into this world and slay whatever you want," Cece said.

Nora cheered. "And you are going to start with that grumpy fisherman. He messed up. He tried to be noble and made everything worse." Part of me knew that. Knew that he wanted to protect me and support me. But part of me was pissed. I was no one's doormat, and I made my own decisions, thank you very much.

"But he thinks he can tell me what to do," I protested.

"Yes, that's a problem," Maggie added. "But I'm confident you can set him straight."

"Of course I can." As the words left my mouth, I knew they were true. Thinking back, I could have been honest with him from the start. I could have explained that I didn't want to go back to the firm regardless of what happened. But I had been so confused and unsure of myself. Walking away from my career was unthinkable just a few months ago, and now I was ready for it. He didn't know that. I had never told him. So as pissed as I was at him, I could recognize the part I played in the confusion.

"So now we need a plan," Emily said, rubbing her hands together.

I made a time out signal with my hands. "Wait. Wait. Why do I have to do anything? He broke up with me. He should be groveling right now."

"But he did. Or at least he tried," Cece said.

Maggie nodded. "Yes. You said yourself you wouldn't speak to him or respond to his texts."

"And there will be plenty of time for him to grovel. But you have to go see him and force the conversation. Lay down the law and tell him to cut the shit," Nora added.

"The Quinn boys are incapable of properly expressing their feelings. Trust me on this one. Especially Declan. He isn't exactly a talker," Emily mused, while turning down the volume on Jacob's iPad.

"I don't see how this is my job," I argued.

"Because you are smarter and more evolved. Plus you have us," Cece said.

"Correct. Poor Declan only has his brothers. And although there is a lot of handsome there, there's not a ton of emotional intelligence," Maggie added.

"Bingo," Cece shouted. "So let's put our heads together, ladies. It's time to plan."

Predictably, my mother had not taken my decision well. When she invited me to lunch I knew it would be tense and I knew it would be miserable, but I couldn't have predicted just how nasty she would get.

Thankfully, we were in her chambers, so I didn't have to worry about making a scene at a restaurant. I almost threw my SweetGreen salad at her when she accused me of giving up my career for a man. She didn't care that I was heartbroken. Didn't care that I had been assaulted. Something inside me snapped, and I just let loose.

I unleashed all of the hurt, all of the disappointment, and all the sadness I had been holding inside me for years. I told her that I would never be like her, loveless and cruel. It was hurtful, but I couldn't help it. I was done with her constant criticism and the unrelenting pressure to live up to some impossible ideal. I needed to be free to live on my own terms, and I made sure she knew it.

I headed back to my apartment, feeling weary. I wanted to put on some sweatpants and cry for the next few hours. I wished I was back at Aunt Connie's cottage, sipping tea and watching the waves crash over the rocks. I walked off the elevator, desperate to get out of my uncomfortable shoes, and found my sledgehammer propped up against my door. There was a note taped to it in a familiar scrawl. *Oh shit.*

I dragged the sledgehammer into my apartment, propping it up next to my coatrack, and stared at the letter. I was overcome with the need to read it and hear his words and also the desire to set it on fire and be done with all the heartbreak. Instead I placed it on the counter while I collected my thoughts.

After losing the uncomfortable clothes and my bra and gaining a large glass of Pinot Noir, I sat down and opened the envelope, bracing myself for the impact of what lay inside.

Astrid,

I am so sorry. I know you don't want to talk to me, but there are things I need to tell you. I love you and I miss you and I shouldn't have pushed you away. That night at the gala I got spooked. First, I let your mom get to me. Her words were cruel but she wasn't wrong. I am not good enough for you. But I realize now that I could be. And I want the chance to prove it to you.

Second, I still blame myself for what happened to you. The caveman part of my brain just wants to protect you and keep you safe forever. I was so overcome with rage at Max and what happened to you, I wasn't thinking straight. I blamed myself and felt like I failed you as a man. I am still tortured by what happened to you. The thought of that prick putting his hands on you makes me see red.

I know you probably hate me and don't want to see me again. But I just had to tell you how sorry I am. I had no right to tell you what you wanted. I had no right to take away your power and your agency like that. And although I'm the idiot that pushed you away, I am also the idiot who is trying to do the work to be worthy of you. I have a long way to go, but I won't stop trying.

No matter what happens, never give up the fight. For yourself, for others, and for justice. It's your superpower and the world needs you.

Love,

Declan

It was a gut punch. I could ignore his calls and texts, but I couldn't ignore this. My stupid pathetic heart wouldn't let me.

I missed him desperately and wanted nothing more than to go back to him immediately. But he hurt me and rejected me and tried to push me back into my old life. A life I hated. I hated Burns & Glenn, I hated this sterile apartment, and I hated feeling so lonely and empty without my friends. And I hated that he was there, and I was here.

I needed to talk to him. I needed to tell him how I felt and what I wanted. He owed me that. But the past few weeks had taught me that I was in control of my own destiny. I was Astrid Wentworth. I never backed down from a challenge. And I always went after what I wanted. And, as angry and as hurt as I was, I wanted Declan Quinn.

38

DECLAN

I DIDN'T DESERVE MY BROTHERS. I COULD ADD THEM to the very long list of people I didn't deserve. Liam and Cal had gone right to work, getting as much info as they could about Astrid. According to Liam, Cece had reported that Astrid was indeed back in Boston and very angry with me. Unsurprising but not exactly encouraging either.

The big game changer actually came from Callum. Apparently he had played basketball with Luke Kim over the weekend, and Luke had mentioned that he had been in contact with Astrid about some upcoming legal projects. My heart soared. Maybe there was a chance that she wanted this life after all? It made me realize I needed to do some housekeeping of my own. If Astrid could go after what she really wanted professionally, I should be able to do the same.

"Thanks for meeting me." The Captain paced around my office in his usual uniform of Carhartts and a flannel shirt.

"No problem, son. Getting out of the house around lunchtime means I don't have to deal with your mother force-feeding me lentils again."

I clapped him on the shoulder. "You look good, Dad."

He rolled his eyes. He would eat tree bark if my mother told him to, and we both knew it. He sat down on the couch and looked out at the view of the harbor. The skies were clear, and we sat in silence for a few minutes, watching the hustle and bustle of a commercial harbor.

I turned to him, gathering my courage. "Dad, it's time," I said softly.

He nodded, not taking his gaze off the horizon. "I know."

I held up a folder. "Did you look at the business plans I sent over last week?" I had prepared and delivered a massive written proposal, outlining my business plans for the next five years. It was all there—budgets, revenue projections, equipment upgrades, and strategic changes. "You worked hard and built something significant. This is how I am going to preserve and improve on your legacy."

He said nothing. Just sat and stared at the water silently.

"I reviewed everything," he said quietly. "Callum came over and walked me through some of it." I made a mental note to thank Callum. I know my dad respected his opinion, and he played a huge role in helping me put the plans together.

"Dad, I know that I'm a disappointment to you."

His neck snapped around quickly. "How can you say that?"

"Because I don't have a degree like Liam and Callum."

He sighed and shifted on the couch. "I don't give a shit about that. I don't have a degree either. A piece of paper doesn't make you smart, it doesn't make you hardworking, it doesn't make you a man of integrity. You are all of those things, Declan."

Wow. For a man of few words, my dad sure had a lot to say on that matter. I sat silently, letting it all sink in. I had convinced myself that he didn't notice how hard I had worked, how devoted I was. Maybe I had been wrong?

"I have had my head too far up my own ass to notice. My heart attack really sobered me. This career has taken a lot out of me, and I'm ready to try some new things. I am still young, and I want to focus on my health and enjoying myself. I took my father's legacy and built on it, and now it's your turn." I was amazed. Who was this man and what had he done with my father?

"I don't agree with everything you propose. And I don't understand some of it either. But I support you and your vision and I know you have a good head on your shoulders."

My heart soared. "Thank you, Dad."

"This is difficult for me. This was my life's work. I started working on boats in second grade. My life has been the ocean, and I spent so many years fixated on success and growth and learning to never rest on my laurels. That's why I'm never satisfied. Because I can't forget where I came from. I can't forget the legacy of our family, coming to this country with nothing and building something."

I nodded. I knew this place meant so much to him. I wanted him to understand it meant just as much to me.

"I don't want to hand the company over to you because I can't let it go, not because you aren't qualified or I don't trust you. This has nothing to do with you and everything to do with me.

"Your mother says I have to start enjoying my retirement. Isn't it bad enough I'm eating vegan and doing yoga? Now she wants to book one of those bus tours of Europe."

I chuckled. A bus tour of Europe was my dad's idea of hell. "Dad, you're lucky that she wants to spend time with you."

"I guess so. And you know me, I'll do anything to make your mother happy."

I smirked. Even as a small child it was clear who wore the pants in our household. My dad may have been a leader outside the home, in the navy, and on his boats, but inside he toed the line.

"Did I ever tell you about the first time we met?"

I rolled my eyes. "Dad, I've heard the story a million times. You were on leave from the navy, and she was a waitress at a restaurant in Boston."

"Yup. And my buddies and I came in for dinner, and I took one look at her and decided that she was it for me." He got up and walked over to the window. "I went back to that restaurant every night for a week and asked to be seated in her section. Every single night I asked her out on a date. And she kept saying no."

I laughed.

"But she finally said yes. I think she didn't want one guy who only could afford to order soup taking up a whole table in her section every night. And the rest is history. I have loved her every minute since."

I smiled. I had heard this story more times than I could count, but it was another reminder that my parents made it work. They fell in love and built a family, a business, and forty years of marriage together. "That's sweet, Dad."

"That's the thing, son. When you find your person you have to be persistent. Once in a lifetime love isn't easy. It doesn't fall into your lap. You have to fight for it and be willing to wait it out if necessary."

"But I just don't know if I'm up for it, Dad. The husband and father thing."

"Why don't you take it one step at a time and be a boyfriend? I doubt Astrid wants a ring or a baby tomorrow. She seems like she has a lot going on."

"That's true. But I doubt she'll take me back."

"Son, you need to believe in yourself. You need to see what the rest of the world sees. You command respect. The crew loves you. Vince hates everyone and barely tolerated me, and he is totally loyal to you. Do you have any idea how many times he's hinted that you should be CEO?"

I had no idea. I was touched. Vince was a tough nut, but he knew everything and was my right-hand man. I trusted him. "Wow." I scratched my chin. Maybe my dad was right.

"I don't want you to think I want Liam and Callum here instead of you. That's not true at all. Would I have loved all three of my sons to take an interest in the family business? Of course. But you, Declan, you love the ocean, you love those boats and the men who work them. This business is in you, in your blood and your bones, just like it was for me. And I'm proud of you. And I will be proud to fully retire and promote you to CEO."

I was blown away. I had spent years being told to keep my head down and work and that I wasn't ready yet. Now he was ready to turn over the reins?

"The paperwork is being drawn up and should be ready by the end of the week."

I didn't know what to say. It was finally sinking in. It was happening. He listened, he understood, and he respected my plans and my vision.

"You have pursued this carefully and strategically and have done your homework. You know your stuff, and although I might not agree with it all, I have confidence in your ability to lead. But you have to apply that same patience, that same focus, to your personal life. You have to be willing to take risks." Oh shit. I knew there was an ulterior motive here. I looked around, half expecting my mom to jump out from behind the furniture.

"Thanks, Dad. I appreciate it. I will do it my way, but I'll make you proud."

He smiled at me. "I don't doubt that." He paced around some more, and I knew what was coming. "You know, Declan, you keep yelling at me for playing it safe, saying we need to adapt and take risks. Follow your own damn advice, son. We all know you pushed Astrid away. You left her before she could leave you."

I was growing weary of talking about this. "Dad. It's not like that. I did what was best for everyone. Fear had nothing to do with it."

"If you are in love with her you figure it out."

"It's not like that."

"Your mother will be devastated."

Now I was pissed. I had reached my limit of parental disappointment. "Why? Because I'm single?"

"No," he snapped. Staring me dead in the eyes. "Because we clearly raised a moron."

That shut me up. My parents were tough, but this was beyond the usual Captain Quinn pep talk. "You are thirty-five years old so I am sad I need to say this out loud. Love, real love, does not come around very often. You cannot take it for granted, you cannot throw it away. You have got to hang on with both hands and ride out every storm together."

"But her career…" I started.

He interrupted me. "Don't shame the poor girl for her ambitions."

"I'm not!"

"It sounds like you are. Women can do anything and everything, and trust me, most of the time they do these things better than we do."

I nodded. He wasn't wrong.

"If anyone can make it all work, it's Astrid. And you

should be by her side, supporting her and helping her build a full, beautiful life. Instead you push her away?"

"Dad, I know I fucked up. I knew before the words even came out of my mouth. But what I feel for her, it's not like anything I've ever experienced before."

"You think you're protecting her, Declan, but you're really just protecting yourself."

Was he right? I had felt pressured to create a fake relationship to make my parents happy. But had that been the real reason? I had always been desperate to please them, but maybe I just wanted a girlfriend. Maybe I wanted a special person in my life but was too messed up to realize it. Since Astrid probably wouldn't ever be in my league, it felt safer to have a fake relationship. To protect myself. Clearly that had backfired spectacularly. I was losing my mind without her.

"I've tried to apologize, to get her back. She wants nothing to do with me."

"You'll figure it out, Declan. Trust yourself and your instincts. That's what I did with your mother."

And with that, he walked out of the office and I was left staring at the ocean, with absolutely no clue how I was going to win back the love of my life.

39

DECLAN

IT HAD BEEN A LONG DAY. I HADN'T SLEPT THE NIGHT before, replaying my conversation with my father over and over and thinking about how I could get Astrid to at least talk to me. I thought after leaving the note and the sledgehammer at her door I would hear something. But Astrid was tough—that was what I liked about her. She was going to make me work for it, and I respected that. I was up at four to get to work, since I was going out on the water today. We had some ground to make up if we were going to make our quotas by the end of the quarter, and I was still covering for Paul. I couldn't afford to keep his boat docked another day.

Also, I had an ulterior motive. Out on the water, working my ass off with the crew, wet and cold and fighting the elements, would keep me from thinking about Astrid, about the business, or about how thoroughly I had ruined everything.

It was after six p.m. when we got back to port. I was exhausted and looking forward to a hot shower and a glass of whiskey. I had a ton of work to do in my office, but I didn't have it in me to slog through a few more hours. I was bone-tired and emotionally spent.

We docked, and I took a look around as the crew and Vince emptied the hull with the crane. I disembarked and made my way up to my office to grab my laptop before heading out. I watched from my window as my crew cleaned the boats, stowed nets, and organized equipment. It was a well-oiled machine, and we would be up early to do it all again tomorrow. It wasn't glamorous but it was who I was. And I loved being CEO.

As I pulled into my driveway, the yard was bathed in a warm, orange glow from the setting sun. I thought I saw someone by the door. Were my eyes playing tricks on me?

Astrid stepped off the porch and started walking toward me. Was I hallucinating? It had been a long day and I was sleep-deprived. But it was her, clad in a black pantsuit, sky-high heels, and red lipstick. She looked beautiful and terrifying.

She stopped a few feet in front of me, her eyes roving down my body and back up to my face. We stood in uncomfortable silence for a few minutes before I broke down and spoke.

"Astrid. What are you doing here?"

She said nothing, just continued to stare. I drank in the sight of her—her long legs, her high cheekbones, and her long graceful neck, highlighted by her trendy haircut. It was her all right, and she was even more gorgeous than I remembered.

"I came to see you," she said in a businesslike manner. "Can we talk?"

I nodded and gestured for her to follow me. We entered the house, and Ginger greeted her like she had been gone for years. In fairness to Ginger, it felt that way to me too.

I had no idea what to say or do. "Can I get you anything?" I asked.

She shook her head and turned around to face me. "I came to talk to you, Declan. I am unhappy with how we left things." Her posture was perfectly straight, and she never broke eye contact. I worried what happened at the gala would break her again—make her retreat—but the woman standing in front of me was the confident, self-possessed woman I had fallen for.

I exhaled. "Me too." I gestured for her to sit down, but she remained standing. I braced my hands on the kitchen island, expecting a verbal assault.

Her face softened slightly. "The last time I was here you didn't give me a chance to speak. I came here because there are things I need to say to you."

I nodded. "I know. I'm so sorry. I hate what I said and—"

She held up her hand. "Stop talking," she barked.

I nodded. Damn, she was hot when she was in lawyer mode.

"You hurt me," she said, pausing to let the words sink in. "I was confused and overwhelmed, and instead of supporting me, you pushed me away."

I walked over to her. "I'm so sorry, Astrid."

She shot me a glare and I shut up. "I didn't stand up for myself, and that is something I deeply regret. Because if I have learned one thing in the past few months, it's that I'm powerful and I will not be pushed around."

"Of course." I could barely get the words out of my mouth. "I didn't mean to…"

She cocked her head to the side and shot me a stern look. I immediately stopped talking and sat down on the couch.

She started to pace around the living room, and I was

mesmerized by her long legs in those sexy-ass pants and heels. I smiled.

"Do I need counsel for this conversation?" I asked playfully.

She stopped pacing and smirked. "Probably. I am a very skilled negotiator."

"Trust me. I know when I'm outmatched."

"You're a lot smarter than you look, Quinn." Her lips curled into a sexy smirk and I was completely sunk.

I loved this woman. There was no denying it, no hiding it. I only hoped she would be willing to give us another chance after I messed things up so badly.

"Astrid. I hate how we left things between us."

"Oh really?" she said. "You didn't enjoy steamrolling me, denying me any agency over my life, and then pushing me away?"

That hurt. It was true, but it hurt. I could see it in her face. Not only had I broken her heart but I had taken away her power, the one thing Astrid held so dear. I had been feeling shitty for weeks. I knew it was wrong. But I thought it was for the best. I now knew just how wrong I was. I hurt Astrid deeply, and that made me feel even worse.

"Stop apologizing and listen," she snapped.

She took a breath and paused, clearly trying to compose herself. "I am Astrid goddamn Wentworth. I go after what I want. I always have and I always will. And you are what I want, Declan Quinn."

I sat there, shocked. Of all the things I had imagined, this conversation was not one of them.

"If you don't want me, that's fine. I'll leave. But if you pushed me away because of some stupid bullshit about not being good enough, then fuck you."

I had to say something but I didn't know what. Instead I got up and put my arms around her. She sank into me and rested her head on my shoulder, and in that moment, I knew I still had a chance.

"You hurt both of us because of your pride and your bullshit male ego," she whispered.

"I'm sorry," I said, holding her closer. "I'm so sorry. I just thought I wasn't good enough for you and…"

She snapped back, breaking the hug, and crossed her arms over her chest. "You are good enough for me if I say you are. Understood?"

I nodded.

"No one has ever taken care of me in my life. And I haven't needed it. I haven't wanted it. But I want you. I want Ginger. I want to read books and smoke meat and sip fine whiskey together. I want to spend hours not talking and then have wild sex."

I grinned, loving her attitude. "But what about the firm?"

She flipped her hair. "Oh, I told them to go fuck themselves. I have multiple other offers. And I have a lawsuit to prepare. I'm not letting this slide. If I'm going down, I'm taking the whole sexist system with me too."

I tried to suppress the grin that spread across my face. I was so proud of her.

"My entire life has been focused on achieving one goal. And coming here and meeting you made me realize that goal was bullshit. It wasn't what I wanted. I was too scared to let myself really want anything. I came to Havenport and discovered great sex and delicious food and how to live. I made friends and fell in love with a really bitchy dog."

I grabbed her again and kissed her gently. I broke the kiss and smiled at her. Before I knew it she clamped both hands on the sides of my head and pulled me into a far more aggressive kiss. Our lips, tongues, and teeth tangled in a clash of lust and frustration.

She stepped back, and I felt a rush of pride to see that she was breathless. "You pretend you want to just sit here alone in your fortress of solitude, but I don't believe you. You are a big softie under that broody tattooed exterior. And I love you for it. I love your hard edges, your cranky attitude, and your soft gooey center."

I knew this was my chance. "Astrid, I love you too. You love fiercely and truly and unequivocally. And I want you to let me love you back."

She nodded. "I know who I am, Declan. I don't need to be a fancy law firm partner." She put her hands on her hips. "I need you. I need my friends, I need this town. And you don't get to tell me what I need."

"I know," I said, ashamed of how I had acted. "Are you trying to get back together, or are you just yelling at me?" I asked playfully, loving how riled up she was right now.

She stomped her foot. "Both." Her eyes narrowed but she was smiling. "I love you because you don't tell me what to do, you help me figure out what I need. The day you bought me the sledgehammer… I knew that day I was falling for you. And that I would never find anyone like you again. I have spent the last few weeks suffering because you weren't willing to give us a chance."

I gathered her in my arms. "Astrid. I was so wrong. About everything. And I will never, ever, ever, do that again. I respect the hell out of you, and I want you to be the person you want to be. I just hope you let me tag along for the ride. Because that's what I want. To be with you every day, getting a front row seat to your awesomeness and taking you home to my bed every night."

She hugged me tighter and my heart soared. "And I am ready to grovel. I am ready to do whatever it takes to earn your respect and forgiveness. Because I know I acted like an asshole and I will do anything to make it right."

She smirked at me. A full-blown, sexy smirk. And I started to mentally calculate how quickly I could get her out of her pantsuit. I slowly eased the blazer down her shoulders and draped it on the couch. I pulled her closer, basking in the smell of her. She carefully toed off her heels, kicking them aside, without breaking the hold we had on one another.

"I met with Lucas Kim yesterday," she said. "I am going to work with him to develop a model for a legal services clinic for the women's shelter here in town. We want to be full service, covering all legal needs. Lucas thinks if we can put the logistics together, we could potentially roll this out to the broader network of DV organizations and shelters statewide."

My heart swelled with pride. "Wow, that sounds impressive."

She looked up at me playfully. "I haven't done anything yet." She took a deep breath. "But it will be impressive. I feel passionately about helping women and children. And, I know you have some weird jealousy thing about Luke, but he's a great guy, and he also asked me if I would be willing to take on some additional legal work for him as well, on a consulting basis."

I began to gently nibble on her long neck, and I could feel her racing heartbeat. "That sounds fantastic. I'm sure he could use someone as brilliant as yourself."

She arched her back, giving me more access to her neck and collarbones. My hands roamed all over her, grabbing her supple ass and squeezing.

"It looks like I'm actually going to be pretty busy for the next couple of months," she breathily whispered.

I paused, my mouth on her neck. "Do you need a place to stay?"

She pulled back and threw her arms around my shoulders. "Do you have a lead on an apartment?" she asked flirtatiously. "I'm pretty picky, and I really like ocean views…"

"I think I can make some room for you," I said, capturing her mouth in a lusty kiss.

And instead of responding, she kissed me back with abandon, giving me everything she had. We had spoken enough words. I picked her up easily, and she wound her long legs around my waist. I carried her into my bedroom and laid her down gently on my bed. I had a lot of groveling to do, and this seemed like a great place to start.

EPILOGUE
ASTRID

EIGHT YEARS LATER

I snuggled deeper into the pillow, clinging to the warm comfort of my bed for a few more minutes. Alas, it was not to be. I felt hot breath on my face, and my eyes shot open.

"Mama," Oliver crooned. His face was inches from mine, and his toddler morning breath seeped into my pores. I closed my eyes again, trying to remember the last time I had a full night's sleep. Probably before I had kids. No, wait, before I was pregnant. I can't really remember that far back, but I bet it was amazing. We ended up not needing those frozen eggs. I got pregnant during our honeymoon to Iceland. I swear it was those hot springs.

"Mama," he whispered again. I looked up at his dark eyelashes and chubby cheeks and smiled. He looked so beautiful and sweet. "Mama, I pooped," he whispered, pointing to his dinosaur pajamas. I lifted my head and was hit with the telltale smell of a diaper explosion.

"Mama will change you." I sat up and scooped him into my arms as I heard footsteps thundering down the hall. The door burst open, and Amelia jumped on the bed with Declan in hot pursuit. He roared like a dinosaur and pretended to take a bite of her leg.

"Daddy, you are supposed to be a Pachycephalosaurus —they are herbivores!" she explained through her giggle fit.

Declan reared up and scrunched his arms in close to his chest. "Nope. I am a daddy T. rex, and I am hungry for breakfast."

Amelia screamed and burrowed under the duvet to hide. Declan looked at me. "Morning, gorgeous," he said, dropping a kiss to my head. "Oh, no." He pinched his nose. "Here," he said, reaching out and taking our boy out of my arms. "This seems like a Daddy job."

I beamed at him. "My hero."

He winked. "You can thank me later."

I laughed and sank back into the pillow for a glorious moment before a tiny blonde head popped up. "Mom, can we have chocolate chip pancakes for breakfast?"

———

Life with Declan was many things, but it was not boring. We had spent the last seven years in a whirlwind of family, careers, travel, and quiet nights by the fire with Ginger.

We ended up adding on to the house up on the bluff. It now housed Declan and me, our two kids, Ginger and our puppy, Elsa, plus two hamsters and three fish. It was a far cry from the pristine bachelor pad I had encountered so many years ago. Now there were Legos and glitter headbands on every available surface and a mountain of laundry that never seemed to shrink. We were busy and tired and happy.

My career had evolved considerably. After the incident with Max Shapiro, I kept working to make sure justice would be served. I found several other women who had been victimized by him and convinced them to come forward. We ended up bringing a lawsuit against Burns & Glenn. They settled with us for a significant sum of money, and as a condition of my settlement, I forced them to implement several remedial measures to ensure female associates were given equal opportunities and sexual harassment was not tolerated.

I donated my portion of the settlement to the Havenport Crisis Center to help set up a pro bono legal clinic. I spent several years working and recruiting other lawyers, and we built a significant operation that was able to assist hundreds of families across the region. Then, I was asked by the National Association of Domestic Violence to travel to other shelters and organizations in the United States to help them grow legal services clinics. It was fun and exhausting, but I loved advocating for the vulnerable. Protecting women and children from violence, discrimination, and anyone that could prey on them filled me with a deep sense of satisfaction. Declan was right—my legal skills were my superpower.

In addition, I kept working for Lucas Kim, becoming his personal general counsel and friend. I helped him buy and sell companies and negotiated his contracts. It was fun and challenging and kept me busy.

Declan had taken over as CEO at Quinn Fisheries and had built a successful beverage distribution company with his two brothers. He was doing things his way and it suited him. CEO Declan was even hotter than ever.

I carefully bundled up each child, going through my mental checklist of hats, mittens, boots, and scarves. Oliver beamed at me. "Mama, I so excited."

"I know, sweetie."

Last week some volunteers had come by to pick up our tree. We never missed the Annual Christmas Tree Burn, not when I was pregnant or even when we had babies. It was our special tradition, and we savored it.

Alas, it was a bit harder with the two little kids. Thankfully, Annie and the Captain were going to take them home for a sleepover so the adults could cut loose a bit later. While I was looking forward to sitting by the fire with my friends, I was really looking forward to having a night alone with my husband.

Declan double-checked the diaper bag, and I felt my ovaries tingle. He was so sexy when he was in dad mode. Despite his surly exterior, Declan was the silliest, most doting dad on the planet. He played every game, read bedtime stories with silly voices, and remembered everyone's constantly changing food preferences.

"Moooom," complained Amelia, "we are going to be late." She was only five but was tall, self-assured, and a tiny bit intense. She spent a lot of time with her grandfather on his sailboat. He called her "the Captain" now and it was adorable. She tapped her boot-clad foot and crossed her arms.

Declan handed me Oliver, who was almost two, and grabbed his coat off the hook by the door. "Can't wait for those teen years," he whispered into my ears before grabbing Amelia and throwing her over his shoulder as he jogged to the truck. She shrieked with joy and I smiled.

————

The tree burn was just as magical as ever. After the kids went home with their grandparents and we had chatted with our friends, Declan and I stood, watching the fire together as fat snowflakes began to fall. He squeezed my hand through my glove, and I felt my heart swell as I stared into the dancing flames.

He turned toward me and gently cupped my cheek. I

gazed up at him, his eyes illuminated by the fire. He slowly lowered his mouth and kissed me gently. "Eight years," he whispered.

I grabbed the back of his neck, feeling the magic of our first kiss coursing through my veins. "How about we head back to the truck?" I asked saucily.

"You want to recreate it?" he asked with a playful grin.

I pulled him so close I could feel his breath on my cheek. "I think I'd like a bit more than kissing," I said, and I felt his grip on my waist tighten.

"Anything for you, killer."

I took a chance, coming back to Havenport, leaving the firm, and going after Declan. I was never a risk taker —I was more of a careful strategist. But I had learned a few things over the past eight years, and one of them was that there were risks worth taking. I escaped to Havenport and found myself. But I also found my person. And I was never letting him go.

WANT MORE DECLAN & ASTRID?

Get the Bonus Epilogue to get a glimpse of their
honeymoon here:
https://dl.bookfunnel.com/4o4veqqpdy
Be prepared to swoon!

SNEAK PEEK

SNEAK PEEK AT HAVENPORT BOOK 3
Coming Fall 2021

Are you in the mood for more small town romantic goodness? Keep reading for a sneak peek at Book #3 in the Havenport Series.

PROLOGUE

CALLUM

OF ALL THE PATCHES OF GRASS ON ALL THE LAWNS IN Havenport, I had to vomit on hers.

My life was shitty enough without coming face to face with the girl whose heart I broke in high school. The girl who was so kind, so generous, so full of life, that I fucked it all up.

I was moving along at a good clip, close to six-minute miles, when the bottle of whiskey I consumed last night instead of dinner began to catch up with me. As I crested down the hill toward the orchards, I began to feel my stomach churning. I slowed down a bit and gave myself a pep talk. I wasn't going to stop until I finished ten miles. If I collapsed on my couch later that was fine. But I wasn't stopping until I achieved my goal. Because what was I if I wasn't that guy? That guy who always achieves his goals? The ambitious guy? That was me. I couldn't afford to be anyone else today.

Things got blurrier. I focused on the road, putting one foot in front of the other. Soon my entire body got cold, and I began to shiver. Next thing I knew, I felt vomit rising in my throat. I veered off into the grass and fell to the ground, retching into the grass. Convulsion after convulsion, my self-loathing spilled out of me, the stench serving to make me even sicker.

My mind was foggy, and my limbs were shaking. I wanted nothing more than to be home in my shower, washing all this bullshit off me. But instead I was here. In a fucking field, wearing my own vomit. My mind was clouded with bad decisions and humiliation as I continued to retch in the thick green grass. Turns out, rock bottom was even shittier than I thought.

"Mom. Mom. Come over here," someone yelled.

From my vantage point on the ground I saw some small feet approach. I looked up to see two boys staring at me.

"Are you okay?" the one with the glasses asked.

"He looks pretty sick," the one with the floppy hair said.

"Let's get Mom." They nodded at each other.

"Mom!" Glasses screamed at the top of his lungs.

"Do you want some water?" Floppy asked me.

I nodded, afraid to open my mouth and further traumatize these children. They looked young. Like five or six. These poor kids did not need to see me in this state.

They scampered off, leaving me to my shame.

As I regained my breath and some semblance of my consciousness, I saw someone approach. The first thing I noticed was that she was wearing flip-flops, and every toenail was painted a different color. I followed the shapely legs up to a flowy dress and then long, wavy, red hair. *FUCK. This cannot be happening.*

I had spent the better part of a year avoiding this moment. Avoiding this interaction and now I was a literal fucking mess and staring up at the one that got away.

The last twenty years had been good to her. She looked like an older version of her high school self. A magical fairy sprite in woman form. Wild hair, lots of jewelry, and a tiny nose ring. I looked into those wide brown eyes, rimmed with thick black lashes, and felt like I was going to hurl again.

"Callum Quinn?" Her face fell as she got closer. "Are you okay? Do you need me to call 911?" she asked, concerned.

One of the kids came back with a bottle of water which she opened and handed to me. She patted the kid on the head, and only then did I see the resemblance.

"Thank you," I squeaked out and sipped slowly.

She turned back toward the kids, crouching down. "Sam, can you go get me some towels from the hall closet? And Henry, can you get my phone off the kitchen table?"

The children dispatched, she stared at me.

"It's great to see you, Violet," I croaked, trying to save face a bit.

"Sure," she said, putting her hands on her hips. "What happened? Are you sick? Did you get hit by a car or something? I'm going to call the cops."

"Don't," I said, raising my hands in surrender. "I was just out for a run."

"Did you get the flu and decide to go for a jog anyway?"

I looked away. "Not exactly."

She put her hands on her hips, clearly not buying my bullshit.

"I am a bit hungover. That's all. Just need to hydrate." Fuck, I hated this. I hated not being in control of this interaction. I knew I would see her eventually, but I wanted it to be on my terms. When I was wearing one of my best suits and had my hair freshly cut. I didn't want to be a wounded animal dying on her property.

She shook her head. "Callum Quinn."

The boys returned shortly thereafter, distracting her

from my pathetic mess. "Okay, boys. Thank you. Can you grab your backpacks and jump in the car? I'll drop you off at camp."

"And you," she said, looking down at me. "I'll take you to urgent care on the way."

"No need," I said. "I'm fine."

"You are not fine. Your skin is gray and you look like you could collapse at any minute. Here." She held out a hand to help me up.

Violet Thompson was maybe five feet two, and I was absolutely humiliated to have to lean on her while walking to the driveway. But this was my life now. *I am such a disappointment. I can't even go for a run without messing things up. I deserve to die alone.*

"I'm so sorry," I grunted while we walked to her car.

"Save it," she said, pinning me with a mom glare.

I buckled myself into her Volvo with the two boys in the back chattering excitedly.

"Mr. Quinn is sick, guys, so I'm going to take him to the doctor after I drop you off at camp, okay?"

"Mom, you said we shouldn't go anywhere with strangers."

"I know, sweetie. And you are right. But Mr. Quinn isn't a stranger. I've known him for a long time." I can't recall the first time I actually met Violet—she was just always around. We went to the same elementary school and our parents knew each other, but we were never friends. I played sports and she didn't. My family lived in town near the harbor, and she lived out here on the farm. So our paths didn't cross until high school. That is when I really met her and immediately fell for her.

"Okay, Mom. It's important to always be safe." Glasses was cute but a bit smug.

"I know, Henry."

"Can you open the windows, Mom? Mr. Quinn smells bad," Floppy hair whined.

"Okay, Sam. I will."

I thought I hit rock bottom lying in a pool of my own vomit on the grass. Turns out, cruising through town in my ex-girlfriend's Volvo while her small children discussed how badly I smelled was even worse.

AUTHOR'S NOTE

Dear Reader,

Thank you for reading my second book in the Havenport series! Before book one was even released, I was receiving multiple messages a day about Declan. It seems everyone, from my beta readers to my friends and my cousin, were all asking for more Declan (and Ginger).

I felt an enormous amount of pressure to get him right. And to give him a woman worthy of him. I love Astrid because we have a lot in common. We are both lawyers, both have resting bitch faces, and both left the glitz and glamour of international law firms to pursue other passions. Because Astrid and Declan have tough exteriors and mushy interiors, it was so much fun to pair them up and watch them grow together.

My favorite scene to write is when Declan gives Astrid a sledgehammer for Valentine's Day. It was so much fun to write Astrid's emotional response to the gift and the personal growth that resulted from it. Seeing her work through her challenges physically and realize her own emotional strength while utilizing her physical strength was a joy to write. I saw this scene playing like a movie in my head for weeks before I actually sat down to write it. If you have not had a chance to smash something with a sledgehammer, I strongly recommend it.

I write romance to make people happy. This is my hobby and my passion and it brings me a great deal of joy to share my stories with you. I had a lot of fun writing this book and I hope you had a lot of fun reading it.

With all my love,
Daphne

ACKNOWLEDGMENTS

Thank you to everyone who joined me in Havenport! I wrote this book while locked down in my house due to Covid. I was trying to work my day job, homeschool my five year old, and keep my toddler from setting himself on fire. I needed a creative outlet to help me get through some of the hard days. At the encouragement of my lovely friends, the world of Havenport was born.

There are so many people to thank.

To my husband, thank you for your patience and encouragement. You have been my real-life romance hero for nineteen years. Thank you for everything that you do. And thank you for thinking that a sledgehammer was a romantic gift idea, thus inspiring me to write the emotional climax of this book.

To my mother, thank you for always having my back. I am so grateful for your support, encouragement, child care, and story ideas.

To the ladies of HoCroWoHo, thank you for your decades of friendship, your continued excellence, and your constant encouragement. You have been cheerleading me from the beginning, and it has been so much fun to share this journey with you.

Erica, you are a wonderful friend and even better book pimp. I appreciate all your hard work and respect your willingness to fight for Declan.

Thank you to my beta readers, Erica, Tegan, Leann, Harley, and Leah. You gave me fantastic feedback and kept me sane while editing this book.

To the amazing ladies who make up my Street Team, thank you for offering your time and hilarious memes. I appreciate the constant encouragement and the hilarity.

To my fabulous author friends, Harley Reid, Tatum Rayne, Skylar Platt, and Lizzie Stanley, thank you for encouraging me, advising me, and talking me off the ledge when necessary.

Kari, thank you for the gorgeous cover.

Ann and Ann, thank you for your thorough editing.

The entire team at Give Me Books Promotions, thank you for helping me bring this book into the world.

Jennifer, thank you for jumping in and helping me with my blurb.

Thank you to my family for being hilarious and loving and silly.

ALSO BY DAPHNE ELLIOT

Havenport Series
Trusting You (Book 1)
Cecelia Leary is looking for a fresh start in small town Havenport, Massachusetts. Liam Quinn is looking for a marketing expert to help save his struggling brewery. Sparks fly in this small town, slow burn romance.

ABOUT THE AUTHOR

In High School, Daphne Elliot was voted "most likely to become a romance novelist." After spending the last decade as a corporate lawyer, she has finally embraced her destiny. Her steamy novels are filled with flirty banter, sexy hijinks, and lots and lots of heart.

Daphne is a coffee-drinking, hot-sauce loving introvert who spends her free time gardening and practicing yoga. She lives in Massachusetts with her husband, two kids, two dogs, two fish and twelve backyard chickens.

daphneelliotauthor@gmail.com

Stay in touch with Daphne:
Subscribe to Daphne's Newsletter
Join Daphne's Reader Group
Like Daphne on Facebook
Follow Daphne on Instagram
Hang with Daphne on GoodReads
Follow Daphne on Amazon
Follow Daphne on TikTok

Made in the USA
Columbia, SC
14 May 2023

16707118R00192